D0191252

Amaia Joy

Geoffrey Crewe

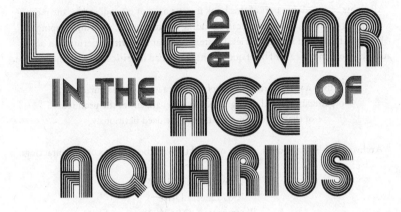

LOVE AND WAR IN THE AGE OF AQUARIUS

AMAIA JOY AND GEOFFREY CARROLL

ARCHWAY
PUBLISHING

Copyright © 2021 Amaia Joy and Geoffrey Carroll.

All rights reserved. No part of this book may be used or reproduced by any means, graphic, electronic, or mechanical, including photocopying, recording, taping or by any information storage retrieval system without the written permission of the author except in the case of brief quotations embodied in critical articles and reviews.

This is a work of fiction. All of the characters, names, incidents, organizations, and dialogue in this novel are either the products of the author's imagination or are used fictitiously.

Archway Publishing books may be ordered through booksellers or by contacting:

Archway Publishing
1663 Liberty Drive
Bloomington, IN 47403
www.archwaypublishing.com
844-669-3957

Because of the dynamic nature of the Internet, any web addresses or links contained in this book may have changed since publication and may no longer be valid. The views expressed in this work are solely those of the author and do not necessarily reflect the views of the publisher, and the publisher hereby disclaims any responsibility for them.

Any people depicted in stock imagery provided by Getty Images are models, and such images are being used for illustrative purposes only. Certain stock imagery © Getty Images.

ISBN: 978-1-6657-0285-0 (sc)
ISBN: 978-1-6657-0286-7 (hc)
ISBN: 978-1-6657-0284-3 (e)

Library of Congress Control Number: 2021902790

Print information available on the last page.

Archway Publishing rev. date: 04/29/2021

NORTHERN
NEW MEXICO

Costilla

Rio Grande

Red River

Tres
Piedras

Questa

Eagle Nest

NEW BUFFALO
(Arroyo Hondo)

Vietnam
Memorial

TAOS

Angel Fire

Pilar

Penasco

Espanola

Chimayo

Mora

I-25

Nambe

Rio Grande

SANTA FE

Las
Vegas

I-25

Pecos

South Vietnam

Cities where major battles took
place, stratigic imortance or
news worthy

QUANG TRI

KHE SAN

HUE

DA NANG

LAOS

TAM KAY

CHU LI

QUANG NGAI

DAK TO

KONTUM

PLEIKU

AN KHE

QUI NHON

HAO BAN

CAMBODIA

TUY HOA

BAN ME
THOUT

NINH HOA

NHA TRANG

DA LAT

CAM RANH
BAY

AN LOC

PHAN RANG

TAY NINH

PHU
CUONG

BEN HOA

MOCK HOA

XUAN LOC

PHAN THIET

CHAU PHU

SAIGON

LONG BINH

SA DEC

MY THO

VUNG TAU

RASH GIA

VINH LONG

GO CONG

SOUTH CHINA SEA

CAN THO

PHU
VINH

BEN TRI

SOC TRANG

MECONG RIVER?
DELTA

BAC LIEU

CA MAU

PRELUDE

1967

THE LOST GENERATION OF THE '20S AND THE BEAT GENERATION OF THE '50S WERE NOW THE LOVE GENERATION OF THE '60S.

Marianne's crayon-lettered party notices for the spontaneous "Rain Festival" had paid off, and it had accumulated about thirty proto-hippie partygoers down by the Rio Grande River. For some, the energy of this misunderstood generation was outrageously explosive; reality was obscured and nonexistent; there were no clear objectives and no known rules; and it was dangerous and diagnostically anarchic. Today's gathering allowed everyone to quickly cultivate a feeling of mental lightheartedness, complete with pious laissez-faire attitudes. Their folly included six bags of weed, a liter of rum, a liter of smuggled Mexican mescal—with a maguey worm—six cases of Schlitz beer, seven pellets of mescaline, a sheet of blotter acid, and the new kid on the block: a saltshaker half-full of cocaine.

Mike Hagger looked out over the crowd. "Ain't it a beaut'?" His voice was dancing full of devilment.

Marianne's voice sang with cheer. "Terri-fucking-rific! Let's part-ee, mahn!" Even after living in the States for seventeen years, Marianne had not yet lost her German accent, and her use of drugs only made her attempt at American slang sound even more raucous.

The hippie fashion rule was that there was no societal catalog. Without warning, this generation had turned the Jackie O fashion trend upside down and inside out. They had brought a tsunami of new styles, including eye-popping neon paisley psychedelic patterns of which the fashion world had never seen.

This troupe of counterculture revelers consisted of a diverse group of old men, young men, boys, braless girls, unclad women, mothers toting toddlers and babies on their breasts, and a flock of dirty half-naked children running about unsupervised, feathers stuck into their sluttish, matted hair. Unequivocally a rainbow of human ethnicity.

The partygoers wore a habiliment of funky masks, colorful headdresses, theatrical capes, long skirts made from patched jeans, long dresses, miniskirts, peasant dresses, see-through tank tops, backless halter tops, and several naked bodies were shockingly highlighted with body paints. To an outsider, it would have seemed that these people were competing for roles in a Fellini movie with the oddest and strangest of caparison. It was Mardi Gras on the Rio Grande.

It was only noon-thirty and the rock 'n' roll music was already becoming noticeably louder; the groove of the dancers became increasing to a frantic pace, and the merriment of voices interruptedly vibrated against the tranquility and enchantment of the river. Most of the attention was being given to a sweaty, hairy-bodied bald man who was handing out acid as he boogied with his barefooted harem of dancers who were reinterpreting the wind as it frolicked up the canyon through the sage, rocks, and across the river, jerking, groovin', and shaking.

The noise level continued to grow until it became a rhythmic tidal wave of sound pressing down around them; the volume enveloping the dancers; and yet louder until body and music fused into one outrageous moment of hysteria where all rules where broken in liberation from control, a poetry of madness escaping into its unique song.

Not wanting to share his picnic of Hamm's beer, bologna, and stale saltine crackers, Mike hoisted Marianne onto his back, providing a piggyback ride farther down the river, as the sound of the music followed them.

"Ya wanna take a trip?" Setting Marianne down by the riverbank, with wicked irreverence, Mike dangled blotter acid in front of Marianne.

"Yaa, bab-bee." She opened her mouth like a pious Catholic taking Communion. "'Tis a boost-ah dose from dah ah-cid I took dis morning."

Mike philosophically rambled, "You know what, man? Taking acid has transformed me from being a devout atheist into being awestruck by God's wonders. We should explore these wonders through human consciousness." Rubbing his whiskered chin, he said, "It has brought me to the most exquisite realizations toward that of unity. I haven't felt so enlightened since I fainted as an altar boy, at High Mass, when I was fourteen." His enthusiasm heightened, he added, "Now that was a trip man."

Marianne said, "Wait a minute, how do ya go from bein' an altar boy to bein' ah devout atheist?"

"Isn't that what happens to most altar boys?" Mike continued to theorize about his most profound insights that came to him when he had taken LSD. "LSD should be used as a religious sacrament. Man, don't ya think it's a powerful tool to access the divine apocalyptic prophecies?"

Minutes passed, and Mike was still long-winded and still going off on his tangents about LSD. Marianne felt the acid begin to kick in, and her senses started down their paths. She was feeling altered and losing control. Flashing lights appeared within her vision, making it hard to focus. Her thoughts and speech became even more disjointed. Her reality was dissolving like the blotter on her tongue. And although she was getting little sparks of sensations, she still wasn't sure if it was the acid or just the mesmerizing waves of the river. "No!" she said out loud to herself. "I'm definitely tripping."

Mike pulled out a joint, lit it up, and passed it to her. With no hesitation, she indulged in the pot, taking in three big hits before passing it back. The wave of the marijuana high quickly rolled over her. She was quite high, and the acid-marijuana mix synergized and intensified her trip.

Mike said, "Wow, man, you should see your pupils." He laughed. "They are so dilated. Far out! Wow, man, are you hallucinating yet?"

They both started to giggle.

Marianne's mind became extremely sensitive to her surroundings. She grew fascinated with a nearby ant colony and began to watch several little ants busy with their daily chores. Laughing, she pointed out the industrious ants to Mike. "Luoke-Mike-luoke, dose ants tis dancin'."

Mike said, "Far out, they are … Wow! They are dancing to the music."

Marianne's immensely stimulated imagination was

transformed into a fantastic dreamlike state in which she perceived that the ants were tripping too. The creatures became three-dimensional tiny humans, busy in their enormous creepy-crawly world. Colors began fusing into their mystical little ant bodies, and patterns from the surrounding sand crept off the ground. Everything was so distinctive with a fascinating kaleidoscopic of bright colors pulsating from them; the ants became an army of dancing little clowns.

"Wow, mon! Yoo tink da moosik from da party wass zright tyear." Marianne felt the music surge within her visuals, she felt infused by the energy of the ants, and she could see them gyrating with the music.

Marianne and Mike began to giggle at the ants, and soon their giggle manifested into hysteric laughter, red-faced, tear-filled eyes, and snot dripping from their noses they laughed into a sheer frenzy and lunacy.

A few minutes later, they didn't quite remember why they were laughing, which of course made it funnier.

Marianne was tripping so hard that the music physically affected her. Her profound high seemed to provide her insight about the music itself. The song coalesced into a distinct character, so defined that it continued as a fitting visual to the moving ants. Mike's continual chatter twisted into an annoying grunting noise. Marianne could still distinctly hear the party's music, and she could unmistakably feel the complicated themes, stories, and the lyrics of "Purple Haze" as if Jimi Hendrix was there with his guitar.

Mike laid back to explore the cumulonimbus spread of clouds.

Marianne zoned out from the party and the ants, and her fascination turned to the river. Now her hallucinations kicked in; the river shimmered in the sunlight, each wave an echo of the rainbow. The serene water called to her, "Come in. Come in." Gracefully she took off her clothes, walked to the riverbank, and quietly slipped beneath the cool and mystically swirling flow of the water. She became a water nymph, infused by the water's transparent efficacy; precise and flowing majestic images soothingly called to her carefree mind.

Her poignantly sensitive state somehow turned her into a submerged submarine. She was effortlessly baptized, her sins and cares washed away while she freely explored the lustrous watercourse. It was an incredible trip. Unknowingly, she became trapped within the controlling grasp of the Rio Grande's powerful currents. The liquid surge suddenly crushed over her, like the lid to her coffin. She felt its watery arms embrace her and the sting of the river sticks, debris, and stray branches. She felt the nipping bites from the river rocks and boulders as she helplessly bobbed over them. Water tightened around her throat; her ears became adulterated with zipping high-pitched screeches. Her joyful tears were instantly diluted by the weighty turbulence. She never fought the current; there was no panic or struggle. As her lungs filled with water, she slipped into a sweet, sweet euphoric state. A final surge carried her into a sweet endless peaceful sleep.

It was dusk when Mike was abruptly awakened by the hard kick from Sheriff Esquibel. Behind him, there were three ugly, red-faced deputies and several angry gun-toting rednecks.

Taos, New Mexico's finest authorities had gathered. Lieutenant Baca of the New Mexico State Troopers, Taos County Sheriff Esquibel, and three of his deputies, along with four of the Taos County Sheriff's Posse.

Mike looked like a wild man. His face was flaming red from dropping acid and mixed with sunburn from passing out by the river in the bright sun; his wild white-blonde hedgehog hair was adorned with twigs and grass. "Hey, man, we were just having fun. We were just foolin' around, drinking, and trying to have a good time. Come on, man. Let me go, man."

The dark black goo of prejudice pumped through his veins as J. W. Weston of the Taos County Posse barked with disbelief, "You stupid fucking hippie. Your evil good times and fun just cost a woman her life." J. W. was still dazed and sickened. He couldn't clear his mind of the horrific sight of the bloated and pale body he had pulled from the river's edge. The woman's staring blue eyes and her pale-white, naked, soulless body continued to stab at his mind.

"Man, man, man." Deputy Chainy spit as he mimicked Mike's words, his mouth foaming with disgust. Deputy Chainy hated the hippies and his words hissed of intense abhorrence. "Ya fuckin' stupid hippie dirtbag, piece of shit, have some respect, man." He threw Mike facedown onto the trunk of his squad car and pressed his .38 service revolver to Mike's temple.

J. W. and several men leaped onto Deputy Chainy. "Hey! Hey! Hey! Easy there, Earl. Stand down."

Deputy Chainy's eyes popped out of his head with rage and instant high blood pressure surged through his obese body.

J. W. quickly stepped in and roughly slapped handcuffs tightly on Mike.

CHAPTER 1

1969 ARROYO HONDO, NEW BUFFALO COMMUNE

"AQUARIUS LET THE SUNSHINE IN," THE FIFTH DIMENSION

The setting sun dripped into the rich, red New Mexican earth as it was peacefully extinguished by the horizon. The angelic woman known as Sunshine sat gracefully on the mesa ledge overlooking nature's tie-dyed spectrum. She skillfully captured the enchanting scenery before her on her worn sketch pad while she examined life's sacred roots that evolved from the omnipotent Rio Grande sun. She drew consolation and God's energy from Mother Earth and her sister, Sun, asking them for guidance. Sunshine spoke softly to the heavens, "Dear God, I invite your serenity into my life and the presence of the Spirit. I feel your love, guidance, and warmth filling me and surrounding me. Any of my worries or fears fade away as I invite you to replace all of my uneasiness."

Sunshine could clearly hear the party at the New Buffalo commune even though it was half a mile away. The voices carried over the soft sounds of nature, calling out in song and laughter.

The past two nights had been the wildest, grooviest back-to-the-earth movement this valley had ever seen. All the members of the sister communes united at the New Buffalo/Taos Valley site for a festival to celebrate their joys together. To most, it was a joy that was from a bottomless well that never ran dry, a reservoir of happiness from deep within. Together, they danced and made music with sleigh bells, rattles, flutes, marimbas, sticks, horns, guitars, and a multifarious selection of drums, including a big conga drum, all in tune with the songs of freedom. The men, women, and children danced wildly, grooving and moving to a rhythm of spirit in expression. They sang and shouted until their lungs and voices gave out. Some sang songs of love, and others made love with a newly freed passion, each in search of the roots of their seething emotions, triumphantly releasing the devil's hot desire. They believed they were united by common humanity, yet they were separated by their individuality.

Turning back to the present moment of her meditation,

Sunshine sat back in the immensity of the earth and sky, wondering if indeed these people journeyed in the right direction. Many of the members and guests spoke with a mystical jargon about their new experiences in the LSD wilderness. Many said that taking LSD opened the doors to one's spiritual destiny. These were the years that the use of drugs spread among the youth. There was a literal buffet of drugs available throughout the counterculture. Abundant and affordable were marijuana, hashish, LSD, mescaline, peyote, a variety of uppers, and also bizarre drugs like DMT, DET, and the most American of all drugs, tranquilizers, but Sunshine felt that life was too beautiful to cloud it with drugs. She hailed a natural high, which was the intoxication of life's energy. She sought to live in harmony with the divine principle of love. She knew God was Love. God was not a distant spirit in a faraway place, but the very breath of life.

In the distance, Sunshine could hear her spiritual brother—Blue—and her giggling friend Yogi calling for her. She responded to herself with an annoyed sigh, "Oh, go away. I'm enjoying this peaceful sunset." She reflected that this shrinking planet leaves few personal oases in which to retreat. Taking in one more glance at the beautiful scenery before her, she sighed and whispered, "*Hermoso lindo.*"

Blue and Yogi's laughing voices continued to stagger closer, for they were the only friends who knew where she could be found; this was one of Sunshine's favorite spots for soul-searching and prayer. This was her sanctuary for meditation, peace, and rejuvenation.

Wild-eyed and laughing hysterically, Blue and Yogi joined Sunshine on the mesa ledge. They had already sampled the abundant libations from the weekend-long party. Blue was Sunshine's closest and dearest friend¾her soul mate. They had experienced most of life's major elements together: friendship, guidance, growth, joy, healing, love, hatred, and death. They understood that friends came and went in their lives, yet some friends became family forever. Although he was not her brother by blood, he was truly her brother in spirit.

Blue was tall with sandy-blond hair, which had been shoulder-length until three and a half months ago when he left for army boot camp. He stood six feet four inches tall, invigorated with strength and force. His piercing blue eyes had earned him his nickname—the same blue eyes that won over many women, young and old. Blue knew he was good-looking, and he was devoted to those good looks.

Blue smiled and said, "Sunshine, you really should be back at New Buffalo groovin' with your brothers and sisters." His statement was filled with pretension and mockery.

Yogi asked, "Sunshine, what are you spacing out on way the fuck out here by yourself?"

Yogi, who was at least a foot shorter, was nibbling gently on Blue's bare arm, hoping to spark desire in him. She chattered with amusement. "Hey! Old Grandpa Tylor sent us to fetch you back. He says you need to stop being such a loner and come join the party. And I think all those bratty rug rats need your help."

Blue guzzled his beer, and in an attempt to sound poetic, he said, "Sunshine, we need your beautiful soul back to the party, and I'm only here for a few more hours, so I'd like to spend more time with you."

Sparking with laughter, Sunshine gave him a brotherly hug and sweetly replied, "Damn, Blue, I am going to miss you."

"I'm gonna miss you too," Blue replied with sincerity as he held her and gave her a lengthy hug in return.

Yogi rolled her eyes and impatiently barked, "Oh, fuck, I am gonna miss you too." She added in a scornful tone, "Okay enough, let's get back to the party."

The threesome walked back together, their bare feet kicking up dust on the trail, arm in arm, singing a song by The Fifth Dimension, "The Age of Aquarius," while keeping in step with the thundering conga drums back at the party.

Yogi was a redheaded Twiggy lookalike with an adolescent body, serpentine hips, small boobs, a knowing smile, and dark eyes that were full of mischief. Yogi and Sunshine couldn't have been more opposite. They didn't have a thing in common, but the two had become close friends over the past few months while Blue was away at army boot camp. Yogi was a living exclamation point; she was a gigantic tease. She could shake you up unexpectedly with her quick wit and audacious remarks, followed by devastating shock waves from her unscrupulous actions. Yogi took full advantage of the sexual revolution: birth control, free love, orgies, and the now-open door of bisexuality. Dozens of men and women had shared her bed. She was a prime symbol of post-voluptuous femininity.

Tylor was the elder of the communal members. Although he was only thirty-five years old, everyone called him Grandpa Tylor because of his long, prematurely graying hair and belly-length beard. He resembled a prodigious troglodyte. He was a deeply gentle and caring man, but he had a dangerously gruff, rampaging rebel side to him. Tylor was a wise mentor and highly respected by all the members and guests.

Three years ago, Tylor had arrived at the commune with a wife and three young sons: nine-year-old Skylor, seven-year-old Raven, and five-year-old Neon. Tylor's wife couldn't embrace the communal concept and didn't like all the hard work involved. As he explained it, "They ran into a little trouble on the highway of forever." She ran off with a fat, bald, traveling life insurance salesman, leaving behind Tylor and their three small rambunctious and inquisitive boys. Being part of a culture that believed in free love, many learned that this practice sadly often created hurt, and there was always someone heartbroken being left behind.

This weekend's party had a dual purpose. It was the summer solstice, the longest day of the year. It was a day when one could lengthen the search of one's soul. It also served as a farewell party for Blue. He had been home on leave after spending the past eight weeks at boot camp at Fort Ord, California. Followed by a short leave, and then back to Fort Ord for specialized infantry training. This was his second leave. Tomorrow he would for Oakland Alameda Air Station; from there, he was bound for Vietnam.

🐓

The people of the Taos/New Buffalo commune came from all over the United States to live the life of a rural community, to organize on a communal basis, and to experience life as a large family. The idealistic said it was to get as far away from society as they could get, to experience countercultures. The original idea was to live in harmony with the earth, sun, moon, and stars. It was 1969. Americans were a few months away from taking an evolutionary leap by invading another heavenly body and pushing the envelope of space exploration by putting a man on the moon. Yet the family members of the New Buffalo commune were still harvesting their food in the way the ancestral Puebloans Anasazi Indians had done more than three thousand years before them. The Anasazi Native American culture held a distinct knowledge of celestial sciences and ethereal spiritual beliefs and worked together closely as a family.

The original idea of the commune was very ancient, but the idea of an egalitarian, nonpatriarchal, nonauthoritarian society was having trouble rebirthing and flourishing. Together, the commune painstakingly built an adobe home out of mud and straw. They dragged long aspen poles for miles from Lobo Peak, above Taos, to use as vigas for the main house and to make tepees for shelter. They grew rows of corn and beans and maintained small gardens with a variety of vegetables. Some grew marijuana for the high, and some grew fresh herbs in hopes of practicing medicinal uses. They toiled by hand in hopes that their effort would create a new way of life closer to nature, make them further from "Mom and Dad's" suburbia.

Sunshine was a quiet, peaceful woman who rarely spoke. She had hopes for harmony and understanding and believed that it could be accomplished through self-love and the love of humanity. Sunshine believed in the inherent goodness of all people. She spent countless hours praying and meditating for an ideal world without hate, poverty, greed, or war. She knew that love was active and generative and that its seeds must be planted if love was to grow. Her beliefs were not mystical or high-minded, they were a simple truth of God's light and love. And although life's conditions may not be exactly what she wanted them to be, she said, "They are what they are." Once she accepted that, she could be lifted into a place where she could see with a clear vision and act with a compassionate heart.

Many members of the commune felt strongly about the communal concept and causes but knew deep in their hearts that it wasn't working. Too many people had taken advantage of their generous hospitality and abused the order they were trying to create. They abused the true meaning of love and turned to sex and drugs. Too many people came needing to escape the plastic and putrefying conditions of the malignant cities, yet few left their evil spirits behind. Many curious people had come just to check out what was happening in the free-spirit world of the commune life; these weekend hippies were called yo-yos.

Life was certainly happening today. Hundreds of people came from miles around for this celebration. The original settlers—brothers and sisters of all New Buffalo's sister communes— along with the yo-yos, the hippie wannabes, interstate visitors, mooches, ingrates, lazy-heads, weirdos, and even the spiritual parasites were all gathered here today. The combination was like a freak circus for the socially manic.

Entering the communal square, Sunshine was greeted

by the children with open arms and loving hearts. She immediately fell to her knees to be on their level, exchanging hugs and kisses as her bright, smiling green eyes loved and adored every single one of them. This love that she so easily shared was what she was famous for among her sisters and brothers of the commune. It was why people trusted her and wanted her close to them. Often, when she felt a lack of love or hardness of spirit, she would go among the children. She knew that their hearts were pure and their ways are guileless. The children offered her a clear window into the pure human heart.

Sunshine was a beautiful lady, not only in looks but in personality as well. Divine life radiated in and through every aspect of her being. Her beauty was beyond that of any made-up Hollywood movie star. She had beautiful white teeth, and you got to see them often because she smiled constantly. Her long, thick, straight brown hair with golden sun-kissed highlights fell freely down her back to her slender waist. She was the perfect illustration of a beautiful human female body.

The hours she spent meditating, worshiping, playing, and painting, and working in the sun had given her a golden tan. Her jade eyes captured many souls. Even though she was wearing a drab, pink, Old Mother Hubbard dress, you could see that her frame was small and elegantly etched. She was a natural beauty, not needing makeup or fancy hairdos to accentuate her lovely features. Sunshine's loving spirit and gentle voice lent her a graceful naiveté.

It made her smile to know she was touching other lives with peace. She knew it wasn't enough to just pray for harmony; she must strive to be harmony. Sunshine's love for the children was as sunny as her name. She sang and danced with them for a short while, calling, "Hey, my little munchkins! What do you say we follow the Yellow Brick Road to Oz and find us some cookies?"

Skylor called out, "I get to be the lion." He immediately started roaring and chasing the other children.

"I want to be the Scarecrow," Raven called. "And Neon is one of the icky monkeys from the mean witch's castle."

Sunshine laughed. "No, poor Neon doesn't want to be an icky monkey! He can be the Scarecrow."

Skylor remarked, "Yeah, if he only had a brain."

Little Joanie declared, "I'm Dorothy." She started singing and marching around. "We're off to see the Wizard."

The children's bright eyes and dirty faces beamed with delight. They sang in unison, "Follow the yellow brick road," and followed Sunshine like ducklings into the hexagonal lodge, which posed as the focal point of the commune. The grand room was made of adobe and possessed a perpetual echo that enhanced the humming of meditation. The room was adorned with psychedelic and tie-dyed tapestries, and posters idolizing rock stars such as Jimi Hendrix, Janis Joplin, Jim Morrison, and the Grateful Dead. The room served many purposes. It was a library, housing around five hundred well-read books, it served as a classroom for the children, in which Sunshine played the role of their teacher, and it was used for the communal council, which faithfully held meetings. The council had no elected officials, and all decisions were made by whoever decided to show up for the meetings. In the long, hard winters, the brothers and sisters of the New Buffalo gathered in this great room and huddled around the warmth of their only woodburning stove. They continually stuffed crumbled-up newspapers and old rags in the drafty holes of the adobe bricks. Last summer, Grandpa-Tylor, and Blue had added a kitchen to the grand room.

Sunshine, along with two of the older children, carried the cookies back into the grand room and placed them on the enormous wooden table, while the children ran around, danced, and played.

Blue arrogantly swaggered into the great room, grabbed Sunshine, and whirled her around in a mock dance.

Sunshine laughed as she tried to keep up with his movements.

Blue teased the children, "Hey, you little rug rats, I'm going to take Sunshine outside to dance."

All the children unanimously shouted, "No! No, you can't have her."

Blue loved to tease the children. "Well, what do you know? You're just a bunch of booger-eatin' little heathens." Picking up Sunshine, he tossed her over his shoulder like a pillow. Irritated by the children's complaints, he added, "That's just too bad." Then mumbled under his breath, "Little shits," and he carried Sunshine outside. Blue placed Sunshine back on her feet, and they immediately started dancing to rock music booming from a nearby van with all its doors open so you could hear his eight-track player, which was scantily rigged to four huge speakers.

"This is far out!" Mocking the lingo of some of the others, he added, "Yeah! Far out, man. And groovy too." As he danced with Sunshine to the tunes of Jefferson Airplane's "White Rabbit," he humorously teased Sunshine, "Hey, you need to loosen up, sister."

Yogi joined them with double-fisted beers and a joint between her fingers. "Out-of-sight party!" She began moving freely with strange gyrations and drollery, her body obeying the ever-changing rhythm. The threesome joined together in a fun balter and danced without grace or skill, swirling, shaking, swaying, clapping, singing, fully enjoying themselves as they jived to the music.

Blue grabbed one of Yogi's beers. "Hey, you Joneser, Yogi,

give me one of those fucking beers." Blue needed to drink more; he was trying to keep his mind comfortably hazy.

"Sure, baby, but that's not the only thing I'm wanting to give you." Yogi giggled seductively. Yogi had supported a wide variety of the party's indulgences, and giving up one beer made no dent in her bumper.

Sunshine, on the other hand, was content to enjoy the company of her brother. She knew Blue would be leaving for the virulent country of Vietnam in the morning.

The following day started quiet and but not restful. The early morning air carried the sounds of awakening life. The noise of squawking, mooing, and bleating animals was mixed with crying babies, giggling children, and the shuffling of the brothers and sisters. Visitors were passed out everywhere, and some were quietly trying to make amends with their bodies after the prior day's indulgences.

Sunshine slept with Blue in their primitive summer tepee as she had for the past two years. Although the two of them sleeping together caused many a questioning brow, the situation was harmless. They viewed themselves as having a true spiritual bond of blood brother and sister. There was no perversion or sexuality involved. The family members of the commune understood and respected their relationship.

Sunshine gently nudged Blue awake. Teasing him, she opened the canvas tepee door and began singing purposely off-key, "Oh, let the sunshine in, let it in your heart," forgetting the words and substituting others, "do, do, do, do, do, oh let the sunshine in ... yeah!"

Blue threw his pillow at her, pretending to be irritated. "What the fuck are you doing? Shut up, girl, and leave the sunshine outside." Yawning, he asked, "Fuck me! What time is it anyways? Oh, man! I feel like a sat-on hemorrhoid."

With false bravado, Sunshine laughed. "It's eleven thirty, and you'd better be getting your scrawny little military butt up and going. Your bus leaves in two hours."

"Shit! Don't fucking remind me." Hostility raged in his voice.

Hugging Blue, Sunshine warned him with tearing eyes. "Blue, I'm scared. I'm so scared."

Blue barked his bitter sarcasm, "Yeah! Yeah! Yeah! I was hoping the fucking Paris Peace talks would do something before I had to get my ass shot at, but they drag on with no fucking end in sight." He rubbed his hand through his stubbly buzzed hair. "Sunshine, we've been through all this."

Sunshine stared up to the roof of the tepee. "Damn it, Blue. The Vietnam War has only intensified. The number of men missing in action and prisoners of war are countless, and their drafted replacements only continue to march in to take their place. All this death and destruction for a damn war we know we cannot win.

"And that asshole, Tricky Dick. Let's not forget his predecessor Lyndon Baines 'Fucking' Johnson who sent us full steam ahead into this insanity." He threw a finger up toward the sky. "Ah, that is ... Ah, Mr. 'Fucking' President." He extended his arms above his head with double-fisted peace signs, making a dignified snarl and trying to mimic the president. "Nixon continues month after month in worthless bullshit and efforts of proposals for withdrawals. It's as useless as tits on a bull."

Trying to keep his cool and camouflage his emotions, Blue released a huge sigh. "Look, Sunshine, we know all this. We know this has become a fucking war endorsed by greedy corporations with huge military contracts, mocked politics, and vain leadership." What he didn't say was that he was scared shitless knowing there had already been thirty-seven thousand men killed in action since the war began, and the news had been posting that so far as of the spring of 1969, it had been some of the bloodiest weeks the Vietnam War.

Blue sweetened his tone and said, "I know you're scared." He cleared his throat. "Now we've talked about this over and over again ..." His words dropped off since he didn't want to add flames to the burning emotional embers.

Sunshine wiped the tears from her eyes, tried to lighten their spirits, and meekly chanted, "Hell no! We won't go!"

Blue joined in with a strong, proud voice and sang a popular Country Joe McDonald song, "I Feel I'm Fixin' To Die Rag," which had quickly become the unofficial anthem of the Vietnam GIs. "And it's one, two, three, what are we fighting for, don't ask I don't give a damn, next stop is Vietnam." The song was medicine to help him to drown the noise that fear was singing in his mind.

The Vietnam War had become a decade cursed upon the nation, sucking up its sons, mainly of working-class families. Hundreds of thousands wanted no part of a war that featured napalm, fragmentation bombs, defoliation, and countless body bags, but in honor of his late father, Blue willingly and proudly joined the United States Army to serve his nation. What most men did not know—and what Blue had found out—was that if you volunteered for the draft, your commitment was only two years. When you volunteered for the draft, you got to choose the date you went in, you got to choose where you went to basic training, and you got your choice of any of the three combat schools: infantry, armored, or artillery.

Tylor tapped at their tepee's canvas. "Hey, lazy-heads, get your asses up. Blue, listen, soldier, you've got a schedule to meet—or you're liable to end up in the brig on AWOL charges."

Blue proudly yelled, "Fuckin' a."

Tylor continued giving orders. "And, Sunshine, Yogi is in need of some help. She's been throwing up the remains of last night's party."

"I don't doubt that, after that disgusting junk she was drinking last night. It probably tasted better the second time." She wrinkled her nose in disgust.

Snickering, Blue added, "Probably tastes like army chow."

Still laughing, Sunshine said, "Okay, okay. I'll be right there. I'll make us all some strong coffee."

Then Blue and Sunshine started chanting, "Hell no, we won't go."

Tylor walked away, pulling on his long beard, shaking his head, and smirking.

Tylor, Blue, and Sunshine squeezed into Tylor's 1965 Volkswagen bug and set off for the bus stop in Taos. It was a scorching summer day, which called for opening all the windows in the deafeningly loud VW bug. They buzzed south down the highway as fast as the old bug would take them. Not wanting to be included in Blue and Tylor's conversation of "money was only a hallucination that banks created," Sunshine gazed out the window. As they drove past the amazing spiritual topography, she hummed a song by

Peter, Paul, and Mary: "I'm leaving on a jet plane, don't know when I'll be back again."

The tiny village of Taos is huddled in a beautiful niche on the western slope of the La Sierra del Sangre de Cristo Mountains, so named because they turn bloodred during sunsets. Many snow-fed rivers and streams flow from the mountains, feeding the alluring and unique countryside below. West of Taos, beneath an enormous sky, a wide plain, the dry flat basin of a lost sea, stretches like the hand of God into the translucent distance.

Tylor, Blue, and Sunshine arrived at Taos's village street corner, which served as the bus station. The bus driver was slowly preparing to leave, edging away from the curb when Tylor pulled his VW bug in front of the bus to stop it. He hollered, "Wait, this boy has got to catch the bus." Changing his tone, he barked out to the bus driver as if he held military rank, "He's a member of the armed forces of this country. Have some respect."

The bus driver responded by laying on his horn.

Blue laughed. "Far out." He jumped out, grabbed his bag, kissed Sunshine on the forehead, shook Tylor's hand, and ran to the bus as he sang the lyrics from the Country Joe song.

A few townspeople stopped and stared at the loud scene, wondering what those damn hippies were up to now.

Disheartened and scared, Sunshine watched Blue board

the bus. She whispered to herself, "Don't leave me alone." As Tylor slowly drove off, she began to cry, in fear of him leaving her alone, in fear of losing him to the war, and in fear of opening another painful wound at the thought of losing him like she had lost her father and mother. She cried, "Please, God, don't let me lose Blue." Desperately trying to add cheer to the sickening situation, she softly cried, "Hell no! We won't go."

Tylor gave her a loving pat on the back, knowing that there was nothing he could say since "I'm sorry" was wholly inadequate. "Hey, Sunshine, I know what will cheer you up. Let's go visit Jerome Naseyowma out at the pueblo." Taylor took a quick right off the Veterans Highway and traveled down a dirt road to the time-honored village of Taos Pueblo.

The ancestors of Taos Pueblo lived in this mystic valley long before Columbus discovered America and hundreds of years before Europe emerged from the Dark Ages. Nestled in the mountain foothills at an elevation of 7,200 feet is the village pueblo, their ancient ruins, and communal dwellings known as kivas. The kivas are still used and are mainly used as spiritual congregational spaces for ceremonial purposes. The people of Taos Pueblo have a detailed oral spiritual history that is not divulged due to religious privacy.

The history of Taos Pueblo indicates that the native people lived in this ancient five-story housing nearly a thousand years ago. The main structures of the buildings were most likely constructed between AD 1000 and AD 1450, and it appears today much as it did when the first Spanish explorers arrived in Northern New Mexico in 1540. The pueblo is considered to be the oldest continuously inhabited community in the United States. The Pueblo is made entirely of adobe. Adobe is earth mixed with water and straw and made into sun-dried bricks. Most of the walls are several feet thick. The roofs of each of the five stories are supported by large vigas, timbers hauled down from the mountain forests. Smaller pieces of pine or aspen wood latillas are placed side by side on top of the vigas, and the whole roof is covered with packed dirt. Like modern-day condos, the pueblo structure has many individual homes, built side by side, and in layers, with common walls but no connecting doorways. In earlier days, there were no doors or windows, and entry was gained only from the rooftop. In keeping their traditions, there is no electricity or running water allowed within the pueblo. Most members live in conventional homes outside the village walls, but they occupy their pueblo houses for ceremonies. Approximately 150 native Taos people live within the original pueblo. Around 1,900 other family members own homes outside the old walls but still within the pueblo land.

As Taylor drove through the pueblo, they found Jerome sitting under a grand old cottonwood tree next to the Rio

Pueblo de Taos River. Taylor and Sunshine were lovingly greeted by him as they joined him under the tree.

With insightful concern, Jerome asked, "Sunshine, my sister, what is troubling your sweet spirit?"

Sunshine shared her troubles and sorrows with Blue leaving for Nam.

Jerome was a spiritual leader and elder for the pueblo, but he was unique in the fact that he gladly shared his wisdom with everyone. He was a zenithal holy man and profoundly humble, and he had a joyful knowledge of life.

The three sat together and held hands as Jerome slowly shared a blessing with them. "We cannot control the circumstances—we cannot control the war—but in the midst of darkness, we can always access the light within us and share the light within us through prayer. We can hold a picture in our minds as we pray for peace. We envision all people working together in love. We envision all people working together in peace. This is our beautiful planet, our Mother Earth, and each of us inhabits this home together. We remind ourselves of our sacred responsibility in helping to advocate peace and live in harmony. Just as the sun rises without fail, we can overcome the darkness within and around us by bringing forth our inner light and sharing our inner light. Say with me, 'Today, we pray for peace, and I make a conscious choice to meet life with optimism because divine purpose inspires me to have confidence and courage.'"

Not a word was shared between them during the drive back to New Buffalo as Sunshine silently wept.

That night, as Sunshine laid alone in her tepee, her heartbeat sounded different. There was a hollow echo in her ears, the sound of loneliness. She clenched her hands over her ears to stop the sound, but she found herself powerless. She wrapped her arms tightly around her chest, but her arms could not mimic the arms she ached for: the arms of Blue or the arms of her father.

Sunshine's grief from the death of her father was still fresh, raw, relentless, and unstoppable as nightfall. A tear fell, traveling the same path it had traveled many times before. Reality seared her senses, and she realized she had nobody. The word *nobody* echoed through her mind. She stood up, took a mirror from the shelf, and studied her face, but she didn't recognize herself. She looked at the image that reflected—only to question who she was or who she had become. She felt as if she was just a little girl: small, fragile, and so alone. Where would she find her loving protection, her encouragement, and her guidance?

Sunshine slid to the floor, pulled her knees up to her chest, and hooked her hands around them, as if to wear armor, only to find it futile. She could hear her heart scream and felt the anguish pulling at her. She lowered herself on to her bedroll and curled up in the fetal position, hoping her grief would be extinguished through her slumber.

Sunshine sighed and said, "Damn war. Dear God, I feel so powerless as I think about the horrible things going on in the world." She took a deep breath. "I am a channel of divine energies of peace and endless love. Love and peace flow to me and through me." As she tried to calm her worries, she reminded herself to touch the presence of God within herself—and then she would never be alone.

CHAPTER 2

SAIGON:
BLUE'S FLIGHT TO NAM

"MRS. ROBINSON," SIMON AND GARFUNKEL

As it turned out, Blue had an adventure all his own just getting to Vietnam. The bus ride from Taos to Kirtland Air Force Base was about four hours. Blue felt compelled to soak in every visual aspect of the magical landscape of New Mexico. He was trying not to contemplate the possibility that this may be the last time he would see the Land of Enchantment. He was worried about leaving his spirit, sister Sunshine, alone at the commune. The love that he had for Sunshine was far more than he had ever felt with anyone in his lifetime. There is a word that the Welsh use for a strong human bond, *"Teulu,"* which is the most precious of gifts. Most people have relatives through blood, but people can have a special family through love. Teulu is where a true friend becomes as close as or closer than family through love, laughter, care, and trust.

It was two-hour flight to Travis Air Force Base, near Sacramento, and then a one-hour bus ride to the Oakland Alameda Air Station, which was the port of call for most of the GIs headed for Vietnam. It was a very scenic trip, especially after the bus crested the Richmond Hills, which provided a magnificent sunset, perfectly framing the Golden Gate Bridge. The San Francisco Bay and surrounding cities provided a spectacular view of color and adventure, except this one little battleship-gray facility near Oakland. Yep, that was the processing shithole to Vietnam.

Of course, in true military fashion, the processing office had closed an hour before Blue arrived. Blue was directed to a bunkhouse facility until morning. *This is not going to do*, he thought. *I'll go crazy before then.* He received directions at the base gate from the MPs to a nearby bar, and off he went to have his last drink or two or three in the United States until he returned home from Vietnam. He thought, *Yes, I will return.*

The next morning, in his uniform, jungle fatigues, Blue went to the processing facility only to find his flight out to Nam was leaving out from Travis Air Force Base, *Shit, man. I just came from there last night. Why did I have to come down to this shithole?*

The sergeant was sympathetic and said, "At ease, soldier. Every swinging dick headed to Nam must process out from here."

He was put back on a bus to Travis Air Force Base.

In typical military fashion, they screwed up his itinerary again—and he missed his flight to Vietnam. A few hours later, he boarded on another flight that would eventually land at Tan Son Nhut Airbase in Saigon.

Blue was getting a nervous feeling that it could be part of a bad omen, but he was relieved to find out the aircraft was a C-5A galaxy equipped with a special passenger compartment for embassy personnel. Walking onto the tarmac to the aircraft, a set of stairs led him into the lower part of the plane's unbelievably massive fuselage. Blue noticed a huge ramp lowered at the rear of the plane onto the tarmac, and he noticed they were loading an enormous deuce-and-a-half truck into the aircraft. The cargo bay had already been loaded with another deuce-and-a-half and other armored personnel carriers.

Damn, Blue thought. *The inside of this plane is huge.* He laughed at himself. *You could put an entire town in here.*

More stairs led him into a beautiful, comfortable passenger compartment adorned with a huge map of the world marked with the routes to all the different embassies the plane traveled to. All the seats were facing the rear of the aircraft, and there were only three windows on each side. *Not too shabby*, he thought. Their first stop would be Honolulu.

Since the seating compartment was only about halfway full, he could choose any seat and spread out a little.

They arrived in Honolulu about midmorning, and what little scenery he could see out the windows was gorgeous. Since they didn't let him deplane, he had to just sit there dreaming about the tropical paradise that was just a stairwell away. In no time, people started boarding—and the seats started filling fast. A very stately couple happened to stagger on last and take the last two seats next to him: a bulkhead and the middle seat. Blue preferred the aisle. The grumpy gentleman extended a hand, introduced himself as General So-and-So, and then introduced his wife, Kitty. The general grabbed a pillow and blanket and was asleep against the bulkhead before takeoff.

Kitty was wide-awake. She had a very lovely friendly smile. Blue thought there was no doubt that she had a flirtatious side to her.

Not even a half hour into the flight, Kitty turned to Blue, smiled sweetly, and said, "Oh my goodness, you have the bluest eyes I've ever seen. I'll bet the girls just love you."

Wow, he thought. *Is that martini breath or what?*

Kitty went on bragging about their time on Oahu. They had been partying until morning at some high muckety-muck party at Fort Debussy. It turned out that he was a general on a diplomatic mission from the Pentagon.

Blue thought, *It seems like the general's wife mission is to flirt and party with as many younger military men as she can.*

Kitty asked about Blue's life and responded like it was the most fascinating thing she had ever heard. She finally dozed off and let her head slowly drop until it rested on Blue's shoulder. Her hand rested on his knee.

Their nap was interrupted by the serving of a meal. *I'll be damned,* he thought. *Check out this kick-ass grub.* It was a chicken breast topped with some fancy tropical fruit sauce and nuts, asparagus, exotic rice, and fresh fruit for dessert.

Kitty glanced over, winked, smiled, and said, "Nice banana ... would you like some of my passion fruit?"

After a crew member removed the meal trays, they dimmed the cabin lights.

Blue reclined his seat and pulled his blanket up to get a little shut-eye.

A few minutes later, Kitty leaned on his arm and let her head slowly drop to his shoulder again.

As Blue was just about asleep, he felt her small hand slide across the top of his inner thigh under the blanket. *Holy shit,* he thought. *Here I am—a lowly enlisted guy—and some upper-echelon general's wife is acting like she wants to grab my dick. And the general is sleeping right fucking there. Fuck-me!*

Several hours later, they landed in Guam. Everyone had a chance to deplane for an hour or so. Since there was a bar in the terminal, Blue took advantage of the opportunity to grab a quick beer.

The bartender served Blue his beer and told him it was paid for by the woman across the bar.

Blue looked up, and Kitty raised her martini glass and winked.

Blue was in total disbelief. *Was that a little tongue out the corner of her mouth? Shit! Really? Fuck! This is getting dangerous. Get a grip, Blue. She's a fucking general's fucking wife.*

After the warm tropical air of Guam, the airplane cabin felt like an icebox. They passed out blankets to everyone, and Kitty rested her head on Blue's shoulder again.

Blue was not ready for what happened next. She bit Blue's shoulder and she ran her hand under the blanket. Under Blue's shirt, she begun caressing his bare stomach. The next downward stroke of her hand went down the outside of Blue's pants. She whispered a barely audible moan and firmly grabbed a handful of the bulge formed by his swelling cock.

As much as he would have loved to unzip his pants for her, Blue knew it was way too dangerous to mess with a general's wife. He had to put a kibosh on Kitty's sexual advances. He sprang to his feet and said, "Excuse me, ma'am … uh … I'm needing the latrine."

When he returned, he tried to position himself away from her to make it clear that her last actions had to stop.

She fell asleep with her head on his shoulder and her hand tucked up between his thighs and against his dick.

It was well after dark when they landed in Manila. They would spend the night there and return for an early departure the next morning.

In the terminal, the general's wife pulled Blue aside and asked where he was staying.

"I was told not to bring much money with me to Vietnam since they have special military money there. I'll be sleeping in the terminal for the night."

"That will not do" she said sweetly. "Let me get you a room in the hotel where we are staying." She stroked his arm and added, "I want to fuck you so bad."

"Sorry, ma'am!" Blue walked away before she tried to be more persuasive. A part of him really wanted to take her up on the hotel room offer. He imagined her horny, slutty body, and he knew she would suck and fuck him to utter exhaustion. Blue snapped himself out of it. *What am I thinking? Firing off of my cock in the general's wife in exchange to face a firing squad?*

The next morning, while boarding the plane, Blue could tell Kitty was put off. With phony politeness, she hardly talked the entire two and a half hours to Tan Son Nhut airport, which was just outside of Saigon.

As they deplaned, she grabbed his arm and said, "Private Cantrell, I hope you will be assigned duty out of harm's way and return home safely."

Blue detected a tear in her eye. He knew he was going to be assigned to an infantry unit—and his duty would be anything but safe. "Yes, ma'am. Thank you, ma'am." He walked away and thought, *What a fucking crazy place this is!*

Blue passed through a simple gate and into a chaotic area that exploded into an overwhelming crowd of people. He could see all nationalities of people and freaky, unfamiliar military uniforms on Asian men. He was at least ten inches taller than the majority of the people there. There was the deafening chatter of differing languages—and not a word of English. Everything was so foreign to him—the sights, the smells, the noises, and the way the buildings were constructed—and even the sky looked different.

A strange sensation swept over him, and he felt like the lead actor in a great military epic movie staged in a foreign land. *What the fuck? What planet am I on?* His humor and his imagination led him to think, *Am I destined to be a war hero and win the Congressional Medal of Honor? Fuck … fuck … fuck!*

Blue realized he was supposed to be checking in

somewhere, but he didn't see a single American. Looking over the sea of people, he finally spotted a foreign MP standing out at the curb in front of the terminal. He didn't recognize the man's insignia. "Excuse me? I'm looking for an American facility in which to report."

In an Australian accent, he said, "There is the bloke you are looking for, Yank." He pointed at an American MP about fifty yards away.

He dragged his heavy duffel bag over to the American MP and said, "Man, am I glad to see you. I was beginning to think I deplaned in the wrong county when I didn't see any Americans."

"Let me see your orders, soldier." After reviewing Blue's papers, the MP said, "You're AWOL. You were supposed to report to Long Bien yesterday. Go stand at the curb near that sign, and a military bus will be by soon to take you there. Good fucking luck, cherry."

The entire day was spent processing in and listening to in-country indoctrination and some gung ho asshole trying to recruit infantry-trained men into becoming snipers.

Blue thought, *I just met the first person I ever wanted to shoot—and he isn't even a gook. What a fucker!*

After chow and a few beers at the enlisted men's club, Blue tried to sleep. *Damn, is it my new Vietnam imagination—or is that artillery and enemy rockets in the distance?* Blue dreamed about battle all night long. The ones with bad endings woke him up. Blue tried going back to sleep and purposely replacing the bad dreams with victorious endings—and with him emerging safely. He made up his mind that he would continue that practice from that day forth.

After little sleep on his first night in Nam, Blue and the other troops gathered for an informal formation outside. They were startled by explosions that sounded like a cross between a whistle and an eerie groan. The incoming enemy rockets were zipping across an airfield less than a mile away.

A chubby sergeant in newly starched jungle fatigues and shiny jungle boots ran out and said, "Not to worry, men. This not unexpected, it's May 19, Ho Chi Minh's birthday. The bastard is seventy-nine today." He cleared his throat. "Just a quick word of congratulations, all of you FNGs, which stands for fucking new guys, you have been assigned to the First fucking Airmobile CAV."

Blue was catching on to the lingo quickly, and he understood that the word "fuck" was strategically placed into every sentence. It was even inserted into many words; the most common was "out-fucking-standing."

The cross fire ceased an hour later, and the base was quiet again. Word came back that air reconnaissance had quickly found Charlie's launch site and taken it out. They headed off to the firing range to witness and experience the weaponry and firepower they would be using. The US was well-equipped with the sheer terror of the red tracer bullets. They concluded the lesson by telling them what Charlie might be throwing back at them.

Just when everyone thought the demo was over, a Cobra helicopter gunship sprayed the strip right in front of them with gunfire at four thousand rounds per minute. Blue almost dropped a sympathy shit in his pants for Charlie.

The following morning, they took Blue and two other guys by jeep up to Bien Hoa to where the 1st CAV was settling in. Things were a bit chaotic. The CAV was still in the process of moving from Camp Evans, which was their base of operation in Phuoc Vinh, which was not far from the demilitarized zone on the border between South and North Vietnam.

Blue walked into a dingy Quonset hut only to find a first sergeant, a company clerk, a supply sergeant, and a private first class.

The first sergeant turned to his clerk and said, "Call the MPs. We got AWOL soldier right here." He turned to Blue and said, "Unless you'd rather go to the bush?"

They all laughed.

"Just kidding, your fucking-new-guy-ass is going to the bush anyway! Let me see your orders. You are Cantrell, aren't you?"

Blue said, "Yes, Sergeant."

"They call me Top because I'm the top swinging dick around here. Set your duffel bag up on the counter." He laughed. "Supply Sergeant Rick is going to dump everything out. Be sure to take your personal possessions 'cause he's going to take everything else. He will issue you a rucksack and show you how to pack it with the things you are going to need. Oh, by the way, do you also want a rifle?"

They all laughed again.

"We think you will—and two hundred rounds of ammo. Your platoon sergeant will issue you more as he sees fit at Firebase Fanning. That's our battalion's shithole."

Sergeant Rick put Blue's rucksack on the counter and started stuffing it with a mosquito net, poncho, poncho liner, olive drab socks, boxers, T-shirt, bath towel, and some other items. Six canteens were clipped to the outside. "Don't worry. Your platoon sergeant is going to dump all this shit out and show you how he wants you to pack it—and what you'll need. Oh, by the way, do you want a rifle?"

They all laughed again.

"And I think you'll need two hundred rounds of ammo. Hey, Top, the colonel's bird is headed out in thirty minutes."

Top said, "You're on it, Cantrell. Jim here will run you out to the chopper pad. You better go shit now, 'cause you guys will probably take on small arms fire, and you are probably going to soil those clean boxers you just put on this morning. And, anyways, it's going to take a few hours to get to Fanning."

Sergeant Top and his crew thought it was fun to fuck with the new soldiers. They looked forward to fucking with their heads and having the last laugh before the jeep ride to the chopper pad.

The colonel's Huey would be the last one Blue would ride in that still has its side doors. No formalities or introduction were given as the colonel, two pilots, and two door gunners boarded the chopper. Blue ended up sitting on a mailbag because there were no seats—and off they went.

Life was going to change forever for Blue.

Twenty minutes later, they were landing on a pad just outside of a shabby, chaotic firebase.

The door gunner yelled, "Hang tight … we have still one more stop before we get to Fanning." Stepping out of the chopper, the colonel went straight through an opening in the razor wire that surrounded the firebase. The two door gunners, the pilot, the copilot, and Blue were left standing there.

The pilot looked Blue up and down and said, "Damn! Look at the cherry FNG. This isn't by any chance your first ride on a chopper, is it?"

Blue nodded.

About ten minutes later, the colonel jumped into the chopper and put on his headgear.

As the chopper was starting up, the pilot turned to the colonel and said something before the colonel looked at Blue and smiled mischievously. The chopper took off, lifting the nose skyward and backward at a forty-five-degree angle.

The colonel looked back at Blue and smiled.

The next firebase they flew over had been overrun by Charlie the previous night, and the colonel wanted to check out the damage. Since there was a lot of activity in the area, they came in very high over the firebase and did what is known as a "Cambodian drop." The pilot wildly laid the chopper on its side, spiraling down in a corkscrew motion.

When they got to the ground, the pilot said, "Are you enjoying his first magic carpet ride?"

The Cambodian drop was the fastest controlled way to get a chopper to the ground from up high. This maneuver prevented the chopper from coming in low and with a long approach, which could expose them to ground fire.

The colonel returned fifteen minutes later. The takeoff was straight up as fast as the pilot could get the chopper up to two thousand feet to prevent them from becoming a small moving target.

Blue got the attention of one of the door gunners and shouted, "How far to Fanning?"

The gunner shouted, "Fifteen minutes—it's about twenty-five miles or so."

After seeing a firebase that had been overrun, Blue was thinking the worst. *A firebase that was closer to the rear than Fanning?* He was imagining a place no better than hell. Shaking his head, he said, "Fuck ... fuck ... fuck!"

Blue was glad to find Firebase Fanning looking somewhat organized and peaceful—at least for the moment. Sure enough, just as he had been told by the supply sergeant back in Ben Hue, the new platoon leader dumped the contents of his rucksack out on the ground and showed him how to load it to be ready for combat. He also showed him how to make a pup tent out of his poncho and mosquito net; issued Blue another 180 rounds of ammo; filled his canteens; and informed Blue that because he was the FNG, Blue would also carry a spare battery for the radio telephone operator.

The platoon leader proceeded to overlap the butt end of two M-16 magazines and duct-taped them together. "When you use up the ammo in one, you just flip it around and insert the other end for an additional eighteen rounds. They only load eighteen rounds in a twenty-round clip to help prevent jamming. Get your ass over to the mess tent and get yourself some grub so you can hit the hay early. We leave at the crack of dawn on a fucking fifteen-day patrol. You just follow your new platoon brothers tomorrow, and when we stop for a break

or lunch, I'll catch up with you to see if you've shit your pants."
The platoon leader smiled and walked off.

Blue was glad to see the platoon leader could smile. These men were the most serious individuals he had ever seen.

CHAPTER 3

SAN CRISTOBAL: SPIRITUAL JOURNEY

"CRYSTAL BLUE PERSUASION," TOMMY JAMES AND THE SHONDELLS

It was a sweltering summer night, hot enough to make the devil grin. After a night of tossing and turning, dawn finally began to peek into the early morning sky. Sunshine lay peacefully, watching the star-studded sky give way to morning and listening to the sparrows greeting the new day. After seeing Blue leave, her heart was left hanging from a fragile thread, her prayers were the only thing left that bonded her to her sanity. She felt lost and forlorn as she wrung her hands and gazed about her tepee, once again alone in her misery and despair. Still grieving, she arose from bed.

She started walking the path to the Rio Grande, crossed the decaying bridge to the other side of the river in search of her spiritual totem and friend. Upon crossing the river, she spotted the horse she called Rusty.

Two summers ago, she had befriended the unsightly equine. She visited him daily at the neighboring ranch known as the Weston Ranch. At the Weston Ranch, the horses in the herd were still unbroken. During her first summer visiting the wondrous animals, Sunshine developed a bond with the tall white gelding, which had an unusual color blend of burnt orange-rust covering his coat. The gelding appeared to be rusting like the old Ford truck abandoned and left rotting in the arroyo below. Sunshine loved the feel of his bristle horsehair, the feel of the power within each muscle that she traced with her hand. She loved the sound of a horse blowing, the smell of him from the hot southwestern sun heating his leatherlike horsehide. The craving juices bubbled inside her, and she longed to ride him, to be a part of him—as one—as only a horse and rider can be.

At first the rusted gelding refused to acknowledge her presence, but after endless days of tender words and caresses, she was able to hand-feed him. She read many books and manuals on horse training and conspired with anyone she thought might have any horse sense to share. Then, day by day, with cool, temperate coaxing, she was able to climb aboard the great rusted steed and attempt to ride him. She was thrown immediately, but she caught the gelding and tried again and again.

For the next twenty days, the horse called all the shots, until she began going with and observing the natural flow of nature and not controlling it. She started closely watching his reactions and his moves, only to discover that a horse could tell you a lot of things if you carefully watched, listened, and followed his signals. She paid attention to all the little signs—the way he moved his body, his ears, his eyes, the little whinnies and snorts—all his way of talking to her. There was his neigh of terror, his scream of rage, his nervous whinny, and his wonderfully rewarding snickers of longing or delight.

After spending an entire week having Yogi remove cactus needles from her backside after landing in a prickly-pear cactus bed, she suddenly saw the big picture. It was like seeing your city for the first time from an airplane. Finally, one afternoon, she led him into a dry creek bed, and in the deep loose sandpit, she looped a rope around his nose, leaped on his back, and rode him bareback to a standstill. She discovered that no horse could be a vicious bucker in deep sand. In the future, when she wanted to ride, she would start in the sand and gently work him into the pasture.

Sunshine became tireless, relentlessly focused on the task at hand and always expecting the unexpected. She devised her own system of breaking the horse, relying on a gentle but fearless approach with simple reward devices.

He became tamer and soon relaxed enough for Sunshine to ride him freely. Eventually, the horse and rider learned to trust one another and move as one.

She traded some of her paintings for an old halter, and he quickly adapted to it. She rode him bareback, with natural skill and grace.

Sunshine uncovered the halter, which she kept hidden in an old abandoned truck at the slope of the arroyo. She began by gently calling for the handsome gelding she had named Rusty. She heard the distant sound of a horse's hooves, which grew clearer as he galloped toward the sound of her voice. The gelding greeted her with a trusting whinny as he trotted up to her. She welcomed him with a hug and gave him his customary carrot from the batch she grew in her garden just for him.

Sunshine gently slipped the halter onto his massive neck, mounting the horse with ease. She wrapped her legs around his body and bent down to hug his neck. "Rusty, old boy, let's go for a ride. What do you say, huh, old boy?" Once again, she realized she was alone, and she began to cry.

Rusty perked up his ears as if he understood her mood. Holding a steady rein, Sunshine urged him first to a meandering gait and then graduated into a rhythmic lope along the open mesa. No longer listening to the chatter of her troubled mind, she allowed her spiritual awareness to give her directions from the divine compass within her soul.

Sunshine had never taken the great steed off the premises of the vast Weston Ranch, but today, she found herself being drawn to the immense mecca of Wheeler Peak. She knew the mountain's timeless tranquility would lighten her sorrows and rejuvenate her energy.

Horse and rider leisurely followed the sage-lined footpath, eventually crossing the Rio Grande by way of the Old Dunn Bridge. They traveled up trail through the rust-blackened volcanic cliffs that lined the river, venturing quietly past the nude bathers at the swimming hole, and then onward, they hazed through the thick brush and cactus of the Llano Arroyo Hondo. The fresh morning scent of the sage and dew began to ease her sadness.

Her lengthy pilgrimage took her traveling past the scar of the once-bustling San Cristobal Village. Using the canyon wall as a guide through the rugged trek, she then trailed steadily up the mountain canyon. This led her to the robust cedar-splashed hills and oak brush pathways that enshrouded the mountain's outpost. She had taken this path before with Blue, and her heart was flooded with his memory.

Hours later, Sunshine paused to look over the territory she and Rusty had traveled. With awe, she viewed the mingling landscape: the monochromatic snubbed desert, the shimmering cottonwoods, the lush green plateaus toward Questa, the basaltic mesas and Rio Grande Gorge, and on over to the southeast toward the great Mountain of Truchase. Upward they traveled to the never-ending carved arroyos and harrowing mountain switchbacks.

She was grateful to be a temporal guest in this preservationists' Eden. She stopped to take a look around, to feel and see the light around her, and to take in a deep cleansing breath. Looking up to the mountainside of Wheeler Peak, she thought of her father and Blue. She began to whisper a chant of sorrow, which led her to sing a song of friendship and love. She was silent. This was her quiet time with God and Mother Nature. She gathered the surrounding energy to enlighten her soul. She released a bottled-up sigh, continued to bask in nature's beauty, and said, "Thank you, dear God, for this beautiful land."

The splendor of the country revived her pioneer spirit just as she knew it must have affected the brave ancestors before her—and the ancient Tiwa Taos Puebloan people. Sunshine was statuesque, tall, strong, and naturally vibrant. She glowed as she sat on the stalwart steed.

She reached the heart of the mountain as the hot, high noon sun-cracked in the clean, clear, azure skies. She found herself entering the conifer gateway of Cow Lake. The lake's clear water reflected the sky, inviting Sunshine to bathe. She tethered Rusty to a bush at the edge of the lake, then gratefully shed her tricolored Roy Roger cowboy boots, frayed cutoff hip-hugger jeans with a blue and white bandanna that she used as a belt, and tie-dyed halter top, and then she gracefully slipped into the cool water, gasping for breath as she sank into the chilling water.

Once in the bracing water, she could feel the sting escaping her sun-scorched skin, releasing the tension of her muscles. She gracefully floated on her back, looking up at the sky, and prayed, "Dear God, heavenly Father, surround me with your light and energy." Sunshine knew that her prayers were her armor.

She climbed out of the lake and found a large, dark rock on which to bask. Lying naked and dazed by the heat, the only sounds she could hear were the energized rustle of the tall pine trees, the jaybirds scolding their rivals, and her own heart drumming. A potpourri of wildflowers and fresh pine-scented air were so pure that she thought she would burst her lungs taking so many deep, cleansing breaths.

She prayed, "Dear God, when I am unsuccessful in accepting things that I cannot change, it is time for me to surrender to you." She knew surrendering was not quitting or giving up; it was setting aside her ego and relying upon the spirit within herself for peace. Like welcoming rain on dry soil, divine life surges forth, tender ideas, nurtured by faith, grow and yield an abundance of good. She whispered, "I give thanks that divine love prevails in my life."

She lay on her stomach; in a daze she watched several butterflies playing tag. As the Sun's rays danced on her slender, tanned body, caressing her shapely buttocks and back, a light warm breeze blew fingers through her golden-brown hair. She was content to be in the arms of Mother Nature and God's golden light. Soon waves of warmth overcame Sunshine as she slipped into a peaceful sleep.

The afternoon passed, as did the clouds. She felt her sleep disturbed by her intuition that someone was watching her. Startled, she quickly sat up and looked around.

A large man with a grotesque rodent-like face was leering at her. His small teeth jutted out of cracked lips beneath a nose that was too large for his pocked face.

Sunshine jumped behind the rock and quickly donned her meager clothing.

Licking his lips, the man spoke with a cotton-thick mouth, slurring his words as if it took an effort to speak. "I didn't mean to startle you; I was just enjoying the scenery." Washing down his statement, he took a big swig of whiskey from the bottle he was hugging to his chest.

Sunshine's face flamed with embarrassment. "I thought I was alone."

The hermit guzzled another drink from his almost empty bottle and scratched his bristled jowl. His leering smile exposed his rotted teeth as he beamed with perverse delight. "I was beginning to wonder if ya was real or just a flashback from an acid trip."

Sunshine was lost as to where to lead the conversation. Sickened, she hissed, "Now that you've had your cheap afternoon's entertainment, I'll be leaving."

His squinting, jet-black, unreadable eyes never released her. "What's your hurry, princess?" The pallid, bloated rodent attempted a gallant bow and then stumbled off balance. "I'm called Jazz."

Too frightened to even blink, she said, "I've got to be heading back." It was all she could manage to say.

The creature's short, plump frame stiffened, and he quickly rushed to her side. His threatening massive grit overpowered her small frame. "Now, uh, there's no need to rush off, princess. We could enjoy this whiskey together, and uh, each other's company."

Sunshine wrinkled her nose in disgust from the stench of stale whiskey and repulsive body odor that filled her nostrils. Combined fear, nausea, and panic caused her knees to weaken; she tried to move away from him, only to be caught by Jazz. Wildly exasperated from fear and anger she yelled, "Let me go!"

As she squirmed, he tightened his grip. With a whining voice, he said, "Now, come on, princess, I haven't had any company to ... uh, uh, well, uh, ... come on, princess, just one little drink." He seemed proud of his smooth logic.

Sunshine cringed. "I don't drink—and I've got to get back home. Now let me go, you creep!"

He responded angrily, "What's wrong, princess? Ain't I good enough for a little hippie chick like you? I don't bite." He laughed at his own statement. "Well, not too hard anyway."

Sunshine quickly scouted around in panic, hoping for someone to help. She tried to flee, but in one quick motion, he grabbed her by the hair with one of his massive hands and instantly took hold of her arm with the other hand.

Frantically, she punched him in the chest and face. The power of her blows did not affect him. She pleaded with him, saying, "No, no, just let me go. Damn it—let me go!"

Piteously wiping the drool from his chin, he said, "Well, princess, I won't do that." He picked Sunshine up as if she were a little rag doll, pulled off his belt, and tied her hands together. When she began to scream, he pulled off her bandanna-belt and tied it around her mouth. He carried her over to Rusty and tossed her onto her horse as if it didn't take a bit of effort. "Now, princess, let us be off to my palace."

CHAPTER 4

MANZANITA: RODENT MAN

"MAGICAL MYSTERY TOUR," THE BEATLES

The clear blue skies vanished and were quickly replaced by overcast clouds as the threatening thunderclouds gathered over the darkening mountain pass. The monstrous rodent-like man staggered along, laboring from every step he took with his burdensome body. He strained from exertion, leading his burro and Rusty, with Sunshine tied on top, to his nearby mountain shack.

The pit of Sunshine's stomach had a sickness that could not be eased, but the ride gave Sunshine time to gather her wits. Appalled by her stupidity for not having prepared herself for her journey, her heart gave a sickening lurch when she realized she hadn't even told Yogi or Tylor where she was going. There was no one to help her.

Wide-eyed and fearful, as Sunshine rode, she continually forced herself to keep a clear mind and gather her courage to handle this disgusting situation.

Among the tall mountain pines, they came to a battered, diminutive shack. With laboring breath, Jazz pulled Sunshine down from the horse. Sunshine could feel his heart pounding as he carried her inside under his arm. He untied her hands and the bandanna from her mouth, as he struggled with every breath, and he tossed her onto a pile of straw in the corner.

Pleased with himself and his afternoon find, Jazz breathlessly bellowed, "Now, princess, let's celebrate. Let's have that drink I promised you!" Gasping for air and continually coughing, he limped over to a wooden box that posed as a cupboard and took out a new bottle of whiskey. He started to clear his throat, which ended in an uncontrollable hacking cough. His shape and posture were reminiscent of an overripe melon that had gone soft. He had a grayish hue to his grisly puffy face; watery black eyes that where outlined in red; and a bluish tinge around his fat lips. Jazz unbuttoned his shirt, exposing his apelike, overflowing belly, scratched his crotch, and said, "Come, princess, and share a drink with me." He sat down at a table made from old wooden crates, continually making grotesque, toilsome grunting noises intermingled with hacking coughs and gasps for air.

Numb and stunned from the afternoon's events, Sunshine sat bravely in the corner. A swarm of busy flies danced around the room, enjoying the smells of rotten food, putrid body order, and rancid liquor, which overpowered the tiny shack. Refusing to look him in his eyes, and unable to bear his lustful stares, she walked slowly toward him. She kept reminding herself that she could outwit this drunk—just as she had proudly done with others many times before at the commune.

Hating him, Sunshine stood proud and tall, yet she was barely able to breathe or even speak; the sound of her brave heart pounded and blasted in her head.

When she grew near the table, Jazz added to her fright by planting a rude lusty whack upon her ass, which brought a screech of pain to her.

"Yeah, you are a lovely little princess," he said, as his enormous hands reached out and yanked off her halter top. Then, using his other hand, he groped her breast.

Sunshine stepped back quickly from his reach.

Jazz was amused with himself and let out a long, loud, growling laugh.

She became livid with rage and struck out at him in her fury.

Jazz caught her wrist and pulled her hard against him. He chuckled unmercifully at her as she struggled to free herself. "Yes, princess, I think I have met my match." His hand moved behind Sunshine's head, forcing her face to slant against his, and his dry, cracked lips twisted across her mouth, hurting her.

Sunshine controlled her urge to vomit as she felt the heavy hammer-like thud of his heart against her bare breast, and she was all too aware of his grotesque body pressed tightly to her slender form. His arm was clasped around her waist in a merciless grip. She felt his hand behind her head, large and capable of crushing her skull without effort, but somewhere deep inside her, her courage was sparked, She twisted her mouth from his and her voice quivered in fright as she said, "Jazz, I think I will have that drink you promised."

Jazz released her abruptly and slurred, "Yeah, princess. I knew you'd come around. I knew you'd party with me. Now let's have a drink."

Sunshine quickly grabbed a shirt that was hanging on a nail on the wall and scrambled to cover her bareness.

Outside, the storm began to open up, rain began crashing onto the roof, and lightning rumbled in the distant valley below. They sat at the table together, and Jazz guzzled down several generous swallows, closing one eye as if trying to focus, and then handed her the bottle.

Living in a commune where some people's sole purpose in life was to see who could get completely fucked-up-blasted-drunk or stoned, Sunshine learned early on that people were thoroughly insulted and often became violent if you did not drink or get high with them. She would take a bottle and pretend to be drinking from it; she would accept the bottle, press it to her lips, and tilt it up only to allow a tiny amount or any of the foul liquor into her mouth.

Her eyes misting, Sunshine held the bottle up to her mouth and pretended to take a drink.

"Good girl, princess." Jazz laughed and gave her a proud, forceful pat on the back, which caused her to spit the whiskey all over the table. This caused such amusement from Jazz that he laughed so hard his face turned beet red. Purplish veins protruded around his reddened, black eyes as he savagely grabbed back the bottle from Sunshine, choking from the swig of whiskey he took. This didn't stop him from chugging down more.

Sunshine played this drinking game with him until the bottle was empty and Jazz was on the verge of passing out. "Let me get us another bottle," she said. "You just stay seated so I can wait on you."

Jazz liked this idea and slapped his knee in delight. "Ooh-kay, princess, get us another bottle."

The lightning outside drew closer, and with each crash, Sunshine's nerves frazzled more. Her mind raged with horror. Mustering up all the courage of a true warrior she possessed, she went over to the wooden box from where he had retrieved the first bottle. Grateful that there was still another full bottle, she pulled it out.

Approaching Jazz from behind, with all of her strength and spirit, she clobbered the full bottle over his head, and the bottle broke into a thousand little pieces, as his grotesque huge head slammed to the table.

In a flash, Sunshine ran for the door, opened it with rage, and ran smack-dab into a man about to enter. Without even looking to see who it was, she started wailing and wildly thrashing at him. Still in a panic, she began to scream and pound her fist at him. "I've got to get out of here. Please … let me go!"

The stranger gathered up her wrists to stop her from hitting him and calmly said, "It's okay. I will not hurt you. I can help you. It's okay. Calm down."

Sunshine broke his hold, ran and jumped on Rusty's bare back, grabbed his reins, and set him in a gallop down the mountain. The stranger flew back in amazement and then ran for his horse. Jumping into his saddle, he dashed after the woman.

He chased the horse and rider for a half a mile. With his superior riding skills, it didn't take him long to catch up. He grabbed hold of Rusty's reins. Sunshine slid off the excited horse and began running down the mountain in the rain.

"What the hell? God damn it. Now what?" he said as he

ran after Sunshine. His long strides had an advantage over hers, and as he wrapped his rock-hard muscular arms around her small frame, he said, "I will not hurt you. I want to help you. What the hell happened up there anyway?"

His words finally sunk into her, and Sunshine tried to slow her breathing. She tried to speak, but no words came out. She sat in the rain for several minutes and tried to clear her mind and catch her breath. She bent forward onto her knees as her fear threatened to turn to vomit. Gasping for breath, she tried to calm herself.

Taking several deep cleansing breaths, for the first time, she looked up at him. He smiled slowly, and a warm shock went through her, which reassured her that she was going to be all right. The rain let up, and bit by bit, her nerves began to calm. Trembling, she stood up and gazed up from his cowboy boots, over the length of his long legs, flat belly, broad chest, and muscular profile, which led up to the most handsome, tanned, clean-shaven face she had ever seen. His features appeared impressively stern and foreboding. He had a tense, almost angry look to the crisp, chiseled line of his jaw and taut cheeks. His grayish-blue eyes had tiny wrinkles around them, which made him appear perplexed with life.

There was something immediately attractive about this man, but she couldn't put her finger on what it was. He just radiated a pleasant demeanor and energy. Looking into his eyes, she could see that they were filled with concern as he searched hers. Completely exhausted, both physically and emotionally, Sunshine sank back onto the floor of the forest and released a huge sigh.

The cowboy knelt next to her, wrapped his damp jean jacket around her, and cocked his handsome brow. "My name is J. W. I'd like to help you get back home. I can deal with the hermit in the shack later." He released a huge sigh. "Let me help you to shelter before we're both soaked to the bone. There is an old homestead cabin down the pass about a mile. Are you able to ride?"

Sunshine was stunned and still unable to speak, but she offered a grateful nod. As they mounted his horse, the black clouds above opened up again as a drizzle began to fall. Sunshine welcomed the rain falling on her; she felt each pure raindrop cleansing her body from the filth she had just experienced with Jazz. She was grateful for the long ride, which allowed her to regain some of her composure.

J. W. placed Sunshine in front of him on his mare, towing the rusted gelding behind as they rode down the mountain to San Cristobal Canyon and the abandoned homestead. The tiny cabin appeared to be frozen in the past and was weathered from the elements. For both the soaking wet riders, it looked very inviting. Sunshine said a quick silent prayer and thanked God for safety.

CHAPTER 5

LOBO: INTRODUCTIONS

"TIME OF THE SEASON," THE ZOMBIES

The rain clouds burst forth, soaking both riders and the rich forest near Lobo Ridge. J. W. swung down off his horse and helped her down off her horse. Sunshine felt as if she was floating down in the soft strength of JW's hands.

He asked, "What is your name?"

"My name is Sunshine," she answered.

He gallantly escorted Sunshine inside.

The tiny abandoned casita proved to be the perfect refuge. The empty cabin was rustic, dusty, and tattered. The large stone fireplace and the small pile of dried wood and brush looked very inviting to their chilled bodies.

J. W. briskly rubbed his arms and said, "Let me get a fire

going." With the skill of a true mountain man, he proceeded to do just that. "Sunshine, I'll be right back. I need to tie the horses."

It was getting dark outside, and the rain surged in a downpour and then relaxed into a comforting song in the forest. Sunshine knelt by the fire, basking in its flames. She combed through her long hair with her fingers and become so mesmerized by the flames that she barely noticed when J. W. returned. She released a sigh and whispered, "Thank you, Mr. J. W., for helping me."

J. W. laughed. "Generally speaking, fancy titles and nightshirts are a waste of time. Please just plain old J. W. is fine. You can forget the 'Mister.'" J. W. stared down at Sunshine. Despite her dilapidated state, she was a fresh and naturally beautiful woman. J. W. squatted next to her, took off his hat, and ran his fingers through his hair. He looked at her apologetically and asked, "What the hell happened up there anyway? And why were you ridin' my horse?"

Still shivering from the cold, Sunshine looked over to him and realized he was J. W. Weston, the ranch owner. "Oh, sir, I'm sorry for taking Rusty off your ranch ..."

Laughing, he said, "Rusty? You mean you've named that ugly rust-colored gelding? I didn't even know he was broke to ride. I was fixin' to sell that ornery critter for glue." Still laughing, he shook his head.

Sunshine said, "Please ... I can explain." Her tongue felt unusually clumsy. "I live near your ranch, and over the past couple of years, I would visit Rusty, uh ... your horse, and every day, I began by bringing him treats, then I gained his trust, working with him a little at a time until, eventually, I tamed him enough to ride him." Sunshine gave him a lengthy description of how she read books at the Taos library about how to tame a horse—and the weeks and months it took to gentle his spirit.

She was afraid she was in big trouble and expected him to call her a horse thief. She gave him a smile, hoping it would calm the storm.

J. W. smiled broadly in return and laughed. "Good God, lady! Let's sign you up for the rodeo." Shaking his head in disbelief, he added, "I can't believe you tamed that old horse."

Suddenly worried, she asked, "You're not going to still sell him for glue, are you?"

Laughing, he said, "No, I guess I can use him as a ranch horse now that you've tamed him for me."

He cocked a handsome brow and gave her a lengthy inspection. "I was checkin' the ranch fences when I saw you leave with that rusted horse. I've been trackin' you for some six hours, trying to unravel the maze of trails you were leaving behind. How the hell did you end up at that wacko hermit's place?"

Blushing and embarrassed, she said, "I am so embarrassed, but I was napping at Cow Lake when that gross, disgusting drunk kidnapped me." Sunshine snarled. "That creep tied my hands and forced me to go with him to his cabin. He wanted me to drink with him." Suddenly embarrassed, Sunshine stared at the fire.

J. W. shook his head. "I'll bet he wanted to have a drink with you! Girl, you could have been ..."

She swallowed hard. "I was so scared. And I think I may have hurt that damn creep. I smashed a full bottle of whiskey over his head."

J. W. laughed. "That blasted, fatheaded old fool well deserved it and more." He released a soft silent snicker. "Darned if he ain't as crooked as a barrel of snakes anyway. I'll send Sheriff Esquibel up to check on him tomorrow—and you don't need to worry about that gross, fat bastard hermit." J. W. leaned over toward Sunshine, and with tenderness and sincerity that even surprised himself, he gently lifted her chin, looked into her jade-colored eyes, and said, "You're okay now. I'll take you back to your home at mornin' daybreak."

Sunshine wasn't prepared for the shock that went through her from his simple touch. His rich masculine voice was as pleasing as his good looks.

"You're still trembling. I'd better build up our fire." J. W.

threw more wood on the fire, scooted next to Sunshine, and began rubbing her arms to help radiate the heat of the fire.

Sunshine said, "J. W., you're soaking wet. Take off your shirt, and I'll hang it by the fire."

J. W. tossed his cowboy hat into the corner, unbuttoned his shirt, handed it to Sunshine, and thought, *Sunshine, you are as sweet as your name.*

She accepted his shirt and spread it out on a pile of pine needles near the fire. In stepping away from the fire, she felt a chilling breeze and involuntarily began to quiver.

J. W. quickly stood up, wrapped his arms around her, and smiled. "Come back near the fire. You're still chilled."

Sunshine had never been affected as deeply by such casual contact. She was stunned by this odd combination of strength and gentleness, which wasn't difficult to find appealing.

His wet hair glistened in the firelight. Removing his shirt only confirmed his broad shoulders and revealed the athletic muscles across his chest. She was actually with a man who, for the first time in her life, seemed to fulfill every letter of her desire. *Surely, there is a flaw in this man; there has to be.* She couldn't help but look into his eyes to search for an answer to her sudden intense desire. The sheer power of him made her tremble.

Once again, he mistook her quiver for her being cold and tightened his embrace as they moved closer together. As their eye met, the attraction was too immense. It was a natural spontaneous response as he gently tilted her head up to his and placed a tender kiss on her lips. That simple kiss only demanded another. He drew her to him and kissed her again. His lips brushed back and forth across hers, nudging, pulling, and pressing open a pathway for his tongue to enter.

Moist heat, silky smooth, on a new swirl of sensations, Sunshine forgot to breathe. She opened her eyes, only to find his in return.

His brows gathered, and a sheer smile touched his lips.

It was a kiss like nothing she had ever experienced or even dreamed of experiencing. She drew in a deep breath and said, "What a wonderful kiss." The wonderment of it all overcame her. Without any shyness, she said, "Kiss me again." She stood on the tips of her toes to reach up to his lips.

Without hesitation, his hand promptly found the back of her head and drew her closer to him. He kissed her with more passion than he had ever experienced. He could feel the thunder of her heartbeat.

Even though their meager clothing prevented any further intimate contact, the ample swell of manhood beneath the snug-fitting, sharply creased Wrangler jeans gave Sunshine bold evidence of his masculinity.

He kissed her tenderly, taking care to slowly arouse her senses. The kiss grew to one of ravishment, their tongues sensuously thrusting and exploring, and then both withdrew, breathless and stunned by the tantalizing desire they felt.

The raw energy about him was undeniable, and the electric current drew her to him. She found him irresistibly exciting. The nearness and his fresh manly scent filled her head. She chided herself for lacking poise and willpower. She realized she had just met this man, yet her attraction to him was so powerful, so heartfelt, and so complete. She stepped over to the window to hide her flushing cheeks. The silence grew long and stilted, and feeling a need to speak, she said, "The rain is refreshing after the heat ..."

J. W. noted her discomfort and stepped next to her, and his smile could have melted the glaciers on top of Wheeler Pike. "Sunshine, you are the most allurin' creature I have ever met." *Damn*, he thought. *She could provoke the most chaste of saints. She is the personification of sensuality.*

In the dim light of the cabin, she looked up to him with purity as if she had every answer he ever questioned.

Her smile made J. W.'s heart skip a beat.

"Kiss me again," she said.

Both felt encased in an inescapable cocoon of desire.

His mind overtook all human reasoning; his male animal instincts wanted to fuck that beautiful pussy till she either exploded or passed out. He kissed her slowly and tantalizingly, increasing the ardor of anticipation.

They molded together naturally and sank steadily in front of the fireplace onto the straw-covered floor. Their kiss became passionate, and their desire increased as he slowly nibbled and kissed her throat, working down to the warm space between her supple breasts.

J. W. paused and looked into her eyes, checking to see if she wanted him to go on.

Sunshine kissed him and removed the huge shirt she wore.

An explosion of desire overtook him at the sight of her beautiful bare breasts. His hands explored nimbly and gently rolled her nipples between his fingers. Sunshine's gasps led to an intensity of eroticism, and he skillfully sucked on her breasts.

In the desperation of hunger, they quickly, frantically removed their clothing.

J. W. gently pulled her on top of him. As her small, exquisite body lay on top of his, she could feel his firm desire. Through passionate kisses, their bodies bonded together. Rapturous waves of pleasure began to roll through her loins, and his hand began stroking the curling of the soft down between her legs, teasing the sweet, moist lips beneath. She moaned in pleasure. Suddenly, as if another worldly entity named passion rolled him on top of her, J. W. intensified his kiss, and then he adroitly drove in the zeppelin of his manhood, penetrating her by exquisitely gradual degrees until she begged him to fill her completely. It was as if the goddess of passion and desire had taken over and was choreographing their every move.

She gasped and said, "Please, I need you." Her arms locked around his strong neck, and her slender legs tightened around him as he penetrated deeper and more forcefully.

He explored every inch of her femininity, eventually forming a wonderful rhythm that didn't end until their passion was used up. Afterward, they just held each other in bliss, basking in the glow and feeling as if they were entwined and levitating.

For the rest of the night J. W. and Sunshine laid on a pile of their clothes in front of a small warm fire in an enigmatic essence, nuzzling, hugging, and kissing as they listened to the soft, steady raindrops plunking on top of the old metal roof as if playing a melody, and coyotes howled in the distance. J. W. shook his head and laughed. "Sunshine, I still can't believe you tamed that rusted horse! What did you name him? Rusty?"

Sunshine's eyes sparkled as she beamed him a smile and nodded.

"Hell, I'll bet you could tame those blasted coyotes outside too. I suppose you've bewitched that horse as you have me." He laughed again. "How many times did he buck you off? I would have loved to watch you."

Sunshine responded, "Oh, I had my share of bruises after the endless times of being thrown." She told him how she saw his horse, earned his trust, continued to try to ride him, and finally used the sandpit to help her break the spirited steed.

J. W. raised his brow in wonder and said, "Did you ever consider rodeo bronco riding? Hell! You could be the next national champion and take away my title."

Her eyes admirably sparkled. "You're a rodeo cowboy?"

His ego beamed with pride and conceit, and he said, "Yes, ma'am, a national champion bronc rider." His laughter led to another long, warm kiss—followed by a night filled with harmonious lovemaking and pure wonderment as the universe unfolded them.

Upon daylight, Sunshine stood and quickly donned her sparse clothing.

J. W. playfully tackled her back onto the pile of straw and said, "Well, this is the funniest way to meet a girl."

She giggled. "It's been said that coincidence is that of God's choosing."

They continued to laugh and tease one another.

J. W. stared with lustful eyes down at the bewitching woman beside him. He couldn't find any imperfection in this sweet, beautiful lady. When he realized the sudden infatuation he held for her, he laughed heartily. "Oh my God, the lovely lady I have found—and who has captivated me—has yet to tell me what her real name is and where she lives."

Returning his smile, she replied, "As I said, my name is Sunshine."

"Sunshine? No, really, what is your real name? Isn't that a nickname?"

She softly answered, "That is my real name. My name from birth is Sunshine McFadden." She paused and looked at him with questioning eyes. "And I'm from the New Buffalo commune on the other side of the river from your ranch."

J. W. sat up, shook his head, and snickered. "You live with the hippies at the commune? You're a hippie?" Images came jerking into his emotions. *What the holy fuck?* A blast of zemblanity filled him—that inevitable discovery of what he would rather not know.

She said, "Yes, I believe in the cause, and I celebrate my life with the brothers and sisters of the commune."

J. W. was stunned; he had built up such a prejudice against his hippie neighbors. He hated hippies. He had never dreamt that he would fall for one! Confused, he wrapped his arms around her, kissed her forehead, and said, "It's okay, sweet lady." Mentally, his emotions clashed. He kept his face immobile. It felt like his emotions were crawling all over him. He thought, *What the fuck have you done? You let your dick rule you over your brain again. Fuck!* It took all that he had to not say those words out loud.

The cabin door flew open and flooded the tiny cabin with bright morning light.

J. W.'s brother-in-law, Joel, stood in the doorway with a huge smirk. "I tracked your horses here. I thought maybe you needed help, but uh … I can see you don't." Joel looked embarrassed, but he was thoroughly amused.

J. W. mumbled, "Miss Sunshine, I'll give you a ride back to …"

They mounted their horses and rode back down the mountain in silence.

J. W.'s prejudice and stubborn pride kicked him square in his chest.

Joel rode behind the two in silence, unable to hide his big smirk.

When they arrived at the Old Dunn Bridge, Sunshine slid off Rusty, patted his neck, and walked off without looking back at J. W. She was confused and hurt. She felt a hurricane blow through her self-esteem; it started in her heart and shot emotional acid through her veins and up into her mind, causing an emotional stroke.

CHAPTER 6

LONG KHANH: FIRST BATTLE

"THE CRUEL WAR IS RAGING,"
PETER, PAUL, AND MARY

Fuck me! Blue hated getting in these Hueys. Perpetual chopper anxiety was guaranteed after hearing all the battle stories from the other battle-hardened grunts. Once they lifted into the air, he couldn't bring himself to look down. He sat with his legs hanging down in the opening of the missing chopper door. All he could do was look around and watch the other guys to see if they were as scared and numb as he was.

He finally summoned the courage to look down between his new boots as the ground dropped farther away. Blue was so self-conscious about his boots and embarrassed because they were so new. New boots were a sure sign of an FNG.

The pilot dropped them in the LZ, somewhere in the abyss of Long Khanh. The platoon wasn't exactly thrilled about being under so much enemy fire. The chopper's skids touched the ground for a split second, and the pilot screamed as loud as he could to the grunts to get the hell out of his chopper.

Blue could hear bullets ripping through the metal of the chopper as the pilot pulled up on the stick and headed for the skies. Not all of the guys had jumped out of the chopper yet, leaving the last three men to jump the six-foot drop to the ground.

As he bolted the hell out of there, the pilot yelled, "Good luck, boys!"

They watched other grunts from the other choppers touch down with the front skids and then bounce back into the air within seconds. It was the classic hot landing zone small arms firepower. From the tree line about three hundred yards away, sweeping AK-47 green tracer rounds gave away the gooks' position. The men dove frantically toward the high elephant grass that hadn't been blown flat by the rotor blades.

Not much to be running for in the way of cover, but it's better than nothing.

The troops dropped into a fast, low belly crawl straight to the tree line. When they'd all reached cover in the tree line, the sergeant made a check. Blue was amazed to see that only one had been hurt; a guy had sprained an ankle jumping from the chopper. When he'd jumped from the chopper into the muck, his best semi-clean uniform was covered with muck. Worst of all, he stunk; it was more than likely water buffalo crap mixed with piss.

The other platoons assembled and moved further down the road toward the base of a hill, south of Xuan Loc with routine rest stops, and took cover in the jungle. Sitting, waiting, and listening, they slowing moved on with a cautious, quiet pace, sometimes taking up to five to six seconds per a step. This went on for hours until nightfall. A dinner of C-rats was pulled from everyone's rucksacks.

There sure wasn't anybody Blue wanted to thank for them, but he was grateful to have something to eat.

Sergeant Cash crawled around to the men and hissed, "No sense in a getting' too relaxed, 'cause that motha-effin Charlie ain't ever goin' to relax. Just when ya get all good and comfortable, he'll come over and take a big old AK-47 shit on us."

Blue was about to light up a cigarette, and just as he stuck the match, all the freaky sounds of the jungle stopped. There was no dwindling or fading away; it was all done in a single instant. It was as though some signal had been transmitted out to all the living creatures. All the bats, birds, rats, snakes, monkeys, and insects had picked up on a frequency that a thousand years in the jungle conditioned you to receive.

Blue wondered if they knew what was coming next. He sat and strained his ears for any sound, any piece of information through the humid air, and wondered if hundreds of Vietcong were coming and going, moving, or had him in their rifle sights. The silence was all-encompassing, almost suffocating. His imagination kicked in, and he began to hear impossible things nearby and in the distance: the damp roots breathing, the ferns growing, the fruit on trees sweating, the fervid action of bugs, and even the heartbeats of tiny animals. He sustained that sensitivity for a long time, every nerve of his body reaching to receive any possible sign of sound until the babbling and chattering and shrieking of the jungle started up again. The prattle of the jungle somehow brought him comfort like a blanket of noise that cloaked him and his buddies in safety, his personal warning system.

As night closed in, the harsh functionings of consciousness played in his head. He looked up at the stars glimmering through the triple canopy jungle in the night sky of the combat zone. He held a cigarette between his lips, unable to light up since the glow would give away his position and make his face the main target. Blue refused to sleep because he couldn't trust sleep, but he could always trust his platoon brothers around him to cover his ass.

His trigger finger and mind were touchy, and he subconsciously squeezed his butthole so tight it was cramping.

He was ready for all hell to break loose at any moment's notice, and he was ready to blow it all to hell—animal, vegetable, or mineral—and especially those gooks, dinks, zipperheads, VC, NVA, or anything else wearing black silk pajamas or an North Vietnamese Army uniform. After all, they had brought him there.

Blue couldn't quiet his mind, and his soldier-trained ego kicked in. *Fuck it all,* he thought. He and every grunt knew that this damn war could never be won; they could only bomb the place into oblivion. They were fighting Charlie in his own backyard. Charlie was fighting for his homeland, and Blue was fighting because he was called to duty to serve his country. His memory file recalled their instructor at Fort Ord quoting John Wayne: "It ain't a good war, but it's the only damn war we got." *Damn gung ho lifers,* thought Blue.

As the last vestiges of light came through the trees, Blue silently watched the other men. He studied the messages in their strung-out, emotionless faces as they stared into the jungle. Their eyes were locked into the dark. All the youth had been sucked from their faces—some only eighteen years old—and all the color was drawn from their skin. He could see their fear through their pursed white lips. Some of these guys were there on their second or third tour, and the war was aging the shit out of them from the overall fatigue and all the adrenaline they experienced. Every sudden flash-bang of intense combat would spike their adrenaline through the roof.

His buddy Troy was eating candy bar after candy bar, and Sergeant Cash obsessively combed his handlebar mustache with his Roy Rogers pocketknife. Blue could no more blink than spit; balls and bowels were turning over together, and his senses were working like strobes.

Not a word was spoken between any of them the entire night; absolute silence was strictly observed. The men took no real rest. Sleep was a commodity that you felt safe in taking when you were on secure ground in an atmosphere of reprieve; sleep kept you from falling apart, the way cold, fat-laden C-rations kept you from starving.

Blue heard auditory hallucinations of twigs snapping, footsteps, rifles cocking, and Vietnamese whispers. It felt like it would be days before he would see the dawn. Blue was violently assaulted when a fire ant flew up his nose—along with the growing feeling of cold even though they were is a miserably hot jungle. When fatigue finally set in, Blue crawled under his poncho, which was stretched tight between two trees with spare boot laces and only eighteen inches off the ground. They were given an air mattress that they inflated just halfway full so it wouldn't make a sound when they crawled in, rolled over, or crawled out. As Blue drifted off to sleep, he thought about the day when this whole terrifying nightmare would be behind him and he would be sleeping in a real bed back in the real world.

Morning stirred them into action. The men grabbed their gear. Most were equipped with M-16 rifles, some carried AK-47s they had taken from dead VC, and a few carried heavier M-60 machine guns. One grumpy old bastard carried an M3, better known as a grease gun, a shorter gangster-looking gun with a long magazine sticking out the side. Everyone left the safety off and set to fully "ought-a-get-em" (automatic) as they started their patrol into the bush.

"Get your asses moving," Sergeant Cash called. "Let's go play Cowboys and Injuns. Let's go put a few holes in some black silk pajamas."

One of the grunts from the other platoon called back, "No slack in the mother-effin' CAV."

Troy said, "Hey, Blue, what's the difference between the CAV and the Boy Scouts? The Boy Scouts have mature adult leadership. Dig it!" He laughed a foolhardy look right into Sergeant Cash's eyes.

They headed out from their night defensive position in a long line of maybe a hundred men. The M-16s, M-60s, mortars, 762 LAAW-portable one-shot rocket-launchers, PRC-25 radios, and corpsmen fanning out into some kind of sweep formation, about a hundred yards apart with small teams of specialists in each platoon.

A Cobra gunship flew close hover-cover until it came to some low hills ahead, and then more Cobras came to the low hills until they'd passed safely through them. Sixteen weeks of training had taught Blue that you could be in the most protected space in Vietnam and still know that your safety was provisional and that blindness, loss of legs or arms or balls, major and lasting disfigurement or death, or any of the fucking whole rotten deal could come in on freaky Friday as easily as taking a shit. Find, kill, search, and destroy. It was more than a tactic from the upper Cracker Jack's command psyche. It'd become a war saturated with death and hatred.

Thirty yards from a small village, all hell broke loose. With his M-16 blazing in a battle for the first time, Blue and his platoon fired cover for a four-man recon team as they tried to get back to the platoon. When they were in the clear, one of them joined them in the gunfire and shouted, "I fuckin' love ya, man!"

Blue put as much fire as his trigger finger would let him, but he couldn't tell whether any of it was coming back or not. The continual rounds of gunfire filled his ears and then filled his head until he thought he was hearing gunfire through his entire being. Adrenaline shot through his body. An unbelievably amazing rocket rush of adrenaline hit him and continued until he was high on war. Woven into this high was an element of fear.

Fear has many manifestations. In combat, it is not as simple as fight or flight. There is an intense urgency of self-preservation that is not like the old water balloon fights. If you get hit, the light goes out forever. Fear in the terrifying experience of battle manifests itself in a feeling that grips the entire body in deep pain, maybe a repulsive smell, perhaps a putrid taste in one's mouth, and sometimes not even realizing they had puked. When the battle ended, a terrifying thought came over you: Perhaps you died and are now in a death dream that you are still alive.

About thirty minutes later, the last cracks of gunfire faded away. Blue didn't know if the action had taken seconds, minutes, or hours—or if it had just been a dream. A wave of confusion and nausea swept over him, and the heat from his rifle reassured Blue that he indeed participated in the return fire.

The village had been taken successfully by Blue's platoon and one other platoon. As they entered the grounds, there were no NVA left except for the dead. Dead gook bodies bobbed in the river, dead bodies littered the grounds, dead bodies sprawled out on the walls, hung over barbed wire, thrown on top of each other, or up into the trees like terminal acrobats. Dead gook bodies littered the area like ants from an ant farm emptied of their plastic container and stepped on by an angry child.

A badass-looking guy with an M-60 stopped to piss into the open mouth of a badly mangled NVA. "Fucking yellow mother-effin' gook." He kicked him and then stumbled back toward his platoon.

Blue tried to clear his head to maintain reality. Something in his chest and stomach flipped over, and he quickly vomited, spewing up his disgust, fear, and hatred. Another passing seasoned grunt offered him a knowing smile. "You just got your battle cherry popped, didn't you?" He patted him on the back and said, "Good luck." Bringing his tone down to a somewhat more serious emotion, he said in Vietnamese, "Sin-loi-bic." This was a common phrase with the CAV, and it meant "sorry about that shit."

Yet another passing grunt laughingly called out to him. "Hang tough, FNG. Good luck!" Good luck was offered often, and it had become the verbal tic of the Vietnam War.

Blue had a flashback of being a kid and staring at the dead bodies from a photograph in LIFE magazine. The picture showed a lot of dead people in a field, often touching, seeming to hold each other. Even though the picture was clear and sharp and clearly defined, something wasn't clear at all, something repressed that monitored the images and withheld their essential information.

Now that he was a man thousands of miles away, seeing the dead bodies legitimized his fascination, letting him look for a long time. His imprinted 1st CAV ego was trying not to feel an ounce of shame from the total impersonality of their group death. Blue could see death everywhere and everything—all dead. Stepping over mangled bodies and limbs, the company commander was tossing out playing cards with the 1st CAV imprinted on the backside.

As Blue's platoon swaggered back to their extraction zone, they passed a Vietnamese man who was sobbing and convulsing as he held out his dead baby.

While they waited for the choppers, Vietnamese civilians kept appearing. Some were smiling, some were crying, and some were struggling to get back to their hooches in the village—or what was left of them. The grunts would try to menace them away at rifle point.

Sergeant Cash shouted, "Di di mau, you sorry-ass motherfuckers. Get the hell away."

The refugees would smile through their terror, a terror Blue had never seen before.

A little boy about the age of twelve came up to a bunch of guys from Charlie Company. He seemed to be laughing and jerking his head from side to side in a comical way. The frightened fierceness in his eyes should have told everyone what was wrong, but it had never occurred to most of the grunts that a Vietnamese child had most likely been driven insane by all that he had witnessed in his youth. By the time they understood what was wrong with the boy, he had begun lunging at their eyes and tearing at their fatigues, spooking the hell out of everyone and instantly making everyone uptight.

Confused, one of the grunts pointed his rifle at the boy.

Blue had flashbacks of Tylor's boys at home in Taos and instinctively grabbed the boy from behind, wrapping him in his jacket. "C'mon, little guy. Let's get you some help." Blue carried him to the corpsmen.

As the chopper lifted into the air, Blue could see the surrounding hilltops. All the ground in front of them as far as he could see was charred and pitted, and some places still smoking. Frail smoke rose where they'd burned off the rice fields around the strike zone, and napalm smoke hovered motionlessly among the trees. Somehow, he felt peace from seeing the smoke.

The chopper fanned over part of the village that had just been bombed from the air.

After spotting some children, the pilot swooped over to them. As children ran from their hooches toward them, a gunner threw several cases of C-rations to them, calling back to the men, "Fucking Vietnam, we bomb 'em and then feed 'em." The pilot laughed heartily.

From a military point of view, it had been a beautiful operation. Few American soldiers were hurt—and even fewer killed. Blue knew he was raw, and he had learned from his first battle. He had learned fear that day, but he wasn't sure what he had learned about courage—if anything. He couldn't ever remember being so tired, so changed, and so happy to be alive. "Fuck me," he called out as he shook his head in disbelief.

Back at the base, an adrenaline hangover took hold of Blue, and he curled up in a ball and slept for fourteen hours straight.

CHAPTER 7

XUAN LOC:
LETTER FROM VIETNAM

"PLEAJE MR. POJTMAN," THE BEATLEJ

Weeks flew by with no word from Blue. He should have been at a firebase where choppers, known as mail-birds, flew in and out on a regular basis. Every day, Sunshine faithfully took the one-mile walk to the highway to check the mail in hopes of a letter from him.

The youthful pioneer life at the New Buffalo returned to its peaceful status and routines. Shortly after dawn, the sharp ring of a Buddhist gong started the day for the family members in the commune. Most of the day was devoted to hard physical labor. They planted, cultivated, and harvested vegetables supplementing their diets, and if they were lucky, they would catch fish from the Rio Grande River or the high mountain lakes. Wood was brought down from the mountains and cut, split, and stored for the long, bitterly cold winter. The adults ranged from seventeen to thirty-six and represented diverse backgrounds and educations.

The commune's founder, Rick Kline, had purchased the 103-acre Arroyo Hondo property in the spring of 1967, using his family inheritance for the down payment. The commune had struggled financially ever since.

Like the Amish, the communal women's duties were strictly dedicated and laborious. Sunshine had nothing in common with any of the other women of the commune. She spent her days helping with communal chores: cooking, cleaning, and gardening. Most of Sunshine's time was committed to her own reading and studies. She was enrolled in correspondence classes at the University of New Mexico. Her goal was to get a degree in teaching. Sunshine also spent time playing with and teaching the children. For her own enjoyment, Sunshine spent her time painting or sketching. However, of late, she found herself continually worrying about Blue or daydreaming about J. W.

She had not visited or ridden Rusty, afraid she would run into J. W. out on the range. She spent countless hours remembering the night they had shared together. She remembered the details of their lovemaking, which repeatedly sent blissful chills throughout her body, and each time, the memories awakened the consciousness of her womanhood, filling her with sparks of erotic thrills.

Her heart ached as she continually wondered why J. W. was so bothered by her being from the New Buffalo Commune. She longed to talk to him. Much of her meditation and prayer was spent trying to understand all the senseless anger and prejudice in the world. She was ashamed for J. W. and prayed for his anger to be released.

Finally, Sunshine received a letter from Blue:

Hi-Ya Sunshine,

Sorry that I've been so long in writing, but I've been adjusting to this new life in hell.

Fuck! It's been quite a trip since you let me off in Taos to catch a bus.

Most of the first guys I met were also "cherries" or "FNGs" (fuckin' new guys). It's very odd seeing some guys going home, and I'm just getting here. It's just one big fucking revolving turnstile in and out of Station Hell.

I just got back from being out on a reconnaissance patrol, and I had my first glimpse of chaos and fear. I am writing this from the so-called safety of Firebase Mace near Xuan Loc, my second firebase, the first one was Fanning not far from here. When not on patrol, we live here in an underground bunker, which has a roof made of huge logs that were cut with a machete, with a double layer of sandbags on top of the logs. The inside is lined with a camouflage parachute where we hang our pictures and posters. Mace is surrounded by a triple-canopy tropical jungle and mountains. I know it sounds nice, but somewhere out there, we're surrounded by thousands of fucking North Vietnamese troops.

Every day, we endure the shocks of dozens—maybe a hundred or more—of mortars and rockets, and every day, we reinforce our positions by adding another layer of sandbags, laying down another roll of triple-coiled barbed wire, German razor tape, and trip flares, and add more claymore mines. Just waiting ... and digging ... and watching ... and waiting ... and digging ... and watching. Some of the guys have done this so much they have developed a blank look in their eyes that

I imagine you'd find in the eyes of men on a chain gang. IT is known as the "thousand-yard stare." At night, we talk or play cards and listen to music, smoke pot, and shoot rats for target practice.

You know, it seems like we spend the entire day defending our allies, the South Vietnamese Army, against the North Vietnamese Army and Vietcong, but in a weird way, we've come to respect those damn gooks too because they never fucking give up.

There is this lone little VC shit, who is officially called the "camp pest." He dug into a spider hole some 180 meters from the perimeter. He rakes us daily with automatic weapon fire, aiming at anything and everything that moves. We return fire each time with mortars—even beehive rounds from a 105 mm howitzer cannon—but Mr. Camp Pest keeps popping up and firing back. The little shit reminds me of a prairie dog in the mesa back home. Well, eventually a napalm strike was called in, inundating his hole with a liquid fire that burned for ten minutes. As soon as the flames died out, he popped up again and fired another round. There is now a reward of five cartons of cigarettes and five bottles of whiskey for anyone who takes him out.

We go out on our second patrol tomorrow, slugging through soggy, muggy jungles and rice paddies, scouting the defoliated jungles and land craters. Please send Kool-Aid—the damn canteen water tastes like shit,

Well, I know I'm still in shock of being here. I will spare you the gory details, and for the first time in my life, I'm not sure what else to say. Ha! I know that's probably very funny to you.

I promise I'll write again soon. Please keep writing. Your letters are the only sanity in this insane war.

Love, Blue

Get this groovy title: Private First-Class Christopher A. Cantrell. Fuck me! But damn it, you'd better just call me Blue.

"When the power of love overcomes the love of power, the world will know peace." Jimi Hendrix

PS. I've been bragging about my beautiful sister, and I read your letters to some of the other guys. Little Joe wants to know if it's okay for him to write ya. I already told him it was because I knew you wouldn't mind.

Oh! PPS. I've explained and made it perfectly clear about yours-and-my relationship ... That we aren't really kind/blood. That we are only best of friends. And that we've never had sex or any kind of intimate relationship together.

More ... PPSS. Who's this cowboy, J. W., you mentioned in your last letter? Ha! And don't go playing spin the bottle with him. Ha! Ha! Ha! I want to hear more about him. Let me know if I need to kick his ass when I get home. And remember the lecture I gave you before I left. Be tough—and don't let people take advantage of you.

Blue had written Sunshine sooner, but he had decided not to send the letter to her. He knew his words were too strong and that he would scare her. Blue loved Sunshine. He knew she was an incredibly strong woman to have endured all the death that she had in her lifetime, and he vowed to take care of her. He only wished she would toughen up a bit. He was afraid people would take advantage of her sweet, trusting soul.

His father, Lieutenant Michael Cantrell, was an army

helicopter pilot for a Special Forces assault team. Single-engine, fixed-wing T-28 Trojans usually accompanied his assault team while scouting into Vietcong "hotbeds." However, the T-28 units became overburdened and were often unavailable for escort duty. Army intelligence decided to provide air support and set up fifteen assault teams of Huey helicopters sufficiently armed with two seven-tube, 2.75-inch rocket pods and high-velocity machine guns known as mini-guns that could fire up to four thousand rounds per minute.

They were often forbidden to engage in offensive operations. The army crews were authorized to use "suppressive fire" only in self-defense. As were the circumstances that day when Lieutenant Cantrell's team was considered to be too far into the DMZ and ordered not to fire. Lieutenant Cantrell and his six-member team were shot down on July 14, 1965.

At the time of his father's death, Blue and his mother had just moved from being stationed in Hawaii to Fort Carson, Colorado. Three months after his father's death, Blue's mother moved them to Albuquerque to marry an old high school sweetheart.

As a child, Blue had been the envy of every mother. His achievements outshined the rest of the boys his age. He had earned the Eagle Scout Guide and County Award, participated in the Latin American exchange program in

Colombia, and perfected his art and hobby in photography. He was a handsome, well-mannered, funny, and quick-witted boy who excelled throughout his education.

Blue and Sunshine had met in high school. Their common friendship flourished into an inseparable bond of their hearts when they discovered their lives had an epic echo. They both were seeking comfort and solace for the losses they suffered as a result of Vietnam. The pathways to both their fathers' graves had been deeply watered by their tears. Few children understood how hard it is to love and lose a parent unless they had gone through it themselves. People told them that time heals the heart, but for Blue and Sunshine, their healing went through a slow recovery. The loss of their fathers left an empty void in their lives.

In sharing their sorrows, Blue and Sunshine intertwined their friendship into a deep brother-sister love and a unique spiritual blend. Sunshine's natural modesty and evangelical spirit balanced out Blue's zany macho conceit and alluring zeal.

Blue's artistic talent, his dazzling characteristic, and compassion for others was cloned from his father. There was no doubt that Lieutenant Michael Cantrell had lived on through him.

Blue never forgave his mother for consoling in another man so quickly after his father's death. Blue and his stepfather fought immensely, making it easy for him to run off to live the utopian life at the commune with Sunshine.

During the time they shared at the New Buffalo, Blue and Sunshine developed an even stronger bond. They joined their efforts in the search for universal truths—through their physical, mental, emotional, and spiritual well-being. They sought out many rainbows, using many soothing universal colors as a positive tool for relieving their stress and anxieties.

As an adult, Blue was the pinnacle of suavity. There wasn't a lady yet who had withstood his good looks and charm. His proficiency in social amenities, alluring ways, dazzling smile, and blatantly blue eyes attracted many a young woman into his bed. However, his eccentric ideas never allowed him to stay monogamous in his relationships. This along with the ego's seductive pull branded him with the role of being a playboy, and he was proud to host the title.

Blue eventually received a draft notice, and although many men refused to comply with the draft and go to Vietnam, Blue had been immensely proud of his father's military accomplishments, and he figured he was going to serve one way or the other. He had a brief window of opportunity before he had to report, and he went out and talked to the air force, navy, and marines. Active service was anywhere from three to four years and few options.

He went to the army recruiter just for shits and grins.

Well, to his surprise, he could do what is called "volunteer for the draft." This would give him the option to choose when he went in before the end of the year, where he went to basic training, and go to armor or artillery training rather than infantry. As it turned out, it all worked out until he discovered after going through artillery training at Fort Sill, Oklahoma, they could still deploy him into an infantry unit.

CHAPTER 8

VUNG TAU BEACH

"A STONED SOUL PICNIC," THE FIFTH DIMENSION

Primarily due to WWI and WWII, the entire world has viewed the men of the United States Army as something more than just ordinary soldiers. It aroused the image of warriors with a proud heritage of one who is expected to be different and above most other soldiers. Americans expect the Army Recon teams to exhibit the best in skills, techniques, and practical abilities that come from resilient training and experience. Being Army Recon is a state of mind that comes from an embedded pride and belief that he is a cut above. Within the army divisions, the 1st CAV has an undeniable proud history of delivering excellence beyond others in all that he does, making them one of the proudest indissoluble brotherhoods of the world.

A lot of marines took exception to the Army Reconnaissance teams for using the term Recon since they considered it exclusively theirs. However, the 1st CAV has an esprit de corps that somehow becomes you the moment you finish sewing the unit patch on to the left shoulder of your uniform. Because the patch is so large, there is a standing joke: You sew your uniform to the patch rather than the other way around.

Fighting the war in Vietnam had become a neurotic passion: the false love object in the hearts of the malignant American military and political command: from the filthiest destroyed landscape of the DMV to the most abstract reaches of the top trinity command and behind the desks of the White House and the Pentagon.

The Tet Offensive began January 30, 1968, and ended in September. The "Tet," which was the Vietnamese New Year, was a massive surprise attack by the North Vietnamese aimed to temporarily gain control over one hundred cities in South Vietnam and to spread propaganda. This attempt did not succeed. However, the other goal—to demoralize South Vietnamese and US forces and bolster the already declining support for the war at home—was very successful. That year, 16,502 US troops died and 87,388 were wounded. An average of forty-three US servicemen died per day.

After the Tet Offensive, the question of defeat was not an option. They knew the war in Vietnam was militarily unwise and even absurd, but more orders came in like a shaken-up bottle of champagne, full of fizz and ready to gush as soon as someone popped the cork. The United States military thought they had seen bad conditions in Korea, but in Vietnam, they had to continually revise their fighting strategies. There were enough Korean War vets in Nam to remind everyone what a total disaster the entire Vietnam conflict had become.

Vietnam was divided into four geographical areas, known as Corps, to delineate responsibility for military operations. From north to south, they were I-Corps, II-Corps, III-Corp, and IV-Corps. The 1st CAV was now designated the responsibility of III-Corps, which extended from the coast to the Cambodian border to the southern ridge of the central highlands about twenty clicks south of Saigon. Blue was assigned to a special team known as Echo Recon, the only company in their brigade that wore camouflage.

In the service, especially in Nam, you are addressed by your last name or a nickname, depending on the creativity of someone. Blue was known as Cantrell or Ocean because of his bright blue eyes.

The landscape of Vietnam varied with dazzling Annamite Mountains carpeted with scrub vegetation; arable forest; narrow village trails; rich delta rice lands; clean roaring rivers that merged into the China Sea; and flat, sandy beaches that surrounded beautiful coastal areas.

However, American troops all too soon discovered the deception of this beauty; eventually, it all turned into the profuse bowels of hell. The bamboo thickets and vociferous streams metamorphosed into deep, thick, impassable, drenching wet rain forests that were infested with mosquitoes and deadly snakes. The joke was that there were three hundred varieties of snakes in Nam; 297 were poisonous, and the other three could crush you to death. Of course, it was not true, but that was the sense of humor and attitude that prevailed in Nam.

Few areas remaining in the 1st CAV's area had enough topsoil to grow rice. Centuries of cultivation had turned much of it into a gluey, red clay subsoil called laterite, which grabbed feet and wheels and slides from beneath buildings and runways. It was also littered with bomb and artillery craters. Water was everywhere. Saigon receives eighty inches annually; up north, the old capital city of Hue drowned in 128 inches per year. Monsoon rains fell in the chilly months of September to January and sometimes lasted until March. The monsoons were amplified by typhoons that roared in from the South China Sea. The winter months brought a damp, numbing cold, and the summers produced unbearable sweltering temperatures near a hundred degrees with humidity at 100 percent.

Returning from a fifteen-day patrol, the filthy men of Blue's platoon were given in-country R&R in what used to be the popular French beach resort of Vung Tau. Blue and his platoon spent the afternoon in an atmosphere of reprieve, lounging around the beach. A muffled Buddy Holly song, "Peggy Sue," played from speakers mounted throughout R&R camp columns, but the air was so heavy that day that the sounds would not carry.

The half-drunk Jimbo danced a staggering dance as he tooted on a flute. He had bought a bamboo flute from an old man on the road near Vung Tau, and he was playing it badly and repeatedly trying to play "Yankee Doodle Dandy."

Blue had just finished studying an exhausted copy of *Playboy* magazine and threw it at Jimbo. "Damn it, Jimbo, get the hell outta here with that fucking flute."

Troy added, "You can't play that fucking flute for shit."

The stoned Mickey tried to pull Jimbo's T-shirt over his head and mumbled, "S-s-stop, mudder-f-a-ker can't p-p-play."

Jimbo continued to play.

Looking like a football lineman, Blue bulldozed Jimbo's massive frame flat on his ass onto the sand. "Get the fuck outa here."

Jimbo laughed and purposely played a screaming high note from his flute.

Blue quickly grasped to cover his ears and said, "Fucking

stop." As he pushed him even further into the China Sea, he added, "You asshole." Blue knew the only reason he was able to move Jimbo's massive frame at all was that Jimbo was half drunk and stoned; otherwise, it would have taken a tank to move him. "Fucking Jimbo, has anyone ever told you that you're a giant, annoying fucking asshole?"

Jimbo smiled and answered. "As a matter of fact, that was my Daddy's last dying words." Jimbo shouted to the heavens, "And may God bless his soul."

Blue's platoon was an ethnic American quilt of young men. His closest bud, Joseph Montoya from Helena, Montana, was a small man with a big fight. He was a short, tough, muscular, and bulldog in stature, with a hard-hitting spirit, and he loved to fistfight. Joe boasted that he had won every barroom brawl he had ever been in—and no one was willing to challenge his claim to fame to find out if he was all bark and no bite. Even though he was a spitfire, because of his size, Joe was quickly dubbed Little Joe. Blue and Little Joe started in boot camp together and developed a noble friendship and respect for each other.

Troy Nickerson was from Gunnison, Colorado. He was a quiet man who loved his hard liquor; he spoke few words, but he said volumes when he did. He loved to read and had his head in a book whenever possible.

Writing messages on your helmet was a common way of expressing yourself in Nam. On Troy's helmet, he had recorded the months he had been in Nam—complete with checkmarks for each month he had survived.

Mike Gordon was from Jacksonville, Florida. The son of a Baptist preacher, it was only fitting that the message he wrote on his helmet hailed a freaky oxymoron: "Thou Shall Not Kill." He carried a five-pound Bible everywhere he went.

Will Willison, appropriately nicknamed Willie, was from Cincinnati, Ohio, and he knew every trivia fact about rock and roll. Willie had drawn a picture of an electric guitar on his helmet and stuck a picture of Jimi Hendrix in his helmet band. He said it gave him power.

Thomas Schmeckpepper justifiably held the pet name Pepper. He was an obsessive luck freak, an evil-omen collector, and the platoon's reporter of any bad signs. He carried around a brownie his mom had sent him from his home in Emmetsburg, Iowa. He said the brownie was his good luck charm, his mom's way of looking out for him. He wrapped the brownie up in protective layers of foil and padded it with two pairs of socks. He took a lot of shit for that brownie; the guys used to tease him that when he was asleep, they were going eat his fucking brownie.

Thomas growled, "Go ahead assholes, 'cause there are three identical foil packs in my rucksack. Two of the foils have my poop in them." He laughed heartily. "So, take the first bite—and you'll know you're in deep shit."

Doug Duncan was born to be a combat soldier. From Coldwater, Michigan, Doug was understandably proud of his Marine father, who'd survived the famous Battle of Iwo Jima. He proclaimed his pride for his fighting Marine father by writing "Semper Fi, Dad" on his helmet. Doug loved, lived, and breathed the military traditions. The fact he had not become a marine is another story.

Mickey Robinson, from North Platte, Nebraska, was the poster boy of the all-American soldier: tall, broad-shouldered, muscular physique; blonde, green eyes, and arrogantly filled with piss and vinegar. He loved motorcycles. He traded ten cartons of cigarettes with some gook for a Lambretta motor scooter. It was probably a VC who was also there on R&R, but how could you know that in Vung Tau? Mickey smugly rode his scooter everywhere on base. He had skillfully drawn a Harley chopper on his helmet.

Emmett Ervin, from Biloxi, Mississippi, was called Mississippi because of his hard-to-understand southern twang. Moe Maddow, from South Carolina; was the platoon's pothead. Don Brown was from Newark, New Jersey, and David Sweeny was from Los Angeles. Bobby Wills had received a draft exemption as a conscientious objector, but he felt an obligation to help the unfortunate brothers who needed medical help. Last but not least, James Schachtner was from the small town of Watertown, Wisconsin. Jimbo was one of the strangest people Blue had ever encountered. His mammoth, inept, fumbling stature and slow speech allowed him to pretend to be stupid, but he had transformed into an amazing warrior: aware, obedient, and ready for battle. In the heat of battle, every American swinging dick was very glad to have Jimbo beside them.

Jimbo's helmet had a score tally of all the gooks he had shot. He continually sang, "Ninety-nine gooks shot off the wall." Jimbo had strapped a grenade to his belly in case he was ever captured by the NVC. He vowed never to be taken alive.

Sergeant Cash left at noon, and with the sergeant away, the boys went to play. They drank whiskey, which they had smuggled out from the adjoining Aussie camp. They smoked ready rolls, which were cigarettes with the filters removed and the tobacco dumped out and replaced with marijuana. You could buy them at any local store using your military payment certificates, which the troops were paid with. The GIs rarely had any hard liquor available to them—only beer and marijuana. They would beat up, trade, buy, or gamble with rear-echelon motherfuckers, known simply as REMFs, in exchange for hard liquor.

The camp's makeshift bunkers had outside primitive latrines. These piss pots were made from fifty-five-gallon drums that half-filled with sand and draped with tarps around them for privacy. After drinking close to his body weight in liquor, Jimbo continued to pester his platoon buddies. Trying desperately to hide from Jimbo, eight of them hid in the empty water tower for hours, smoking pot and drinking Vietnamese beer, which the troops had dubbed "Tiger Piss."

There was so much smoke inside the water tower they couldn't see one another from one side to the other.

Willie said, "Say! That Jimi Hendrix is my main man. I sure wish they would play his music on the AFVN. Did you know that Hendrix was once in the 101st Airborne? The Airborne in Nam is full of wiggy-brilliant black brothers like him? I'm not shittin' ya."

Emmett took a big hit off the joint and said, "I can't see Jimi Hendrix in the 101st. It's too bad he wasn't good enough for the CAV."

Willie said, "Yeah! Too bad he wasn't in our platoon—wouldn't that have been out of sight."

Blue said, "Well, if he was as good with a fucking gun as he was with his fucking guitar, he would have been a hell of an asset." After taking a hit of a joint, he added, "Fuck yeah!"

Don said, "Who the hell is Jimi Hendrix?"

Not wanting to hear Willie's story again, Troy quickly changed the subject. "I hate this war. We should just blow Vietnam all to hell: animals, vegetables, and minerals. We should load up the friendlies onto ships and take them out to the South China Sea and then bomb the entire fucking country flat, return the friendlies, and be done with it. You know this war cannot be won. It cannot be exhausted; it can only be destroyed. And dig it! 'Cause it's destroying the fucking the US-of-fucking-A."

In a delightful state of misery, after what seemed like hours of evading Jimbo, hoping he'd surely had passed out, they returned to their bunker to play poker.

Jimbo soon staggered in, too sloshed to even speak.

"I can't believe he's still able to stand," Willie said as he took a hit of the joint they were passing around.

As Jimbo approached the makeshift card table, the overwhelming stench of urine pierced their nostrils. Jimbo had fallen into the piss pot while trying to take a leak. The men all jumped up and ran outside to escape the disgusting stench. They went back in and dragged Jimbo down the beach and threw his ass into the North China Sea.

When Jimbo crawled back to the hooch, they dug a hole in the sand and buried him from his neck down. Oblivious as to where he was and why he couldn't move, in the height of his prodigy, he sang at the top of his lungs: "The Magical Mystery Tour is waiting to take you away. Waiting to take you away, waiting today."

The next morning, Sergeant Cash rudely awoke Blue along with his platoon. "Who was the wise-ass who buried Jimbo in the fucking sand?" To add torment to their pounding heads, the sergeant turned up the radio full blast. A song by the Rolling Stones, "I Can't Get No Satisfaction," was playing, but Sergeant Cash barked his orders over the song. "Gordon and Ervin, get your fucking army-owned asses up and get Jimbo out of the sand. And make sure he takes a shower and get him fed. Cantrell and Nickerson, hop in the jeep. I need you to take Sergeant Keller into Vung Tau to the 35th evac hospital. Move it. Move it ... *Didi mau.*"

Sergeant Cash radioed into the 35th Evac that they were bringing Sergeant Keller. Sergeant Keller, Troy, and Blue were waiting by the jeep when six long-range reconnaissance patrol swaggered into camp carrying one of their dead men over their shoulders. Their weariness had gone far beyond physical exhaustion. Every torpid movement they made showed that they were tired. Their eyes were dim, and their faces were puffy.

Every man in sight stopped in silence to stare in awe at these hardened combatant men. The LRRP was an elite reconnaissance team composed of five to seven men who went deep into the bush to observe enemy activity without initiating contact, although they constantly tempted fate and got close enough that they could report they were just defending themselves. Wearing rumpled fatigues, no shirts or flak jackets, only ammunition belts strapped crisscross over their burly, naked, muddy, tattooed chests, and on a shoelace hanging from their belt, dried up shriveled ears, one taken from every gook they killed. They were known as the "Bush Beasts," and they were undoubtedly the baddest asses of all. Total respect was given to each of them at all times; all the troops who had been in battles were humbled in their presence.

These Bush Beasts had been successful on their recon patrol and discovered a large arms cache. While taking cover, they fell into an NVC cache pit filled with a lottery of ammunition, guns, and explosives. They crawled out of the pit, found safe cover, and then blew it all to hell. However, their good fortune didn't hold because less ten minutes later, one of their men fell into a punji pit and was killed instantly. A punji pit was one of the primitive but effective guerrilla warfare tactics the VC and NVC used. The pits were lined with stakes constructed of sharpened bamboo sticks smeared with excrement to cause infection. Very few made it out alive.

Blue couldn't look at the Bush Beasts any longer. "Fuck me! Those guys give me the creeps. The shit they've been through is not even human."

Troy moved his attention and turned the jeep radio up as high as it would go. A Creedence Clear Water Revival song was playing: "Bad Moon Rising."

Sergeant Cash turned down the music and said, "Hey, Nickerson, there is something I've been meaning to ask you."

"Yes, Sarge, what is that?"

"Are you any relation to General Nickerson?"

General Nickerson was the general for the III-MAF command.

"Nope, no relation, Sarge."

"Good ... because I think he's a supercilious prick," Sergeant Cash barked. "I thought you must be because I think you're a prick too, a real fucking dumbass, and you'd better fucking listen to me when I'm talking to you."

Troy snickered. "Yes, sir."

"And don't call me sir—I work for a living."

Cash handed an article of paperwork to Sergeant Keller. "Bill, these boys are going to see that you get safely to the 35th evac hospital." Sending a challenging glare to Blue and Troy, he added, "Aren't you, boys?"

In unison, they said, "Yes, sir ... I mean Sergeant Cash." They laughed as they drove away.

The trip to the 35th was thankfully uneventful, although every jarring bump the jeep made had Sergeant Keller holding his head in agony. He had been suffering from a headache for three weeks now, and Sergeant Cash had finally talked him into having it checked out.

Once they got to the hospital, they had a confrontation with the hospital's army guards because Sergeant Keller, Troy, and Blue refused to check in their guns and ammunition.

Their insistence prevailed, and Blue and Troy sat in the hallway of the hospital and waited for Sergeant Keller.

As it turned out, Sergeant William Keller had suffered a concussion from a bomb blast in a battle three weeks earlier. Bill was one tough son of a bitch. He possessed a silent-secret-survivor's smile because he had witnessed and undergone more than most warriors could probably withstand. Between a tour in Korean and three previous tours in Nam, he had been shot three times, stabbed twice, and blown into the air several times by mortar, artillery, and rocket blasts. He had outlived what was considered one of the most grueling battles in the Korean War: the Chosin Reservoir. He had withstood one of Vietnam's bloodiest and most maddening battles, the battle of 1965 Ia Drang, which ended in a pure slaughter. Bill was currently on his fourth tour in Vietnam. The words "survival miracle" couldn't even apply because he was truly beyond that.

One of the head nurses tried to throw Blue and Troy out. "You boys, get outta here. You're in the way. Get!"

Blue shined his baby blue eyes at her, using all his charm with a foolish and cheery countenance. "No, Mama, we have strict orders to stay here and wait for Sergeant Keller."

Troy said, "Yes, ma'am, that's right ... strict orders."

They had only waited in the hospital to check out the nurses. They were told the hospital was filled with dozens of pretty Red Cross volunteers, better known as "Doughnut

Dollies." There had been an unsuccessful battle in Tay Ninh. In a joint offensive, the 1st CAV, First Army Division, and the marines had intercepted an NVA incursion over the Cambodian border, taken over four hundred casualties, and killed nearly two hundred. There had been so many casualties brought into the hospital that the Red Cross was contacted to bring in the girls to help cheer up and comfort the survivors.

The nurse strutted away, and Blue laughed. "I think she wants me. She wants some of this."

CHAPTER 9

SANTA FE: ART ON THE PLAZA

"SUGAR, SUGAR," THE ARCHIES

General Moonbeam held the highest education title of the commune family. At the young age of twenty-five, he had earned a doctoral degree in philosophy from Harvard University. He was a diminutive, mousey figure, all beard and beads. He had thick, fuzzy Elvis sideburns, thin, brown straggly, early balding hair, and thick, rectangular coke-bottle glasses. He respectfully had earned the title of being the commune's poet.

General Moonbeam was planning a trip into Albuquerque; he was to be the guest speaker at a seminar hosted by the University of New Mexico. It was early dawn, and as the general was loading his van for his trip, Yogi ran up and gave him a big hug. "Hey, General! Since you'll be passing through Santa Fe on your way to Albuquerque, can Sunshine and I bum a ride from you to Santa Fe?"

He replied, "Sure, no sweat. You'll have to thumb a ride back. I'm not coming back until next week."

Yogi jumped up and kissed him. "Thanks, man. That's far out!" She ran off to tell Sunshine.

The general called after her, "Hey, girl, you chicks get your sweet little asses a move on. I'm leaving here in ten minutes—with or without you guys."

An art festival was happening in Santa Fe Plaza that morning, and Sunshine and Yogi decided it would be a good opportunity to sell their artistic creations, hopefully making some money. Yogi had tie-dyed many different articles of clothing—everything from scarves, T-shirts, and skirts to underwear. Sunshine gathered several of her best watercolor paintings and sketches, leaving behind a few of her favorite paintings of Rusty.

Yogi and Sunshine loaded up their artwork into the general's 1963 Ford van, and they were on their way. The general's van was brightly decorated on the outside with dozens of neon-colored, fat-pedaled flower decals; hand-painted, bright, psychedelic symbols of peace and love; and endless messages in protest of the war. There was so much depiction adorning the van that you couldn't even tell its original color. Its interior was much the same style. The back seats were substituted with two yellow beanbag chairs, wall-to-wall bright orange shag carpet, and cotton fabric curtains with a psychedelic pattern and green dingle balls.

The general's van roared with an earsplitting rumble from the time-honored and fatigued engine, making their bodies vibrate and their teeth chatter. The van was so loud that they practically had to yell at one another for their conversations to be heard.

The general hollered, "Sunshine, why don't you drive Blue's car. I heard that he left it at the commune so you could use it."

Sunshine shrugged, "I don't—"

"It's 'cause she's afraid to drive that fucking monster," Yogi yelled.

Blue had left his souped-up 1968 muscle car, an Oldsmobile Cutlass 442.

Sunshine laughed and said, "It is pretty powerful and scary to drive. You just give it a tiny bit of gas, and it peels out."

Yogi shook her head and said, "She's afraid she'll crash it."

To pass the time of travel, the three passengers listened to an eight-track tape of Bob Dylan's music and cheerfully sang along. "The answer my friend is blowing in the wind, the answer is blowing in the wind."

Once past the village of Taos, Yogi pulled out her stash,

rolled up a joint, lit it up, took a huge hit, and then tried to pass it to Sunshine.

Sunshine yelled over the van's engine roar, "Dang it, Yogi, you know I don't smoke pot, drink, or do drugs."

"It's okay, sister! Jesus! Don't freak out. I thought I'd be polite and offer anyway. I forgot we had Saint Sunshine with us today."

As the general and Yogi shared the joint, Sunshine sat in the back of the van enjoying the music and the beautiful drive that unwound along the Rio Grande watershed, passing villages and pueblos where the old and new mixed.

Just outside the tiny town of Espanola, a state policeman pulled them over. He walked up to the general's window and said, "Let me see your license please."

The general meekly pulled out his driver's license and handed it to the officer.

The officer viewed it, handed it back to the general, and said, "Mr. Haberkorn, you are driving too slow. Try to keep up with the speed limit—and be sure to stay in the right-hand lane when you're driving so slowly."

Yogi and Sunshine started cracking up. "General, what did he say your last name was?"

The police officer said, "Are you two young ladies all right?"

In a fake southern drawl, Yogi said, "Why, yes, Officer, we'll be just fine." She batted her eyelashes at him.

Nervously, the general turned around and whispered, "Damn it! You two, mellow out."

Yogi and Sunshine quietly giggled like little girls.

The officer said, "Be on your way—but drive safe."

Yogi held up her hand and offered a peace sign to the officer. As soon as he had his back turned, her gesture turned to flip him off.

The general slapped Yogi's hand and pushed it out of sight. "Maintain. Damn it! You're going to get us thrown in jail!"

Yogi laughed out loud. "Let me see your license." She grabbed it from him and rolled on the floor laughing "Hey, Sunshine, guess what the general's real name is? It's Hershel Haberkorn!"

Sunshine was laughing so hard she had tears in her eyes. "Mr. Hab-ba-corn? Now we know why you changed your name."

"Now, Sunshine, I thought you—of all people—would have more respect."

Sunshine laughed. "Don't worry. Your secret is safe with me."

When they arrived in Santa Fe, the general was only too grateful to drop off the two giggling females at the art festival on the old plaza.

The legendary city of Santa Fe is nestled and enthroned

in the arms of a miraculous mountain province. The city sits at 7,198 feet above sea level where the air remains cool, crisp, and clean year-round. Santa Fe's meaning is "Holy Faith." It is located along the watershed from the Santa Fe River, below the southern end of the omnipotent Sangre de Cristo Mountains, which translates to the "Blood of Christ Mountains." Visible to the west are the Jemez Mountains, and to the southeast is the Sandia Mountain range.

Santa Fe is one of the oldest cities in the United States. It was established in 1610 by the peerless Spanish conquistadors as a trade outpost among the ruins of a Native Indian pueblo.

As soon as Yogi slammed the door to the general's van, he sped off, eager to be free of the two women. Their cheerful spirits continued as they scampered off to find their awaiting friend and designated booth in the plaza.

Santa Fe's plaza or "city square" was originally the center gathering place in town. To many, it is still said to be the "heart" of Santa Fe. The plaza is located next to a National Historic Landmark, the "Palacio de las Gobernadores," or Governors Palace, which was originally constructed in the early seventeenth century to house Spain's seat for the government. The picturesque ancient adobe dwellings and structures now operate as one of New Mexico's history museums.

Yogi was wearing her favorite bell-bottom pants, which

flared out at the knee; it was a fashion steal from the traditional navy uniform. She also wore a braless, bare midriff, tie-dyed halter top, leather sandals, and a Christmas tree's worth of love beads around her neck. Completing her persona, she reeked of patchouli oil.

It didn't take them long to find their friend from Santa Fe and exchange hugs. Yogi said, "Hey! Megan, good to see you! How is your life's journey?"

"It's out of sight, sister," Megan said,

Sunshine said, "Peace, my sister. It is so good to see you again."

"Megan, wait until you see the far-out paintings that Sunshine brought to sell today."

"Lay it on me, man; let's see what you've got."

Always needing to be the center of attention, Yogi said, "Check out these tie-dyed T-shirts, undies, and junk that I've brought. Now all I need is some groovy beaded jewelry." She was jumping up and down like a little girl at Christmastime. "This is so far out. I'm so excited to be here today."

Sunshine said, "Thank you, Megan, for sharing your booth."

Megan was a fun-loving, robust black woman, who had big, smiling coal eyes, a contagious love for life, and an overwhelming knowledge of astrology. Megan also had an enormous addiction to barbiturates. Quaaludes was her choice of downers.

Just a year prior, on April 4, 1968, Megan was working at the front desk at the Lorraine Motel in Memphis when Martin Luther King Jr. was assassinated from his motel room window. He was shot in the jaw by a sniper bullet that traveled to his spine, severing it and killing him. New Mexico had predominately a Hispanic culture with very few black people living in the state, but Martin Luther King Jr.'s virulent death had an immensely suffocating impact on New Mexico and the entire nation.

Martin Luther King Jr., an African American Baptist minister and activist, had become the most visible spokesperson and leader in the civil rights movement from 1955 until his assassination in 1968. His legacy will always be treasured for his nonviolent calls for racial equality. He envisioned a world where his children would not be judged by color of their skin but by the contents of their character.

People took heed his messages laced with truths from the Bible and the US Constitution. He was a master orator and a brilliant wordsmith, and he put pressure on President Lyndon B. Johnson's administration to push for civil rights laws to pass through Congress.

During a tumultuous time, his actions unified all races together under a common goal. Although prejudice remains in the hearts of the wicked, the tide had shifted in a way where the racists of the world were scorned. He played a pivotal role in lending the legal segregation of African American citizens in the United States and the creation of the Civil Rights Act of 1964 and the Voting Rights Act of 1965.

Megan had previously shared the terror of having lived through the assassination, and it was a severe loss for our great nation and all of humankind.

Sunshine and Yogi beamed with pride as they set up to sell Yogi's electric mix of tie-died wares and Sunshine's watercolor paintings. For an amateur artist, Sunshine's paintings included an alluring, unique collection of expressive realist work. Her natural skill could be seen through her loose, moody, yet whimsical vibrant brushstrokes, combined with keen attention to detail. Her talent gave testimony to her interest in portraying the indigenous relationships she found in New Mexico. Sunshine's years of dreaming—along with her ability to show the essence of the moment—expressed her true love for New Mexico's landscapes, animals, and culture.

Santa Fe has always been committed to its New Mexican cultural and artistic sustainability, and the creative hustle and bustle of the plaza was an enterprising event to take part in. It was a festival rich with unity and spirit of three cultures: the Hispanics, the Native Americans, and the newcomers, the Anglos. The festivities showcased mariachi music, felicitous dancing, and the tantalizing, pungent smells of roasted green chilis, Indian fry bread, and all the other inviting varieties of Southwestern culinary delights. All this made the art festival an intriguingly, exciting place to be.

The morning rushed by, passing beyond the high-noon sun, into the closing afternoon. Sunshine decided to take a break and walk among the many talented peddlers and watch the beautiful people. As she roamed around the plaza, she stopped on the sidewalk of the Governor's Palace to talk with an old native Jemez Indian woman who was proudly selling her beautiful handcrafted turquoise and silver jewelry. She talked and laughed with the Hispanic children who were selling their grandmother's *empanaditas* and *biscochito* cookies on the street corner. She respectfully bowed to the Hare Krishnas on a recruit. She talked to the young and old alike and enjoyed visiting with every single one of them.

Sunshine found a vacant park bench and sat back to watch the community. She had an unquenchable love for people, and to simply sit and watch the world made her afternoon. As she sat on the park bench in a euphoric daze, spacing out on the festivities, she heard a familiar voice. Her heart did a quick somersault, and she looked up to see J. W.'s gray-blue eyes.

"If you want to forget all your troubles, just take a little walk in a brand-new pair of high-heeled ridin' boots." He smiled. "It sure is a beautiful day!

"Yes, it is indeed." She returned a beaming smile.

"What brings this flower child down from the Taos Mountains?" He took a seat next to her on the bench.

Even though his bullheadedness, J. W. could see the real beauty in this woman. She was wearing a simple yet chic granny dress that was made from refashioned vintage table linen. She wore it as an elegant fashion statement with a necessity for a lightweight, durable, and comfortable summer dress. Around her slender, tanned waist, wrists, and ankles were adornments of silver native Indian jewelry, but J. W. only saw her face—and he could not take his eyes off this intriguing, simplistic angelic vision.

Her flashing green eyes fixed their glance upon him, and she said, "I'm here for the art festival. How have you been?" Sunshine's emotions raged; she didn't know whether to slap him or hug him. Her heart felt tight and sore in her breast, and her mind turned like an electric fan. She smiled and said, "My girlfriend Yogi and I came in hopes of selling some of our artwork."

Rubbing his tanned chin, he said, "Ah, you're a woman of many talents. You can break horses, and now I find out you're an artist? What kind of art do you do?"

Sunshine noticed the two small paintings in his hand and said, "Well, do you like the two paintings you have there?" She pointed to the unframed paintings in his hand.

He smiled. "Yes, I just bought these from a booth around the corner. Why, do you paint also?"

"Yes, sir, I surely do. I painted those two paintings." She laughed. "In fact, that pinto horse and rider are you and your horse. I painted them this past spring out on your mesa."

"Well, I'll be damned!" J. W. shook his head in amazement. "You're pretty talented. Where did you learn such a skill?"

Sunshine smiled, "I've always enjoyed painting. I've been painting since I was a little girl. I started painting pictures to send my father who was overseas, and I just continued over the years. And what brings you to Santa Fe? Shouldn't you be home on the range, rounding up cattle or something?"

J. W. gave a small snicker. "I was in Albuquerque yesterday to pick up a new horse trailer. I was on my way back to Taos and thought I'd make a quick stop at the Santa Fe Plaza Hat Shop. You see, this one here kinda got ruined in a rainstorm last month when I was out chasing a pretty little woman who took off with a rusted gelding of mine." He smiled and tried to sound irritated.

Grimacing, Sunshine said, "Oh … uh … oops! And how is Rusty?"

They spent some time chatting about the festival and the fun things going on there.

J. W. enjoyed watching Sunshine and the joy that was evident in her eyes.

Yogi waltzed up and said, "Hey, Sunshine, who's the good-looking goat roper?"

Tension and prejudices sprang into J. W., immediately destroying their peaceful aura. Instantly he felt anger toward the rude little hippie.

Sunshine said, "This is our neighbor, Mr. J. W. Weston. You know, the Weston Ranch from across the river?" She briefly paused when she noticed J. W.'s irritation. "And J. W., this is Yogi."

J. W. stayed seated on the bench. Without looking up, he said, "What kind of name is Yogi?"

Yogi quickly made up a western accent to accompany the occasion, "Golly, I'll be, if you ain't a fine specimen of John Wayne? Or is it Hopalong Cassidy? Sunshine, I hitched us a ride back tomorrow with that groovy Peter Wood dude I was hanging on earlier. He has invited us to party with him at his place here in Santa Fe tonight." Yogi leaned over and whispered, "He's got some great home-grown, and I'd love to have the opportunity to get in his pants if you know what I mean." She laughed tartly.

Sunshine was embarrassed and hoped J. W. couldn't hear what Yogi had whispered. "Yogi, you know I don't party. Can't we thumb a ride tonight?" She turned to J. W. and said, "J. W., could I bum a ride back to Taos. You did say you were on your way home, didn't you?"

J. W. had a clean-cut, distinguished look that people trusted. He tipped his cowboy hat and said, "Yes, ma'am. I'd be honored to give you a ride back to Taos."

Yogi said, "Dig this fucking cowboy! Ain't he a smooth one? Sunshine, are you sure you'll be okay?"

Sunshine laughed and said, "Yes, Yogi, I'll be fine. You don't mind packing up and bringing home what we haven't sold, do you?"

"No sweat, 'cause all your shit sold anyways." She giggled and whispered, "Megan said the moon and some groovy stars are in line tonight, and women should feel a ragging spiritual sense of eroticism." She lifted her brow toward J. W. and said, "Oh, baby, I hope you get some of that." Yogi put a lot of energy into her jive.

Yogi quickly hugged Sunshine and ran off, yelling back to J. W. with her silly, made-up country drawl, "Nice to meet ya, neighbor! And happy fucking trails."

J. W. was grateful to be rid of the tramp. "We'll have to hike a ways back to my truck. With that horse trailer on it, I had to park a ways away. Are you ready to go?"

"Oh, wait! I need to run and get my bag. I'll be right back." Sunshine ran back to their booth, gathered her earnings and her duffel bag, and then dashed back to the bench. "Okay, I'm ready!" She beamed as sweet as sugary icing.

"Then let's go," he said with a slow smile that said he was never in a hurry. "Let me carry your bag."

Sunshine handed him the green army-issue duffel bag.

"Shee-it! What the hell you have in here—rocks, horseshoes, or bars of gold?"

"Well, the bars of gold of course." Sunshine laughed. "No! I went by the library earlier and checked out a dozen books."

CHAPTER 10

CHIMAYO DE RIO ARRIBA

"TAKE ME AS I AM," RAY PRICE

Leaving Santa Fe Plaza, J. W. and Sunshine leisurely strolled past the vast array of stores, window-shopping, and people watching, and stopped along the way to pick up his new hat.

As they were approaching J. W.'s truck, Sunshine said, "Wow! This is your truck? It's beautiful ... and this must be the new horse trailer you picked up in Albuquerque yesterday! It's huge! How many horses does it hold?" Sunshine walked around inspecting the truck and trailer.

J. W. followed her around like a puppy. He was beaming with pride as he said, "It's a Johnston gooseneck horse trailer; holds up to ten horses. I've had the truck for a couple of years. I bought it with the money I won from the rodeo championship." He held open the door for Sunshine.

When they were both settled, J. W. skillfully drove the truck and trailer out of Santa Fe.

Sunshine studied the interior of the truck. It was a white Chevy custom sports truck with air-conditioning, AM and FM radio/stereo with an eight-track player and four speakers mounted behind the seats and under the dash. Hanging in the back window was a gun holder equipped with a rifle and lariat. A little plaque dangled from one of the dash knobs: "Don't squat with your spurs on."

J. W. and Sunshine felt awkward being alone together again, not sure of any emotions created from their first and last encounter. J. W. kept fighting with his thoughts. It was like a cartoon with two states of conscience arguing back and forth. He hated hippies and everything they stood for, but his heart kept overriding his head as this amazing woman mesmerized him.

Sunshine finally said, "Gosh, I didn't know they made such fancy trucks; it even has carpeting! It's so shiny and clean. Do you always keep it this clean?"

"Yes, I guess I do!" He turned on the radio and said, "I don't suppose you listen to country-and-western music?"

Sunshine said, "Why, yes, I love country music. I was raised on country music. My father was from Montana, and country music is all we'd listen to. We'd listen to everything from the traditional old-time gospel country, to good old hard-core honky-tonk. Every Saturday evening, we'd have the Grand Ole Opry on the radio. We'd listen to Bob Wells, Patsy Cline, Dolly Parton, Hank Williams, George Jones, Porter Wagner, and—"

"Well, I'll be gawl-damn if you ain't as surprising as a sidewinder. Pick out a tape there for us to listen to."

Sunshine picked a tape and handed it to J. W. "It's been a while since I've listened to any country music. How about if we listen to Merle Haggard?"

J. W. put in the tape, "The Fightin' Side of Me," and a song about Vietnam played: "If You Don't Love It, Leave It."

In leaving Santa Fe, at the edge of town, they drove past the National Cemetery. Sunshine stared out the window, quietly watching the perfectly formatted, axiomatic rows and rows of white headstones. She said quietly, "My father is buried in the National Cemetery over there. He was one of the first airmen killed in Vietnam in 1964."

J. W. said, "I'm sorry. I know it's hard to lose a father."

Sunshine tried to change to a cheerier note, saying, "Can we turn up the music? I love this song."

J. W. laughed and said, "Go ahead and turn it up as loud as you want."

Sunshine was like a little girl playing with a new toy. She

slowly turned the volume knob, giving an attentive ear as if listening to find the perfect volume, and laughed. "Cool!"

They traveled without making conversation and listened to the music. In their ascent north toward the Santa Clara Indian Reservation, the western skies over Santa Clara Peak were luminescing with vivid, bright colors, reflecting on the accumulated clouds. Soon, it developed into a breathtakingly beautiful sunset.

J. W. said, "Darn if that ain't the prettiest sunset I've ever seen. It's as pretty as the lady sitting next to me." He even surprised himself by confessing to the last part of his statement.

Sunshine said, "Yes, it is a beautiful sunset; it would be a wonderful landscape to paint."

"You could paint that sunset?"

"Sure, sunsets are very easy to capture with watercolors."

"You could paint that easily? All's you would need is your paint and paper?"

Sunshine laughed. "Yes … as a matter of fact, I have everything I need right here in my duffel bag."

"Really? Would you paint it for me?"

Sunshine smiled and nodded. "Sure."

"Well, then, let's pull over." J. W. crossed over the highway, pulled onto a dirt road, and stopped the truck in a spot with a clear view of the spectacular, panoramic sunset. He hurried to the other side of the truck to help Sunshine with her bag.

Sunshine found a comfortable spot, sat down, and skillfully set out her tools: a pad of watercolor paper, a tin paint box with a variety of well-used tubes of paint, a palette, a handful of brushes, a charcoal pencil stump, and a Tupperware bottle with water.

J. W. plucked a blade of grass, chewed it, took a seat beside her, and silently watched her artistically duplicating the brilliance and radiance of the sunset above the magnificence of the Santa Clara Mountains. A soft summer breeze blew, spreading a fragrance of wildflowers. The clean, crisp, arid skies began to dim with the setting sun. Dark clouds gathered as if magnetized to the splendid mountains, highlighting the diverse richness surrounding the lands to the west and the northern length of the Sangre de Cristo Mountains and the hills below. The clouds threatened rain.

Sunshine sat in the open mesa, humming to the music J. W. left playing in the truck, and painted with ease. Neither Sunshine nor J. W. spoke during the time that it took for her to capture the parade of colors from the magical, tranquil setting.

After Sunshine finished the painting, she proudly signed her name and gently handed the painting to J. W. "It will take a couple of hours to dry, but here you go. It's yours."

"Damn, that is some talent you have, lady. I'm honored to have such a beautiful gift. Thank you!" He gave a sweet, gentle kiss on the forehead and helped her back into the truck, and they continued their journey.

Hidden in the waves of the desert and the surrounding mountains between Santa Fe and Taos, then quickly jaunting east of Española, they headed toward the tiny town of Chimayo. The small, winding road took them past the historic Tewa Santuario de Chimayo Mission and the Rio Arriba River to a quaint New Mexican restaurant filled with culinary treasures.

J. W. pulled into a dirt parking area in front of the Rancho de Chimayo restaurant. "Let's stop and get something to eat. I don't know about you, but I'm hungrier than a goat in a dumpster. They make the best chile rellenos here, and their sopapillas are huge."

As soon as they walked into the restaurant, a short, chubby, elderly New Mexican woman with rosy cheeks rushed over to J. W. "*Mi niño,* Julian." She hugged him, followed by a kiss on his forehead, which he had to bend down to receive. "*Como has estado? Ven, sientate en tu mesa favorita.*" ("How have you been? Come, sit down at your favorite table.")

J. W. said, "*Es un placer verla, Mamá Josefina, su comida ha sido mi antojo todo el dia.*" ("It is good to see you, Mamá Josefina. Your food has been on my mind all day.")

Sunshine quietly watched the two and smiled at their exchange of happy greetings for each other.

Mamá Josefina graciously ushered them over to a table in the corner and said, "I run and get my sweet little Maria Elena to take your order." Pinching J. W.'s cheek, she said, "You remember my Maria Elena? She's the one I want you to marry." She grinned. "She's still single and still the prettiest girl in town. "Oh ... I'm sorry, *niño...* I hope I did not offend this lovely little lady?"

J. W. smiled and said, "This is Sunshine. Sunshine, this is Curandera Mamá Josefina. She is the best cook in New Mexico."

Sunshine said, "*Es un placer conocerla. Su restaurante es muy bonita.*" ("It is nice to meet you, you have a lovely little restaurant here, and J. W. informs me that you have the best New Mexican food in the Southwest.")

Mamá Josefina smiled heartily at Sunshine. "Gracias, *niña.* Now I must get back to my kitchen so I can make you some food. I have Maria Elena come to take your order."

J. W. lifted his brow and said, "*Donde aprendiste hablar Español?*" ("Where did you learn to speak Spanish?")

Sunshine said, "While I was taking lessons in high school, my best friend, Blue, and I would play a game speaking only in Spanish to practice—so our mothers wouldn't know what we were saying."

Maria Elena brought out their sodas and water and gave J. W. a brotherly hug. She was a beautiful, petite young native New Mexican woman, and by the gleam in her eyes, she adored J. W. Maria Elena gracefully took their orders and promptly returned with their food, shyly returning to the kitchen after serving them.

"You're right, J. W. This is delicious food, but the chile is really hot!" Gasping from its heat, Sunshine quickly took a drink of water and fanned her mouth with her hand. "They say that chile is the fire in New Mexico's soul."

J. W. let out a hearty laugh. "Yes, good and hot! One time, I was on tour passing through to a rodeo in Santa Fe, and I stopped here with a friend from Oklahoma. You should have seen the look on his face while he was eating Mamá Josefina's green chile stew. His face turned beet red, his eyes started watering, and he broke out into a sweat. He nearly drank the well dry trying to cool down. I know he'll never forget this restaurant!"

Sunshine continued to eat, although she had to stop every once in a while to drink her soda or suck on an ice cube to cool her mouth. "So, you were a rodeo cowboy? Do you still compete?"

J. W. smiled. "I started when I was a small boy. I practiced riding the bronc horses on the ranch. I knew I wanted to be a rodeo cowboy. I craved the chills, spills, and thrills of the sport and all its pageantry. I practiced and practiced ... and practiced. I had a fierce determination to compete at the rodeo." He shook his head. "As the saying goes, if I had a dollar for every time I was thrown from a horse, I wouldn't have had to worry about the prize money. I'd be dancin' the two-step on golden floors. Shortly after I got out of high school, I left home to follow the rodeo circuit, but I couldn't make up my mind about which trail to follow. I'd work at home for a while, run back to the rodeo, run back home again with my tail between my legs, and run back off to the rodeo. The rodeo was an elixir in my blood. Two years ago, I finally spun into the professional circuit and followed the rodeos from Idaho to Oklahoma and from the Dakotas to the tip of Texas. I traveled thousands of miles ridin' hundreds of broncs, but this time, I was winning. My future looked like it was lit with neon. That fall, I won the daddy of them all when I finally made it to the National Rodeo Finals in Oklahoma City. I took first place in bareback ridin', and I was nominated New Mexico's Rodeo Athlete of the Year." J. W. heaved a big sigh. "Two weeks after the national finals, my dad had a heart attack and was unable to keep up the ranch. I returned home, hopin' that my dad would recover so I'd be able to return to the rodeo. A few months later, he suffered another heart attack—and that one was fatal. He passed on last summer."

Sunshine gave him a gentle smile. "I'm sorry."

J. W. said, "Hell, to every backside there's a bright side, and I learned a rodeo cowboy don't look to the future or the past. If you get slammed down into the dirt, you're supposed to get right back and cowboy up because when you put that cowboy hat on your head, you're representing a tradition. For most, that's the reward. Money-wise, the risks aren't worth it."

"I'm sure your father was very proud of you." Sunshine smiled.

J. W. said, "Well, now that's another story." He shook his head again.

"Are you still involved in the rodeos?"

"The closest I get to the rodeo nowadays is from the contact I have with the New Mexico Rodeo Association in providing the livestock for their events. The state fair is coming up in September. I'll be rounding up and shipping off my herd for that. Hey! It's startin' to rain. We'd better head on up the pass before the thunderstorm hits."

The two went to the door of the kitchen to say goodbye to Mamá Josefina. As soon as J. W. left Sunshine standing outside the doorway while he went in to find Mamá Josefina, a middle-aged, tall, sinewy man approached Sunshine and yelled, "Hey, we don't allow fucking white-trash hippies in our restaurant. Get the fuck out of here!" He mumbled, "Hippies are only good for kicking."

Sunshine stared in disbelief and said, "I was just leaving."

J. W. heard the commotion from the kitchen and hastened back to her side. "Wait a minute, partner. She's with me!"

Mamá Josefina came running from the kitchen, and she reprimanded her nephew in Spanish and English, saying, "Watch your tongue! These people are my guests."

Her nephew said, "A hippie and a cowboy? Whoever heard of such a fucking joke?"

J. W. suddenly wasn't sure if he was angry with Mamá Josefina's nephew or with himself. He quickly bid his farewells to Josefina and escorted Sunshine out to his truck.

CHAPTER 11

ORILLA VERDE PILAR

"COME TOGETHER," THE BEATLES

J. W. and Sunshine continued on their journey to Taos in silence. J. W. was angry with the confrontation in the restaurant and questioned his raging emotions. *What the hell is wrong with me anyway? How could I be falling for this hippie chick? Why did I take her to Mamá Josefina's? For that matter, why did I even offer her a ride home?*

Although it was dark outside, the drive through the winding pass provided exhilarating strobes of lightning. A light rain splashed to the ground, with sudden bolts of light highlighting the chiseled land formations of the Embudito Mountain pass and Rio Grande River below.

A few miles before Pilar, J. W.'s truck gave a big kick,

followed by a loud bang. J. W. pulled the truck off the road and let it coast down the highway, onto a dirt road, then came to a stop. "What the hell?" Turning off the ignition, he grabbed a flashlight from under his seat and went out into the pouring rain to check out his truck.

Sunshine could hear him spitting out a long procession of cuss words.

He climbed back into the cab of the truck, soaking wet and madder than a hornet. "It's the drive shaft. I've broken a U-joint." He sighed. "And it's not something I can fix on the side of the road."

Sunshine asked, "Should we try to thumb a ride?"

J. W. shook his head in disgust. "No, at this time of night, there aren't many travelers on the highway—and it's probably another twenty miles to the next homestead. We'll have to wait it out here until dawn and then see if we can hitch a ride."

Sunshine offered a sweet smile, hoping to calm the tension. "It'll stop raining by then."

They sat in silence for several minutes and listened to the rain.

The soft strumming of the rain was calming to J. W. "We could at least go get comfortable inside the trailer. I've got some blankets behind the seat. Well? Should we make a mad dash to the trailer?"

Sunshine nodded.

J. W. said, "Ready? One, two, three!"

They dashed out of the truck, through the rain, and into the trailer.

Inside the trailer, J. W. began to laugh. His laughter lightened the mood, and in that uneasy moment, he made a truce with himself. He spread out a blanket onto the trailer floor and sat down on the blanket.

Sunshine joined him. She was beyond grateful for his amusement and the breaking of the tension.

He said, "For having a name like Sunshine, the rain sure does like to follow you."

Sunshine threw the blanket at him, and then she joined in on the laughter. "That's not funny."

"Sunshine, if your father was military, why did he bless you with an unusual name like Sunshine?"

"I was born in Hahn, Germany, in an air force hospital. Shortly after my mother gave birth to me, my father was admiring his new daughter and rocking me in his arms. He started singing, "You are my sunshine, my only sunshine. You make me happy when skies are gray. You'll never know, dear, how much I love you. Please don't take my sunshine away ... and the name just stuck. It was a popular song written by Jimmy Davis and Charles Mitchell in 1939."

"Your father was killed in Vietnam?"

Sunshine said, "Yes, he was a lieutenant in the air force

in the 615th Tactical Fighter Squadron, known as the Yankee Team. He was flying an F-100 Super Sabre based out of Da Nang. While on an intelligence-gathering patrol off the North Vietnam coast, he and one other pilot were shot down by North Vietnam MIGs." She paused as a whirl of memories swept through her mind. "That happened six months after President Kennedy was assassinated. My mother went crazy. She was trapped in his memory. She convinced herself that she was dependent on my father, and she could not live in reality without him. Her pain was too much; she never did recover, and she started binge drinking ..."

J. W. said, "And your mother, where is she now?"

Sunshine said, "My mother was born and raised in Hahn, Germany, where she met my father. My father found out later that she purposely got pregnant with me so my father would marry her and take her back to the States. My father was a happy-go-lucky guy who everybody loved. He always tried to make the best of every situation, but he did love her. I never could understand her, and I'm ashamed to say I didn't have much respect for her. I've always thought that we should strive to become the things we loved most about in the people who are gone. Carry forth the good from the past generation." She shook her head in disgust. "But she didn't have much good in her." She sighed. "I never did call her Mom. Ever since I was a little girl, I called her by her name, Marianne. My mother became a raging alcoholic. The three years after my father died, she got progressively worse, and she started including drugs in her collection of highs.

"We lived at many different air force bases while I was growing up. We were living on base at Kirtland in Albuquerque when my father died. After my father's funeral, we moved into the city for a short time because I wanted to finish high school there. I never did get to be a teenager. I was forced to be ten years older to take care of my mother. I was too busy taking care of my mother. I took on all her responsibilities: paying the bills on time, cooking, shopping, and cleaning. She continually challenged me, and I continually tried to keep her sober and out of trouble. One day, she got a crazy idea that she wanted to be part of the counterculture—and we moved to the commune a few years ago.

"Two summers ago, my mother went swimming in the Rio Grande near the gorge. She was drunk and tripping on LSD. I guess she thought she could breathe underwater. Carelessly, she drowned. She was such a foolish woman."

J. W. was shocked to realize he had been the one who found her mother's dead body, but he couldn't bring himself to tell her that. The truth in his tender heart allowed him to show compassion. This selfless compassion was melting away his prejudices. J. W. held her close and stroked her hair, wishing with all his heart that he could stroke away the pain with each movement of his hand. "Why do you stay at the commune?"

Sunshine said, "I guess I have nowhere else to go. My family has become the people of the commune. I don't have any other family, and I love the children. A couple years ago, my best friend, Blue—who I call my brother—came to live with me at the commune." Through misting eyes, she added, "Last winter, he was drafted into the army and is now in Vietnam. He's really all I have left."

J. W. looked at her with sincerity and said, "I'm sorry. I didn't mean to bring on an avalanche of emotion." He gently pulled her to him, placing her head on his chest, and hugged her.

Sunshine responded to his hug and wrapped her arms around his muscular frame. It felt good to be in his arms. She was conscious of how warm his body felt through his shirt. "Really, I'm all right. I've learned to deal with it. In the meantime, I believe in God and all his miracles. I continue to put my faith in him. I figure what we are is God's gift to us—and what we become is our gift to God." She looked up into his eyes. "Thanks for your concern."

J. W. said, "Makin' it in life is kinda like bustin' broncs: you're gonna get thrown a lot. The simple secret is to keep gettin' back on and keep ridin'."

Sunshine laughed at his analysis and instinctively traced

her fingers over his lips. "J. W., where the hell do you come up with all this wonderful cowboy logic?"

J. W. responded to the familiar yearnings, which she had evoked with her touch. His hand lifted to the back of her head. He drew her to him to meet his lips, and then he kissed her tenderly. Moist heat, silky smooth, with a swirl of sensations, his tongue began flirting and caressing her sweet mouth. Their breathing deepened, and an electric current rose through their bodies and minds, tightening their embrace.

As their lips parted, Sunshine gasped for air. She could feel her face was flushed with desire.

J. W. could feel his heart beating wildly; his need for Sunshine was unbearable. He said, "What is this hold you have on me, Sunshine? Gawl damn, I want you, lady." He swiftly drew her lips to meet his—all the while exploring and trying to find the answer to his overwhelming desire for her.

Every nerve ending sprung to life in their bodies with an exploding gratification of corporeal delight. Their lips parted from their sultry kiss, and J. W. continued to kindle their desire by nibbling on her ears and neck, adding to the sensual delight.

In a blissful daze, Sunshine fumbled with the buttons on his rain-soaked shirt and removed it from his strong frame. Sunshine gently pushed herself from his grasp and began to softly knead his muscular shoulders, continuing to his chest. Her mouth began to explore his neck and chest. She needed to taste him, to run her tongue over and explore the invigoration of his enthralling stature.

The luxuriousness of her exploring caused J. W. to inhale a soft hiss. "Jesus, woman, you've bewitched me!" He craftily drew Sunshine's dress over her head and tossed it to the side. His rough hands tenderly fondled her breasts, sending her heated flashes of desire. J. W. stood up and quickly discarded his boots and jeans. Then, with great strength, he pulled Sunshine up to kiss him. The kiss deepened their passion, and J. W. slowly and tantalizingly kissed her neck and then her breasts. Dropping to his knees, he continued his caress and kiss her stomach as he gently removed her panties. He kissed her thighs and briefly licked her sweet, heated essence. Then tracing his path back up to her neck and back to her lips, their sultry kiss once again blustered into rapture.

Without interruption to their kiss, taking no strength at all, J. W. pulled Sunshine onto his lap. She straddled his body, instinctively wrapping her legs around him. Sinking back onto the blankets, Sunshine was wrapped in her rising lust, and she could feel that J. W. was wildly hungry for her. She stroked his face with her breasts, rotating her moistened groin over the tip of his probing zeppelin, and then she softly eased herself onto his throbbing erection. Slowly, she lowered herself deeper and deeper, gasping a breath with every penetrating degree, slightly withdrawing and then lowering until she, at last, rested on his lap. Her body welded to his; he was completely buried within her.

With mastered stamina, J. W. slowly moved in and out of her, thrusting them into a frenzy of passion. She was unaware of the pleasurable, soft mewing noises she made. Invincibly and unknowingly, they kept their sexual rhythm to the raindrops hitting the top of the trailer. Persistent to rise to a stupendous climax, they were entwined in a great spiritual dance. They became unaware of the passing of the night. The dance continued through waves of passion that took complete control of their senses, ending with no choice but to yield. Sunshine stayed mounted on his lap, and J. W. held her head to his chest and wrapped his masculine torso around her, their hearts racing in tune with one another's. When their haze returned to consciousness, they relaxed in each other's arms on the blanket.

Sunshine traced her fingers over his chest and teased his stomach. "What do your initials stand for?"

J. W. gave her a light kiss and replied, "Julian Weston, my full birth name is Julian Coalton Weston."

She smiled and said, "Julian? That's a classy name. Well, Mr. Julian Coalton Weston, let's go out and play in the rain. I love the rain."

J. W. laughed. "Lady, I would love to lick the raindrops

off your sweet little body." He stood up, picked her up, and carried her out into the rain. Under the canopy of rain, they embraced one another and giggled, feeling the soft raindrops fall in an enigmatic pattern over their shimmering, naked bodies. Sunshine intuitively began softly biting, nibbling, and licking the water from his body, renewing their sexual energy for each other. The fleeting lightning brilliantly illuminated the sky in a continual strobe of flashing lights, and crashing thunder rumbled, echoing through the mountains beyond.

The trees, flashing sky, rain, and crisp air were all part of their erotic flight. As they stood locked in each other's embrace, there wasn't another soul in their universe.

In this dreamlike sequence, J. W. watched the lightning flash illuminate the silhouette of Sunshine's lovely face and the slender graceful outline of her form. He knew this beautiful woman in his embrace was taming his heart, but could she tame his mind as well?

J. W. said, "You're going to catch a chill out here." He picked her up and carried her back into the trailer. They wrapped another blanket around themselves and cuddled until lust renewed itself; they made love over and over again until their stillness finally settled into an untroubled sleep.

The morning sun exploded with a flash into their slumber.

Joel flung open the trailer door and laughed. "Well, I see

you've picked up the new horse trailer. It's a beaut, but did she come with the trailer?"

J. W. was jolted back into reality. "Oh ... uh ... my fucking truck broke down last night on the way home."

CHAPTER 12

BIEN HOA: LETTER FROM BLUE

"PURPLE HAZE," JIMI HENDRIX

The ride home from Pilar with J. W. and Joel was uncomfortably long and quiet, but at least J. W. had the nerve to make general conversation. They talked mostly about horses.

Joel was amazed and amused that Sunshine had tamed the old gelding that she called Rusty and kept the conversation going about that. Joel and J. W. agreed it would be okay and gave Sunshine permission to ride the rusted gelding whenever she liked. He dropped her off at the commune without giving her any indication about seeing her again.

Sunshine tried to settle back in at home, but she was unable to keep J. W. off her mind. He would work his way into her head like an annoying song you can't stop thinking of. She forced herself to take a walk to the highway to check the mail, being thankful the box was a bit of a walk down the road, which gave her time to think. She tried to keep her mind off her troubles. She tried dancing about in the road, looking for guidance in the sky, and counting clouds. She sang "Amazing Grace," but she lost the words halfway through. She picked flowers from the fields, enjoying their colors, fragrances, and beauty of the blooms, but nothing could clear her mind. She felt so alone with her footsteps.

She prayed and sought peace in her spiritual center. She recited, "God is the source of the air I breathe, the food that nourishes my body, and the spirit that comforts my soul. I breathe in this truth. I exhale, releasing any thoughts of scarcity or lack. I return to that deep, abiding inner peace that fills me. I am infused with peace, strength, joy, and gratitude." Her prayer helped her for a short while, but her mind kept wandering back to the memories of the night before with J. W. She kept replaying J. W.'s kisses. She replayed the passion of his hands touching her and the way his body felt against hers, which sparked surges of passion. She wanted to crystallize the night in her head so she would have it there forever, the way a photograph freezes time.

She was startled by a jackrabbit darting out in front of her on the road. She wondered what he was running from—or to.

Was he running toward a dream or from a nightmare? "Damn it! Get a grip on yourself. I will not let any man get to me." As she kicked small stones in the road, she muttered, "I trust in God." She looked up to the sky. "You hear that, God? I'm putting this situation in your hands."

In the mailbox, she found a letter from Blue. Excited to hear from him, she read it as she strolled back to the commune. In no hurry to return to the commune, she dragged her feet in the dirt, becoming more and more absorbed in Blue's words. The more she read, the less aware she became of the scenery around her. She was soon transported to a far-off land.

Hey Sunshine,

I've been out on patrol, and I finally have the opportunity to sit down and write. It sounds like life at the New Buffalo is pretty much the same. I sure do miss everyone.

Trust me when I tell you I am counting the days until I come home. We all set up what is known as a "short-timers' calendar," and every day, we cross off the days we have left in this hellhole, but damn it! The days left on my short-timers' calendar seem anything but short. Fuck! Every day here is one day closer to home.

Thanks for sending the care package with cookies, candy, Kool-Aid, and stuff. I shared it with everyone; it's kind of an unspoken rule with the guys here. A kind of "all for one" thing. A cookie here is more than just a cookie. And Tabasco sauce is liquid gold, a drop goes into every C-rats to either add flavor or kill the taste. Oh, what I wouldn't give for some New Mexico green chili.

Every three days, a chopper resupplies us with C-rats, water, clean clothes—well, sort of clean, ammo, and mail. Our squad leader passes out the mail, and we each shake any package a guy happens to get and try to guess what's in it. It becomes a funky ceremony, and its contents are often the subject of obscene conjectures. If it contains any kind of edibles, etiquette requires that we share it immediately—and then we all give it a rating. Our letters are the bridges between Vietnam and our worlds back home. With the possible exception of our rifles, nothing is more important to the guys than their mail. I know that might sound silly to you back there, but as I said, things are different here. You'd be surprised at the simple things we get a kick out of. It's those silly small moments that help keep me together. If it weren't for some of those things, I think a man could get lost out here. I don't mean lost without a compass—I mean lost without sanity or a soul.

Little Joe appreciates your letters. We all read them—so be careful what you put in there. I think all the guys have fallen in love with you. Mickey is the only one in the squad who's married, and Doug and Jay have steady girlfriends. So, there's an ongoing game as to who will be the first to get back to the world and marry you. You're the best, Sunshine, and I'm proud to have you as my sister.

Everyone in my platoon holds a weird natural allegiance to the CAV, and even not particularly wild with patriotic feelings, we do respect and watch over each other. When you're out on patrol, it's your ass they're covering for as well. There's a lot of joking and kidding that goes on, trying to keep our spirits high on our three-day break between patrols, but when we're out in the bush, it's a different story. There is no playing around; we depend on each other to stay alive. I can't explain it, but when you've allowed yourself to place your life in another man's hands, you build a bond with that man. After a while, words like "me" and "myself" quickly start being replaced with words like "us" and "we."

In some places, the scenery is beautiful here—so lush and green—but the death and destruction far outweigh the beauty. We've been out on one-week-long recon missions in the Xuan Loc area, twenty-five clicks north of Bien Hoa. The small rivers have lots of bamboo bridges used by Charlie that we take photos of and report to the demo forces. They blow them up along with everything around them until the area has been reduced to a bleak, fucking, smoldering hellhole. It's hard to see the beautiful countryside demolished like that. On the other hand, we would love to see this entire place blown out of existence. No matter the number of bombs and shit we drop on them, those damn gooks keep rebuilding. I swear they're half ant!

When we are out on patrol, our job is to scout out the territory for well-used trails and bunkers so that we can report back to the base—and they bomb them to hell.

Fuck me! I've killed more monkeys, birds, lizards, and snakes, thinking they were gooks, than I can count. I'm not sure how the war's going, but I know one thing: the wildlife of Vietnam has suffered dearly at our hands.

There is a fucking incredible massacre of humanity here. The human damage is unreal, and it's not just the dead. It's the GIs who can't talk in coherent sentences anymore, the sick bastards who have found they love to kill, and even the gentle, graceful Vietnamese people who have known nothing but war their entire lifetimes. A lot of those same people have turned into thieves, black marketers, and prostitutes. The few South Vietnamese soldiers we have had working with us seem all too content to watch us "gung ho round eyes" carry on the fight with the North Vietnamese.

Hey! I heard on the radio that a man successfully walked on the moon. That's amazing. Just think, while I was out walking through fields riddled with so many bomb craters, making it look like the surface of the moon, Neal Armstrong was out walking on the moon. Fuck me! That's cool as shit! Can you imagine being up on the moon and looking down at our planet? "That's one small step for man, one giant leap for mankind." That statement sure holds true.

Anyway, I'll look up at the moon tonight and wave hi to ya. Hey! I guess I better get over to the mess tent before the hot food is all gone.

I'll write again in two weeks. We're scheduled for a three-day in-country R&R in Vung Tau.

Please keep writing!

Love,

Blue

P.S. Send me some more of your amazing cookies, please.

P.S.S. Enclosed is fifty bucks I won at poker last night. Buy yourself something groovy.

After reading Blue's letter, Sunshine stopped to think about how his words didn't sound like him; these words sounded like those of a warrior. She released a huge sigh. "Dear God, please keep Blue safe." She broke down sobbing until her stomach cramped. She could hardly bear to read the news from Blue's current world.

She began to reminisce about their last summer together: the time they spent together exploring, meditating, and reading about the way to spiritual enlightenment, trying to live in a world without material accumulation, in search of a higher truth. *Dear God, is it working? Is it all a comic game of pretending?*

Blue had sent money, and she had sold some of her art. She knew she had enough money to rent a place of her own, but where should she live? And if she did move, she knew she would be alone.

"Dear God, please lead me to the path of my future. Help me make the right decisions. Angels, be with me. And while you're at it, God, please surround Blue with a whole battalion of angels. Dear God, I want and need your guidance. I know God has given us all free will on earth, but I want my angels' intervention. Please guide me."

Sunshine stopped to pick the wildflowers that lined the dirt road, and then she returned to her world at the commune.

CHAPTER 13

VUNG TAU: THREE-DAY R&R

"THE THRILL IS GONE," B.B. KING

Dear Sunshine,

I'm writing this from our R&R center in Vung Tau. Really? Rest and relaxation? It's more like this: "Get your shit together—or you're liable to get it blown off when you get back to the bush." It's a little vacation that Uncle Sam sends us on.

This is the first time since I've been dumped in Nam that I've slept with both eyes closed—let alone in a bed. Holy shit, we have flush toilets. Like I said in my last letter, it's the simple things you learn to appreciate.

The guys all say hi. Little Joe loved the sketches of Wheeler Peak with the Taos Valley below that you sent in your last letter. We have them hanging in our bunker. Little Joe stared at those pictures for hours. While he stared at them, I knew what he was thinking. He escaped for just a little bit into those pictures, and for just a few moments, he was there in Taos and not here in this hellhole. He says he wants to come check it out in person when we get back.

We got a new guy, Danny, and the poor fucking guy never stepped a foot out of his small town of Cushing, Oklahoma, until he was drafted. He's so cherry that he fucking scares me. His mom sends us lots of great candies and cookies, and she even sent us some brownies. So, we're all doin' our best to take real good care of him. I'm half kidding about that. He's as important as every other man in my squad—but his mom's brownies really do help me to like him.

This fucking country is spinning out of control. Vung Tau is dinky-dow-crazy. Bombs continually go off in the distance just outside of the city. Children are hanging on you and begging in the streets. Keep your money stashed in inside pockets; otherwise, the kids will run off laughing, and you will be instantly broke. Damn thirteen-year-old little girls are advertising themselves as prostitutes: "GI, you like me, want number 1 boom-boom only ten dolla." Mothers are selling their young daughters; you can't imagine how low a culture can sink during war. I tell myself they're just trying to make the best of a situation that is unthinkable and unbelievable to most of us.

Oh, yeah! I've had my baptizing with "Saigon Tea" at the Palace Hotel bar. This place was a trip. You no more than sat down, and a Vietnamese girl would be unzipping your pants: "You handsome, take me to bed?" She tries to talk you into buying her a drink. The drinks seem to be watered-down whiskey. The price is high, but it's worth it. Most of the guys just go there and pay the high prices to be close to another human being who doesn't stink of gunpowder, C-rats, or rotting combat boots. And they have a band of young Vietnamese guys trying their best to imitate an American rock band. One steps up to the mic and says, "We rike to pray for you popuder American song, 'Fry Me to da Moon.'"

I've been reading the *Stars and Stripes* and listening to AFVN radio newscasts about what's happening back in the States. Sounds like the same fucking bullshit in Washington—politics, with them coloring the information that they give to the American people. Fuck it! Sometimes I feel there are two different wars going on: the one we're actually fighting here in Nam and the one being fought in some other country in the world, also named Vietnam, and that's the one that gets presented to the American people. It's all such fucking bogus bullshit. The commanders of the American forces say they have feelings for the Vietnamese, but we sure the fuck never see it. There is an awful lot of ego in the military hierarchy and an awful lot of guys kissing ass to get ahead so they can get promoted so they can get the hell out of Vietnam. We should give any officer with more than two bars the task of spending one day filling fucking body bags.

Captain Mayer is our commander. He's the biggest piece of shit of them all. I can respect the knowledge he has as far as "academics." Hell, that bastard probably could recite every battle since the Civil War, but as far as good old common sense, he doesn't have a fucking clue. You can't imagine the division between officers and enlisted men. It's like the difference between serfs and royalty, but you take some hot-shit Annapolis grad, with a pair of silver bars on his collar, and toss him out into a skirmish with some persistent gooks, you'll soon find out he froze up in the heat of it and never fired his rifle, but when the first green tracer passes between his legs, he quickly finds out that all those fancy-ass battle classes were no good to him. Ha! After the gunfire, the officer yells out to the platoon, "Which one of you GIs shit in my pants? Ha! Ha! Ha!"

The highlight of my three days of R&R so far has been last night. We scored some great Thai weed, and we all got stoned and drunk.

We went to the movies to see *Beach Blanket Bingo* with Frankie and Annette. All the voices were speaking Vietnamese, and we laughed our asses off.

Love,

Blue

P.S. Please keep writing!

Several hours later, Blue reread his letter. He questioned whether or not to send it. He decided that it would just scare Sunshine, and he rewrote it and sent her a softer version of the letter. He knew this war was hardening him forever. He knew he'd never be the same man.

Each member of Blue's platoon was given a letter written from children at a junior high school in Abilene, Texas. Blue read his letter and got a big kick out of it:

853 Lexington Street
Abilene, Texas

Dear friend,

I just wanted to write to tell you how much we appreciate you being over there.

We know you are risking your life every day for us and our freedom.

I am a student of Lincoln Junior High. I hope we can become good friends! We had to write this letter for our English class. I'm taking Summer School Classes because I failed my English class last year.

I played eighth-grade football last year, and we just about had the championship. If I get my grades back up, I'll play ninth-grade football. Hopefully, we can take the championship this coming year.

Please write me back. I have a lot I can say. If you write, give me your address—or even better, tell me how I can get my next letter to you!

I have always wanted a pen pal. I hope you will write.

Oh! I forgot to tell you that I was vice president of the seventh grade. Well, I was elected by default because no one else ran against me.

Best of luck!! Keep your head down.

Your friend,
Scott Dillingham

P.S. I hope you can read my writing!

Sunshine tried to send Blue something every day. She sent him a daily letter. Sometimes she would send him a magazine article or a newspaper clipping she felt he would enjoy. She even sent him homemade cookies sometimes, but it was her sketches and watercolor paintings that Blue enjoyed the most. They kept his soul in touch with the reality of home and his instinct for survival intact. They were a reminder that through all the ugliness, there was still beauty.

After completing her routine chores and the lessons she spent teaching the children, Sunshine spent many an afternoon taking walks to meditate and pray for the safe return of Blue. She prayed for J. W.'s acceptance and understanding of all God's children. She also prayed that he would overcome adversity and find the ability to see beauty, compassion, and joy.

Sunshine followed the path to find her favorite colorful, spirited place on the Rio Grande River. She would spend hours praying and painting the landscape so she could send her paintings to Blue.

While sitting at Cedar Springs, the brilliant golden rays of the sun offered her the potential for splendid change, healing, and renewed balance. She felt the rays of the sun on her face. It was not a harsh and burning ray, but it was slightly muted and diffused, like God's whisper. This inspirational light brought happiness to her soul. The light gave a promise of splendid change, healing, and renewed balance. There was more than just warmth in those soft waves of sunbeams. There was hope: hope for her future, hope for Blue's safe return, and hope for J. W.

"Dear God, surround Blue with your protective light, giving him your comfort and keeping him safe. Let him feel your arms around him. Let him know that you are always with him."

As she meditated, she was reminded of when she and Blue first arrived at the commune with her mother. They had both journeyed to find the answers to life's "internal trip." They spent hours studying and researching many different religions, consoling in each other, trying to weigh out the answers, and finding a spiritual center in the greatest of all classrooms: humanity.

CHAPTER 14

CERRO DE LOS TAOSES: WESTON RANCH

"WORKING MAN BLUES," MERLE HAGGARD

Weston Ranch was homesteaded by J. W.'s grandfather in 1901, eleven years before New Mexico became a state. With meticulous attention, J. W.'s father, Owen, had rebuilt their home in 1947 as a birthday gift for his wife, Katie. Among the tall, dignified cottonwood trees, the Weston hacienda stood proud at the northeast end of the property.

The territorial-style adobe home glistened with Southwestern charm. The south and east sides of the house hosted portal porches with panoramic views of Wheeler Peak and the Taos Valley. The home entertained a great room with a twenty-two-foot raised viga ceiling and Saltillo-tiled floors. Each room was adorned with a cozy kiva fireplace, adding to the warmth and elegance. The furnishings had an incredible sense of heritage. The durable, handmade pieces were timeless and noble, captivating the frontier's past along with the sophisticated present.

The Weston Ranch had ideal western landscapes, which were profoundly beautiful and unique. God had painted the land with a multitude of celestial colors and light shades that could be found everywhere—simplistic sagebrush-scattered mesas, wildflowers, remote pastures, arroyos, and towering mountains adorning bellowing luminous clouds—and it was rich with the history of the native people of Taos.

All the responsibilities of the ranch were shared between J. W., his sister, Wendy, and his brother-in-law. The neighboring old-timers said they would never be able to handle the responsibilities of running the ranch when Owen died two years ago, but they had showed them differently. They had several cowhands come and go, and none stayed more than a year at a time.

The Weston Ranch was 3,883 acres, which kept thirty-seven rough-stock horses, six well-trained, saddle-broken riding horses, and give or take seven head of cattle. The Weston Ranch-registered brand was recorded at the state of New Mexico Livestock Board as the "Rocking W."

Spending time there assured silence and audible quietness that few could ever imagine. One could witness and experience nature's quintessence and ever-changing moods and fill their lungs with clean air while experiencing the fragrant smells of the earth.

Mother Nature had gifted the land with elk, bighorn sheep, antelopes, coyotes, bobcats, prairie dogs, jackrabbits, cottontails, lizards, and snakes. Every now and then, a black bear or cougar would venture down from Wheeler or Lobo Peak.

J. W. held a deep God-centered connection to this land; the connection grew to be an intrinsic response that was steeped in nature. This connection became his natural meditation and soldering relationship with God. It was a daily vitamin for his psyche. And even though his father was a hard-headed monster to be raised by, and lacked any tender fatherly qualities, Owen Weston was a deeply religious man with a strong continually evolving faith in God, and he conveyed and instilled that faith to his children, J. W. and Wendy.

J. W. was known as J. W. only to his friends and the rodeo world. His birth name was Julian Coalton Weston. When he was at home, he was known as Julian. And although he yearned unmercifully for his rodeo days, J. W. loved and respected his family's ranch. He spent most of his time out on the range or at the family home with his younger sister, her husband, and their two children. Justin was four, and Kayleigh had just turned three. He adored his niece and nephew and spent as much of his free time as he could afford playing with them. When Justin was a toddler, he couldn't pronounce Uncle Julian. Instead, he called him "Guncle Julie."

Joel and Wendy were in the process of building a new home for themselves on the south end of the ranch. J. W. wasn't sure if he'd get used to living alone in the main house and wasn't looking forward to them leaving.

J. W. and Wendy had always been very close. When J. W. was five, their mother passed away soon after giving birth to Wendy, which left Owen Weston and J. W. to raise a baby girl. Although Owen hired a full-time nanny to help with the baby, J. W. worked hard to help out with his new baby sister.

Their nanny was from Chihuahua, Mexico. Her name was Maria Gutierrez, but they both called her Mama Gutchie. She was a tall, thin, elegant woman with a magical matriarchal ability about her. Even though her dark eyes were unreadable, her love for the children shined through.

Mama Gutchie spoke mostly Spanish, and the children had learned to speak it fluently. When Wendy began elementary school, she had a hard time adjusting because she spoke better Spanish than English. Mama Gutchie's only child, Joel, was the same age as Julian, and since the ranch isolated them from any other children, Julian, Joel, and Wendy bonded together like the Three Musketeers.

While Julian was galloping around the Southwest, tracking the rodeo circuit, Wendy and Joel fell in love. However, Owen Weston's deep prejudices insisted that Wendy was too young to be in love, and he refused for her to fall for a "Mexican" boy. Wendy was only sixteen when she became pregnant with Joel's baby. Owen was outraged, and if J. W. hadn't calmed the storm, Owen would have shot Joel.

Only after a heated confrontation with J. W. and against his will, Owen consented for Wendy to marry Joel before the baby was born. Even though he knew how much Wendy and Joel loved each other, he never did accept them together—although he deeply loved his grandchildren.

Wendy shared her love with everyone. Her sweet, chubby frame reminded everyone of a cute little baby doll from a toy store. She was a foot shorter than Joel. Wendy had sparkling blue eyes, and her long, silky hair was light blonde.

Joel was a quiet, peaceful, profoundly humble, jovial man, and he was by far one of the most handsome Mexican natives in New Mexico. He was a wiry six foot four, lanky and slender, and he gathered many a gaze from girls and women.

After J. W. and Joel towed his truck from Pilar, life settled back into its normal routine. The ranch always needed attention. During the countless hours J. W. spent in solitude, riding the ranch and checking on livestock, he couldn't help but ponder his feelings for Sunshine. She provoked a whole range of emotions, and his mind whirled like a dust devil twirling in the wind. He admired her honesty, her natural modesty, and her infectious, positive outlook on life. He lusted for her sensual, provocative body and her blazing green eyes, but what he couldn't get past—and what he couldn't understand—was why the hell she had to be a gawl-damned fucking hippie! With his emotions so tangled up, he felt like an imposter. He felt like he was living with his father's prejudiced soul, and he hated the thought of resembling his father's imperfections in any way. His prejudices were as twisted as the old juniper trees in the nearby hills and valleys.

While Julian was out on the range one afternoon, he saw Sunshine riding the rusted stallion. He stopped and watched her for several minutes, trying to get up the nerve to ride over and talk to her. He upset with her being a hippie, and his embarrassment chased him like a wild bull. He was extremely embarrassed by the way he had treated her. He wanted to talk to her and see her, but he stalled, amazed at the amount of courage he had to dig up. He spent a couple of hours storing it up and losing, arguing with his ego about his feelings for her and his motives for talking with her. He had practiced what he would say over and over, but he never got up the courage to go talk to her.

Finally, a week later, he waded through his bullheaded hick ego and pride and got up the nerve to ride over to the commune to see her. He even got as far as the east side of the river when he found a group on male hippies sitting around naked and sharing a joint. Two the men were making out. As J. W. rode by, the pair of gay hippies held out a lit joint and invited him to join them for a hit of their joint. This instantly set him off, and he quickly turned his horse around and went back to the ranch.

Julian couldn't help but remind himself about the horrifying event that took place with the psycho cult leader, Charles Manson, and his followers and the massacred actress Sharon Tate and her guests. And the thousands of hippies demonstrating throughout the United States burning our American flag and flaunting their slogan of "Sex, Drugs and Rock-n-Roll." J. W. had lost one of his rodeo buddies to the Vietnam War. He didn't believe our men should be in there fighting the war, but he didn't agree with the way the hippies went about protesting either, and the severe harassment of the servicemen when they returned home.

Even though Sunshine was only miles away, J. W. continued to dig up memories of her and find traces of her. While he was out checking the horses one morning, he found a string of wildflowers around the rusted stallion's neck. *Damn, how she has captivated my soul.* He kept telling himself that it was only lust—just a new blanket companion. Of all the cowgirls he had ever tossed in bed with, none of them fascinated him enough to haunt his mind as Sunshine had. Sunshine's physical images were inscribed in his mind so clearly. He kept shaking his head and thinking, *Damn it! Why can't I keep my mind off of her?*

On a hot, late summer evening, Julian was on the porch, watching the sunset and reminiscing about the sunsets he had witnessed from this ranch.

Wendy said, "Julian, you've been quieter than a cricket without legs. What's bothering you of late?"

J. W. said, "I learned a long time ago that it's best to keep your troubles pretty much to yourself 'cause half the people you'd tell 'em to won't give a damn—and the other half will be glad to hear that they're your troubles and not theirs."

Wendy's eyes resembled wonderful bits of the spring sky, glistening as she laughed at his cowboy logic. "Remember that even a kick in the ass is a step forward. Julian, I know who's been on your mind. Joel told me about her. Why don't you go talk to Sunshine?"

Julian laughed, hugged his sister, and said, "There's a lot more to ridin' that horse than just sittin' in the saddle and lettin' yer feet hang down."

The two siblings sat on the porch and laughed and teased each other until the children came running out to see what was so funny. Julian had his sister wrapped in a headlock, messing up her long blonde hair, and Kayleigh and Justin playfully yelled and pulled at Julian to stop messing with their mama.

Julian looked up and saw Sunshine sitting on the rusted stallion. She was embarrassed to be interrupting J. W. at his home. She had spent the past week trying to get up the nerve to go see him—and then finding him at such a playful moment with this other woman, her mind tumbled and fumbled. *Is this his wife and children? Is this the reason he became so distant?*

Julian released his sister and briskly walked over to Sunshine. "Sunshine, what brings you here?"

Sunshine suddenly became incredibly tongue-tied. "I, uh, I came to ask you a question, uh ... I didn't mean to interrupt."

Wendy came over to Julian and said, "Hi, I'm Julian's sister, Wendy. Please, won't you come join us for some iced tea or lemonade?"

Sunshine was suddenly very relieved. "Yes, uh, iced tea sounds wonderful. Thank you." She dismounted from Rusty.

Justin came over to Sunshine and offered her a handshake. "Hi, my name is Justin, and that's my baby sister, Kayleigh. You sure are a pretty lady."

Sunshine smiled and shook Justin's hand. "It's nice to meet you, Justin. My name is Sunshine."

Wendy said, "Good, I'm glad you will join us. I'll be right

back with some iced tea. Come help me, Justin and Kayleigh, and leave your Guncle Julie with his guest." As she started for the house, she said, "*Guarda su lengua y portese bien trate de mantener un conversacion mentras estoy afuera. Oh! Esta bonita como dijeste.*" ("Put your tongue back in your mouth and try to carry on a conversation while I'm gone. And yes, Julian, Justin's right, she is a very beautiful woman.")

Julian tried to sound angry as he said, "Yes, I agree, Wendy, but just so you know, Sunshine also speaks Spanish." He shook his head. "A lesson every cowgirl should learn is where her business ends and someone else's starts."

Julian offered Sunshine a seat on the porch. "Well, what a surprise. What brings you here? Are you all right?"

"Yes, I'm fine. The last time we were together, uh, I mean ... the last time when we drove from Santa Fe, you mentioned you were planning a business trip to Albuquerque during the state fair. Well, I was wondering if I could bum a ride from you? I mean, ride with you to Albuquerque? I would like to visit an old friend of my father's, and I have some business I need to do at UNM."

Wendy returned with their iced tea, and when Justin handed Sunshine her glass and sat next to her, Wendy laughed. "Hey, partner, don't get too comfortable. You're coming with me back in the house so we can leave your Guncle Julie with Miss Sunshine."

Justin said, "No, Mom. I want to stay here."

Joel came out of the house and tipped his hat to Sunshine. "Hola, Sunshine! It's good to see you again." After Wendy gave him a jab in the ribs, he added, "Justin and Kayleigh, why don't you come with your mom and me to check on the new colt." He gathered the children in his arms and began to walk toward the stables. "Adios, Senorita Sunshine. It was good to see you again."

Wendy said, "It was nice to meet you. Please come back."

Sunshine smiled and said, "What a wonderful family you have, *Guncle Julie*."

J. W. laughed. "Yes, I'm very lucky. So, you want to go to Albuquerque with me? I'll tell you what. I'll do you that favor if you do me a favor?"

"Sure, what's that?" she asked.

He thought, *Aw, shit! Why not?* "Every year, during the fair, the New Mexico Ranchers Association has a Cattlemen's Ball. I guess I need a date to take with me. I couldn't go alone. Would you do me a favor and accompany me to the ball?"

Sunshine was stunned. "What? You want *me* to be your date?"

J. W. smiled. "Yes, Sunshine. I'm asking you to return my favor and accompany me to the ball."

"Wow, I guess I could ..."

J. W. laughed and lifted his brow. "It's not that big of a deal."

Sunshine said, "Okay! Okay! I'll go."

J. W. said, "Good, I will be leaving on Friday morning. I'll pick you up at nine o'clock."

CHAPTER 15

CAMBODIA BORDER JUNGLE

"MAGIC CARPET RIDE," STEPPENWOLF

Dear Sunshine,

After returning from R&R, we were sent out somewhere near the Cambodia border on a patrol to scope out some of the NVA action. Keep in mind we're not supposed to cross over into Cambodia, but honestly, that's horseshit, 'cause I have no doubt that's where we were.

My God! The epic poems I could write about the horrors of this nightmare. Sometimes I think it's so bad it must be a dream, a nightmare that I'll wake up from, lying in my bed back home, covered in sweat and thinking, *Thank God!* I'm not trying to worry you, but I'm tired and I'm scared. I thought I was scared when I first got here. I'm not sure how much of this a man can be expected to handle.

Of the men in my original squad, only Doug, Troy, Mickey, Jimbo, Little Joe, and I are left alive and unharmed. A squad normally has five or six men each. All good guys, and I'm proud to stand with each of them. We hear fucking artillery wherever we go; there is no peace in this godforsaken land. Even right now they're firing eighty-one-millimeter mortars in the background. In a weird way, you get accustomed to it. You develop a sense as to when it's something you need to worry about—or if it's some other poor fucker who needs to worry about it.

My days go something like this. In the early mornings, I put on my fighting gear. It consists of a web belt with ammo pouches, hand grenades, smoke grenades, first-aid pouch, and canteens. I put two bandoliers of ammo around my neck so that it crosses my chest; running out of bullets is never a good idea. Then comes my thirty-pound rucksack, poncho, poncho liner, five C-ration meals, rain jacket, extra canteen, extra ammo, and other extra paraphernalia. Sometimes we'll leave gear behind to carry extra rounds. I'd rather be hungry and wishing I had that one last grenade than the other way around. So, with all that, I follow my squad leader through the soggy mud, up and down hills, and through the thickest jungles I have ever seen. I had no idea so many plants could grow so close together. Fucking a! I've never seen so much mud! There's mud on the roads, mud in the rice paddies, mud in the fields and mountains, and there is even mud in the jungle. The jungle, with all the layers of foliage that are so intermeshed, that whatever sunlight penetrates is but a diffused glow. All this walking is done in wet socks, blistered feet, jungle rot, and sprained ankles. We live in mud and rain. I look like a fucking human prune. I'm so sick of the fucking mud and rain. Ha! We sure don't see this kind of rain in New Mexico, do we?

There are leeches all over, and during what little time we get for a siesta, the mosquitoes storm you and suck out so much blood that you need a fucking transfusion when you get back to camp. Even while I'm lying with my poncho completely wrapped around me, those fucking tiny bastards eat at me. I swear, Sunshine, if I ever get out of here, I'm never leaving New Mexico again. I don't want to see another jungle, I don't want to live where it's humid, and I especially don't want to live anywhere where there's an abundance of mosquitoes!

Once again, thanks for your letters and sketches. Whenever the mail comes, the guys all check out whatever comes from you first. You've become somewhat of a celebrity around here.

You mentioned in your last letter that you were worried about us getting so high over here. Hey, you needn't worry. I can assure you if we're anywhere near danger or headed to the bush, we're all very straight. You have to be to keep up a keen survival sense. We've got a job to do, and we do it well. We depend on each other to stay alive—to cover each other's asses. My squad doesn't play any games, and no one gets high if we're headed out on patrol.

If you get careless out here, you end up zipped in a green body bag. The only reason we get high during the stand-down time is to stay numb to this hell; otherwise, you spend all your time thinking about what you *just* went through and worrying about what you're *about* to go through. Don't worry. I'm not taking any chances. I'm taking care of myself and taking every chance I get to stay out of danger. No one here wants to make it home worse than I do. We're the 1st Cav—some of the best-trained fighters in the world. Of course, every military division thinks that, but I plan to put every bit of that training to good use. To be quite specific, the saving of my ass!

Two weeks ago, before I went on R&R, we were out on a recon patrol, we went into a cool tiny VC village, and although there were only old men and women and children left, the Vietnamese people were incredibly warm and friendly. It kinda stuns me to see people who, after the hell, they and their country have been through, can find it in their heart to be friendly and kind. We met up with the 2nd Battalion, 5th Regiment, 1st Marine Division and helped them inoculate the villagers with some vaccines they needed. We left them with some extras out of our C-rats and whatever else we could scrounge up. It wasn't much, but geez, Sunshine, you'da thought we'd left them a prime rib dinner for everyone in the village. I think there's something we can all learn from the people in that village. Remember us studying together? Remember coming across passages that talked about being careful not to overlook things and people you wouldn't think you could learn something from? I think about those times, Sunshine. Although I'll admit at times it's hard to be grateful for a learning experience out here.

Hey, thanks again for your letters you've been writing. We all read them until the pages are worn and torn, although I didn't share the last one about this cowboy J. W. I sure hope you don't get hurt. Please take care of that precious heart of yours. You know how I feel about you.

I know now that I've taken for granted a lot of the simple things in life, including the cool, clean snowfall over the mesas above

New Buffalo and the spring showers that are followed by a clear and colorful rainbow over Wheeler Peak. Ha! Even Tylor's little rug rats! All of this means so much, and how little I've appreciated them until now. And I wonder, why it should take something like this to force us to appreciate those things. Gawd, I can't wait to be home.

Most of our days are fairly uneventful, but the nights are pure fucking hell! There has only been one night that I have been able to see the stars, but when I looked up at them, it was so hard to believe that the same stars shine over you. Fuck me! It seems as if we live in two different worlds. I don't really know the reason I'm writing this … actually I'm writing because I have to write or go out of my mind. Hope you don't mind the ramblings of a homesick GI.

Thanks for being there for me.

All My Love,
Blue

PS. Ha! I read in the *Stars and Stripes* that last week, the US House of Representatives approved a proposed constitutional amendment guaranteeing equal rights for women. That damn bill had been introduced every year since 1923 and finally passed? Who knows, this may signal a new crusade for total sexual equality—and maybe they'll start drafting women for Vietnam.

What Blue didn't tell her was they went back through the village the next day—where they had fed and inoculated the old men, women, and children—and found that the NVA had come through the village during the night and left a pile of severed arms. They were the arms of the villagers. They were the arms of old men, the women, and even the small arms of innocent children who hadn't done a thing to deserve that kind of animalistic treatment. Blue looked, and on each arm, he could see the place where they were inoculated. Blue took pictures of it, but when he submitted his film back at the developing tent, Lieutenant Shithead confiscated it and burned the negatives and photos. "We have to censor any hardship from the American people." Blue thought, *None of the so-called propaganda is to be seen by the American people at home. They get to see only the roses growing from our asses in Vietnam.*

Blue didn't tell her the truth about how many GIs were high on heroin. Heroin was dirt cheap and easy to find.

Blue truly believed that the American people had no idea

what went on in Vietnam, and that if they did, there would be more war protestors and their protests would hopefully take on a different form. It was all a sick game between the high-and-mighty government leaders, the greedy investors who gained to make more money, and the egotistical upper echelon of the US military.

Blue felt the brothers and sisters who were currently protesting back in the States were only doing so because they were riddled with bratty self-interests, and most where only protesting because it was the hip, groovy thing to do. He shook his head in disgust as his thoughts drifted to one of the GI returning from the States and telling him that he had been spit on by the protesters.

Looking up into the night sky, a blanket of peace fell over him. He thought about a story his Native American friend from Isleta Pueblo had shared with him. The stars in the midnight sky were the souls that have gone to heaven. Each star had been pierced by a soul who had pierced a hole in the veil of heaven, and the light that shines through is the light of God—the Great Spirit.

CHAPTER 16

ALBUQUERQUE: THE BIG CITY

"SUMMER IN THE CITY," THE LOVIN' SPOONFUL

Sunshine had stayed out at the Weston Ranch for a while, and J. W. invited his sister and brother-in-law and their kids to join them. Gunkle Julie informed his family that Sunshine was the talented artist and that she was the one who had painted the pictures he had recently displayed in his room. When Justin found out she was an artist, he ran into the house and brought back a pad of paper and colored pencils. Sunshine had a blast with the kids, drawing pictures of the ranch animals for them.

On Friday morning, Sunshine was up at the break of dawn and ready to go. She was excited about her scheduled trip to Albuquerque with J. W. They agreed that J. W. would take Sunshine to Albuquerque if Sunshine would accompany J. W. to the Cattlemen's Ball.

J. W. pulled into New Buffalo right as scheduled to pick up Sunshine, and she ran out to his truck to greet him. J. W. was apprehensive about going to the commune. He stepped out of his truck and helped Sunshine with her bag. As he was opening the door for Sunshine, Yogi ran up to them. She was wearing a long dress made up of a gauzelike material, and with the morning light behind her, her dress became perfectly transparent and showed her nakedness beneath. Her hair looked like she hadn't brushed it in weeks as it sprouted outlandishly all over her head. The makeup under her eyes left streaks down her washed-out face. She looked like a character from skid row.

Yogi had been waiting to get another peek at that good-looking cowboy who was stealing Sunshine's heart. She quickly walked up to Sunshine and J. W. and said, "Far out, Sunshine! I see your handsome goat-roping redneck is here to take you away from this hippie-ville commune." She could see that she had irritated J. W. and was loving his reaction. "Hey, cowboy, I'll bet you can bust a cherry as good as you bust a bronc."

J. W. tried to ignore her as he helped Sunshine into his truck. As he walked to the other side, Yogi blocked his way. She loved to fuck with people's minds and was getting off on irritating him, but for Sunshine's sake, she refrained from lifting her dress. Snarling her nose and petting her crotch, she said, "Don't you ever wonder why your precious little cowgirls always make such a fuss about protecting their hymens? You don't need to worry about that with me because this hippie chick loves to fuck like a rabbit." She put her hand over her mouth in feigned innocence.

Sunshine yelled out the window, "Yogi, that's enough. You can go now."

J. W.'s heart was pumping hatred, and he felt a need to spew some hostility, but without a word, he shook his head, stepped aside, and went around her.

Yogi leaned her head inside the cab of the truck and giggled. "Oh, come on, cowboy! Just because you are acting like a dick doesn't make yours bigger." Her giggles quickly changed to a triumphant laugh. Yogi loved the response she was getting from J. W. and howled and laughed until they drove off.

J. W. spun his truck tires in the dirt drive, leaving behind a huge cloud of dust.

Sunshine said, "Look, J. W. I'm sorry. She gets a little carried away sometimes."

J. W. gave Sunshine a quick look and an amused snicker. "Damn if she ain't a wild little bitch." His mind considered whether or not he was right to follow his heart in falling for this beautiful woman. *Damn her anyway! Why does she captivate me? What is her hold on me? I had so many girls chasing after me in the rodeo—and now I'm chasing the tail of a goddamn hippie!*

For an hour, they traveled in silence. Sunshine was getting bite marks on her tongue from fighting back the words she wanted to say. Finally, she couldn't take the tension anymore. She knew she had to try to break the ice. She heaved a big sigh and said, "Hey, listen, we didn't get off to a very good start. Can we start over again and forget about Yogi's little head trip?" She gave him one of her infectious smiles and held out her hand to propose a handshake as a peace offering.

Mocking the hippie gesture, he gave her a peace sign.

Sunshine laughed and returned the peace sign. Giggling, she blew him a kiss.

J. W. said, "Damn it, you're right." Her brilliant green eyes had softened him. He accepted her hand and kissed it. "Most folks are like a barbed wire fence. They have their good points, but you have to take caution 'cause they can scratch your ass too." Rubbing his chin and shaking his head, he laughed. "But durned is she enough to make a preacher cuss. She's a *desgraciada sin verguenza.* That ornery little slut sure does get under my skin."

They both laughed. When the laughter died, an easy feeling remained between them.

J. W. asked, "Why don't you pick out a tape for us to listen to? We've got a long ride ahead of us."

One of the modern-day entrainment sound systems was an eight-track player that played tapes of music. The first dash-mounted eight-track stereo was introduced by Ford in the Mustang, Thunderbird, and Lincoln.

Like a little girl in a toy store, Sunshine went through J. W.'s boxes of eight-track tapes. "Johnny Cash? I love Johnny Cash." She put in the tape and began to sing "Ring of Fire."

J. W. soon joined in the singing.

Like the generations of struggling pioneers who had journeyed before them, they traced the path along the life vein of New Mexico: the tumbling Rio Grande River.

Sunshine viewed the scenery closely as they passed through the Sangre de Cristo Mountains to the east, divided by the highway, with the opalescent Santa Clara and the rich vista of the Jemez Mountains towering above the spacious skies to the west. A vast array of colors greeted them, rich verdant greens, deep blue greens, along with a splash of aureate and pale yellows beneath the expansive, clear, crisp, azure skies. Sunshine said, "It is so beautiful here. God sure did good work. Didn't he?

"Yes, he sure did."

Sunshine said a silent prayer. *Dear God I see the beauty, the mystery and majesty of your creation. I thank you for the wonder and splendor you have gifted us. Thank you, dear Lord.* She continually tried to view the world with childlike wonder. She prayed that humankind could shift into a spiritual awareness and recognize the oneness of the tapestry of life in harmony with all creatures on earth. *We should honor all life on earth: the rain forests, oceans, and the icy reaches of the polar caps. The ecological actions we take ripple out to support elements on this living organism we call earth.* She prayed that everyone would be grateful for the bountiful home we share. *It shouldn't be Mother Earth's responsibility to take care of us. It should be us taking care of Mother Earth.*

The trail they followed was like taking a tour through time. It was easy to visualize how it had been one or two hundred years ago. The memories of old New Mexico are captured through the culturally rich, tiny communities: the remnants of old abandoned adobe homes, dilapidated trading posts, and graveyards of decaying automobiles cluttering the mesas.

September is the highlight of all seasons in the Land of Enchantment, and the countryside bursts with exploding colors of wildflowers in bloom: brilliant yellow sagebrush, purple asters, bright red Indian paintbrush, coneflowers, and brilliant yellow sunflowers lining the roads and highways.

South of Santa Fe boasts a geological variety of terrains. As they continued to follow the Rio Grande watershed, they passed villages and pueblos where the old and new combined. Barely a century ago, settlers had followed the same route on horseback and in carretas. Three hundred years earlier, the Spanish settlers, in great caravans of merchant oxen-pulled wagons, had rumbled through the same pass. Spain's terminal point from Mexico concluded in Santa Fe.

The rolling hills to the southeast are freckled with dots of cheddar brush; it looks like God sprinkled them on the hillsides with a saltshaker. The volcanic-formed, picturesque Jemez Mountains flow into the timeless atmosphere of rustic cliffs and hills, ending in the bottomlands along the Rio Grande River with its rich veins feeding the acequia irrigation to the serene farmlands and ranches below.

Though the tension was broken, J. W. and Sunshine traveled mostly in silence, introducing small talk about the scenery or the country-and-western music they listened to. They spoke in English and Spanish. Sunshine told J. W. about the letters she had received from Blue, and J. W. had even gotten his nerve up and asked some questions about the commune.

Sunshine said, "What's your sign?"

"Sign of what?"

"What star were you born under, you know, your zodiac sign?"

"I never believed in that horse crap. I guess I was born under the star of Taos."

Sunshine carefully searched for another question. "Are you going to teach your nephew Justin to rodeo bareback ride?"

J. W. realized that Sunshine was trying to soften the tension. His eyes briefly looked into hers. He smiled at the beautiful image she left him as he watched the highway. His mind moved through time and memory. "I'd love to teach Justin the ways of the rodeo. I miss the rodeo and would love to run back to it. I crave the fame and glory, the carefree travel, the action, and the danger—and being able to spend my money on whatever I fancied." He released a huge sigh. "It's time to grow up and give it up. I have a ranch to run now." He laughed. "Well, I guess I'd better clear it with my sister before I turn Justin into the next rodeo hero. Where were you planning on staying while you're in Albuquerque?"

Sunshine said, "An old friend of my father's lives on the base. I thought I'd ask him if I could stay there. If not, I'll check into a cheap motel."

J. W. said, "I'm not sure if I agree with your carefree attitude or your choice of places to stay the night." He raised his brow. "Look ... uh ... the Cattlemen's Ball is tonight at eight. It's being held at the Western Skies Hotel. I have reservations for a room there for the next two nights. Those big, fancy hotels usually have two beds anyway ... why don't you stay with me? At least for tonight ..."

Sunshine smiled and said, "Maybe for tonight, and then tomorrow, I'll see if I can stay with my father's friend, Sergeant Woods. I don't want to be in your way."

J. W. smiled and said, "Sunshine, you won't be in the way. I'm honored to have you with me." He had never known such an uninhibited woman; she was the sweetest creature he had ever met.

Albuquerque's colorful past was rivaled by its zany present. The mysticism of the majestic Sandia and Manzano Mountains towered over the busy city, exploding with expansion and development, sweeping out between the western desert hems of the Isleta and Sandia Indian Pueblos.

The thriving city houses half of the state's population, and the cultural influences from the Native Americans, Hispanic, and the Anglo settlers all try to balance out against the thriving contemporary metropolis.

Their drive took them east through the city's busy historic Highway 66 and Central Avenue, and people were buzzing about the streets.

As they passed the state fairgrounds, he said, "It looks like the fair is bustin' with excitement."

"It's been many years since I've been to the fair. Maybe I

can make it by here tomorrow. Gosh, I feel like such a stranger here. It's only been a few years since I lived here."

At the far eastern edge of the city, nestled at the foothills of the Sandia Mountains, J. W. parked his truck at the Western Skies Hotel. After he checked in, he drove around the back to park near his room.

He helped Sunshine out of the truck and escorted her to his room.

Sunshine remained wide-eyed and quiet.

When J. W. opened the door, Sunshine stepped inside and exclaimed, "Wow! Look at this place. It's so big ... and beautiful." She walked over to the sliding glass door and looked out. "We're right next to the pool!" She walked into the bathroom and joked, "Hey! Check it out—it even has indoor plumbing." She flung herself onto the bed and said, "It's been a long time since I've slept in a real bed." She started jumping up and down on the bed like a happy child.

J. W. laughed. "I don't want to find you wanderin' outside to find the outhouse. I take it you will be comfortable staying here tonight?"

Sunshine said, "You're damned right I will! This place must be costing you a fortune; let me help pay for it."

J. W. smiled. "No, darlin'. Just seeing your enjoyment of the place is payment enough." After seeing Sunshine's amusement, he was glad he had asked the front desk clerk to upgrade his room to an executive suite.

Sunshine went back over to the sliding glass window and said, "Wish I had a bathing suit. I don't guess they'll let me go skinny dippin'?"

J. W. smiled. "No, you can't go skinny dippin' in the pool!"

"J. W., do you mind if I take a shower?"

He laughed and said, "I suppose it's been a long time since you've done that as well?"

Sunshine answered, "As a matter of fact, it has! I go down to the river or the hot springs to take a bath every day."

Sunshine was in the shower for such a long time that J. W. began to worry. He peeked his head in the bathroom door and called out, "Are you all right in here—or did you go down the drain?"

Sunshine poked her head around the shower curtain, "Oh, sorry. Am I taking too long? It just feels so good. Why don't you come in and join me?"

J. W. felt his zeppelin stir in his pants and mumbled. "Hmmm ... temptin' ... very temptin'."

Sunshine asked, "What was that?"

J. W. said, "It's a temptin' offer, but I'll wait till you're done." He left the bathroom.

Sunshine came out of the bathroom with only a towel wrapped around her. Using another towel, she bent over to dry her hair. "Gosh, I've forgotten how good a shower could feel."

J. W. sat in a chair near the window and watched the beautiful woman before him. He found himself unable to respond. He thought, *That's what makes her so sexy. She's completely uninhibited. Damn, she is beautiful.* Just from watching her, he could feel the passion stirring in his Wranglers. "Well, I think I'll take a shower now," He quickly went to take a cold shower.

When J. W. returned, Sunshine—wearing only a sundress—was propped up against the headboard in one of the beds, lying tantalizingly among the pillows. She had the television on and was engrossed in an episode of *Gunsmoke*. "*Gunsmoke* is on. I love this show." Her eyes never left the TV. "Come join me!"

J. W. was wearing jeans and no shirt. *If she can walk around naked as a jaybird, I should at least try to relax a little as well.* He watched Sunshine for a minute. She looked like a little princess on a throne. She was lovely with her long hair draped over her shoulders, and the bedsheet gracefully covered her slender frame. He sat down next to her on the bed, and her sweet fragrance drew him nearer. "Damn, you look beautiful sitting there."

Sunshine was so caught up in TV that she didn't hear him. He said, "Let me guess—you're a fan of *Gunsmoke*."

"I love watching all westerns." She laughed. "When I was a little girl, I was a huge Roy Rogers fan. I've seen every movie he's ever made. I even belonged to his fan club when I was a kid."

J. W. reached his hand up to the side of her face and then gently kissed her lips.

She was surprised by his action, but she was also grateful to be kissed by him again. She responded meekly to his first kiss, but her response soon escalated to a deep, sultry kiss. Their kiss heightened their yearning for one another, and their embrace tightened as they sank onto the bed together.

J. W. had run his feelings for this woman through his mind countless times, questioning whether or not it was lust or love he had for her. However, their simple kiss was leaning toward his erotic appetite. *Damn, I want her.* He said, "Lady, you feel so good."

Their kiss deepened, taking them to a whirling ecstasy. There was no time or need for slow, sweet caressing; their need was too great. They quickly removed the few clothes that were between them and joined their bodies together. Their combined sexual desire was too great to allow foreplay. The spontaneity of the moment drove them right to the deed.

J. W. tried to enter her slowly, but Sunshine's desire was too overwhelming. She arched her hips high, inviting J. W. to thrust himself within her, filling her. Their hot, glowing vitality escalated like wildfire, burning out of control, only to be accelerated by a blazing kiss that deepened their rapture and ignited their lust. Both were rewarded with lusty sensations neither had experienced before. It was a thunderstorm of passion, lust, and profound intimacy. Their bodies quickly became a symphony of lust; their hearts intertwined and pounding wildly; their every breath bellowing with ecstasy; their moans and cries singing satisfaction; their skin blazing with splendor; every thrust closer to rhapsody.

J. W.'s stamina was as great as his sexual appetite, and they continued the sweltering blaze of lovemaking until their passion was spent.

As they remained locked in one another's embrace, J. W. said, "Damn, you're a helluva woman! If you only knew the effect you have on me!" He lifted the sheet and added, "I guess you can see!"

Sunshine smiled with her head on his chest. " I think you have the same effect on me! As handsome a cowboy as you are—and all the traveling you did—I'm sure you've made love to many women."

J. W. had a quick flashback of the many buckle bunnies he had fucked. "Yeah, only a few buckle bunnies."

J. W. gently pulled her head up to meet his and looked deep into her eyes. "I've never been with a woman who I have found as passionate and exciting as you. You're really putting a spell on me. Besides, I'm sure you've dazzled many a man yourself."

Sunshine said, "No, I haven't ..."

J. W.'s head was sent spinning by her statement, but he didn't offer any response.

She laughed, "What's a buckle bunny?"

He replied with a hearty laugh and a sultry kiss.

His desire sparked again as he looked at her beautiful bare breasts. Unable to resist exploring more, he nimbly and gently rolled her nipples between his fingers.

He sucked on her nipples skillfully, and Sunshine's gasped.

Satisfaction allowed them to lay quietly in each other's embrace for several comfortable minutes, not talking, only exchanging a kiss every so often. Sunshine rolled away from his embrace and said, "Lay flat on your tummy so I can massage your back."

J. W. followed her order.

Still naked, Sunshine climbed onto his back, sat on his legs, and poured cold lotion all over his back.

"Damn, that's cold!"

Sunshine laughed and began to massage his tanned, hard, muscular back.

J. W. moaned his approval.

She continued to massage his back and then moved to

massage his shoulders and arms. Finally, she moved toward his buttocks and upper thighs.

"Sunshine?"

She gently bit one of his butt cheeks and said, "Yes?"

"Sunshine, you're giving me another hard-on." He flipped over on his back and playfully pulled Sunshine on top of him. "Sunshine, I need you again." He gently tossed her onto her back and playfully climbed on top of her.

She laughed and said, "Well, gawl-damn it, cowboy, you'd better put your hat on for this next ride."

J. W. stopped and quickly sat up. "Groovy, man, you're right!" He ran to get his hat from the chair, placed it on his head, and dashed back to the bed. He hopped back on top of her and said, "Never was there a horse that couldn't be ridden. I wonder if I can tame this little filly with my lovemakin'." Turning her swiftly so he could lightly slap her ass, he tossed his hat onto the other bed.

Sunshine was laughing so hard that she couldn't see through the tears in her eyes. She seductively pulled J. W. down to meet her lips and gave him a sweet, sultry kiss. In a voice she had never heard from herself, she hissed, "Well, ride 'em, cowboy."

Again, they made love, but this time in a tender, playful manner—with no sense of frantic urgency. Their pace was comfortable and tentative, and he filled her with his strength until they were totally satisfied.

The high afternoon sun prompted J. W. to check on the time. "Holy cow paddies, I'm late for my appointment." He hopped out of bed and threw on his clothes. "Sunshine I hate to uh ... make love and gallop off." He tipped his hat. "I'll be back about five."

Sunshine stood up, grabbed his hat, and put it on.

He grabbed her, gave her a passionate kiss, and asked, "Will you be okay?"

She laughed, smacked him on the ass, and said, "Yes, cowboy. This buckle bunny will be fine. I might catch the Central bus and go down to the Wyoming Base gate to see if Sergeant Woods is home."

J. W. took his hat off her head and put it back on his own. "A cowboy hat ... the cowboy's proudest, most personal, precious possession. Next to the Stars and Stripes and the Statue of Liberty, the cowboy hat is America's most famous symbol." He handed her a key and said, "Here's your key to our hotel room for when you get back." He picked up her naked body, gave her a quick kiss, and playfully threw her on the bed. "Now be a good little filly while I'm gone!" He rushed out the door, still tucking in his shirt.

CHAPTER 17

MANZANO WESTERN SKIES

"I WALKED ALONE," MARTY ROBBINS

When J. W. returned from his business appointment, an old flame who had been waiting for him in the lobby intercepted him. He didn't want to talk to her, but out of politeness, he stopped to pay his respects. Rebecca Warner was the spoiled daughter of one of the state's richest ranchers, and she had tried many different games to capture J. W.'s attention.

J. W. tipped his hat and said. "Miss Rebecca, what brings you here today?"

Rebecca batted her thick fake eyelashes and said, "Now, J. W., you knew I'd be here lookin' for you." She wrapped her arms around him and kissed his lips.

J. W. squirmed away.

She pouted and said, "Oh, J. W., I've missed you so much. I was hopin' we could spend some time alone before the Cattleman's Ball this evening." She batted her eyelashes again. Rebecca was known for wearing tight clothing, and she wore a western-style snap-up shirt that was too small and too tight for her plump stature. It appeared that her overly large, fatty breasts could come busting out with her next move. It made J. W. nervous because at any moment her boobs could come exploding out. The male in him amusingly thought, *Those sweater puppies could take an eye out.*

J. W. wasn't up to playing her game, and he said, "Well, Miss Rebecca, I figured a pretty girl like you would already have a beau lined up for tonight. And it just so happens I already have a date for tonight—and she's probably waiting back at my room now."

He could see the anger in her face, yet she continued to play the role of the sweet child. Tracing her chubby little finger over his mouth and grabbing his rodeo buckle, she asked, "Now J. W., you're not telling me a story just to get rid of me, are you?"

"Miss Rebecca, half your troubles come from wantin' your way, and the other half comes from getting' it." The only reason he didn't toss her into the lobby sofa was that he was currently involved in some livestock business with her father. He pushed her away again. "Miss Rebecca, I need to get goin'.

I'll talk to you tonight." He walked away, shaking his head in disgust. He was grateful to be rid of her, and his emotion turned to excitement as thoughts of Sunshine came back to him.

When he reached his hotel room, Sunshine was sitting outside the door. She was wearing a halter top made from three bandanas and a skirt made from an old pair of blue jeans that had been split up the legs. Brightly colored material sewed into a triangle made it a shirt. Sunshine was sitting on the sidewalk with her back against the door and her knees drawn up to her chest. She appeared to be upset.

J. W. knelt beside her and drew her to him. "Sunshine, are you okay? What happened?"

Sunshine tried to laugh. "Oh, I guess I had a pretty shitty afternoon."

"Well, I guess it must have been 'cause that's the first time I ever heard you say a curse word. So, what happened?"

"I took the bus down to Kirtland to go see my dad's buddy, Sergeant Woods. There were war protestors at the base gate, and the MPs were trying to get them to leave. The protesters were yelling and screaming, 'You are denying us our constitutional rights of assembly.' When I tried to get on the base, the guards wouldn't let me. I guess they thought I was one of the protesters." 'We don't let hippie radicals or protestors on base.' I tried to reason with them and asked if they would call Sergeant Woods because he knew I was coming, but they wouldn't help me—they wouldn't even budge. Like a dummy, I left his phone number back in Taos. As I was leaving the gate, some of the protestors wanted to know if I wanted to join them. I told them no. I explained that protesting the war didn't make sense. How can you be against war and for peace? What you resist only attracts and carries on. You would have to have a peaceful demonstration to promote peace. To stop the war, you'd have to be pro peace—and act and think of peace. Well, I guess my statement set one creep off, and he started yelling in my face. 'Stop war. Stop the baby killers." She teared up as she thought of Blue in Nam. "I told them they were misinformed about the war and how we should be supporting our honorable men over in Vietnam, who are proudly serving our country. I continued to argue with them, and some of the protestors started shaking the base gate and throwing things." She laughed. "When the MPs showed up, I ran all the way to Central. And then, to top it all off, when I was walking back to the hotel, some drunk on the street gave me a hard time. And it gets better. I left my hotel key in our room before I left, and that jerk at the front desk wouldn't let me in. He said that the room was registered only in your name."

J. W. tightened his embrace and laughed. He kissed her forehead. "You're right. You did have a shitty afternoon."

Rebecca laughed behind them and said, "J. W., don't tell me this—this hippie trash—is your date for tonight." She walked over to them and laughed. "J. W., I think you've been kicked in the head by horses too many times." She held her head up to the sky and let out a fake laugh.

Sunshine looked up at the short, chubby, dyed redheaded cowgirl with too much makeup. She wore white lipstick on her pouty lips; pale blue eye shadow, and bright pink blush on the chubby cheeks of her washed-out, deathly pale complexion. She looked like a corpse awaiting a funeral.

J. W. seemed immensely irritated as he unlocked the hotel room, helped Sunshine inside, went back outside, and closed the door behind him.

From the chair, Sunshine could hear the woman's fake laughter. She peeked out the window to find her with her arms around J. W. She could not see J. W.'s face, but the cowgirl seemed to be having a great time.

Minutes later, J. W. came storming into the room.

Sunshine was afraid to say anything. Her mind reeled with confusion. *Who is that woman? Why is J. W. so angry? Is that woman his girlfriend? Maybe an old girlfriend? Maybe a previous buckle bunny?*

J. W.'s anger quickly changed to amusement and laughter as he tossed his cowboy hat onto the chair and combed his hands through his hair. "Damn, that woman drives me crazy. I'm going to take a shower and try to cool down a bit."

When he walked into the bathroom, Sunshine turned on the TV, blankly stared at it, and tried to decipher the situation.

J. W. took a cold shower to calm his temper, and then he walked out into the room with only his towel on. He was embarrassed by the confrontation and said, "Sunshine, why don't we get ready for the dance?"

Sunshine asked, "Do you still want me to go with you?"

J. W. cocked his brows and said, "Yes, of course!"

Sunshine quietly got up from the bed and walked into the bathroom.

Nearly an hour later, she emerged—standing proud and beautiful in her evening dress.

He said, "Wow! Look at you. You look prettier than a newborn filly."

She replied, "I picked it up at the western-wear shop on my way to the hotel. Do you like it?"

"Yes." J. W. walked over and placed a sweet, loving kiss of approval on her lips.

She was a stunningly beautiful combination of hippie and elegant western flair. She had braided her long hair back into a classy French braid. She wore a plain silver concha and elegant pieces of silver Indian jewelry that richly accompanied the black panne velvet broomstick skirt, along with a simplistic black velvet scoop-neck blouse. The low neckline allowed a glimpse of her ample breasts.

J. W. said, "Turn around—and let me get a good look at you."

Sunshine complied with his request.

J. W. shook his head, put his hand up to his heart, and said, "Be still, my heart! You look stunning." He whistled his satisfaction. "Hey! Look at those boots!"

Sunshine giggled. "I'm even wearing a little bit of makeup."

J. W. smiled and gallantly made a mock bow. "Hell, I'm honored that you splurged for the occasion and—and that you even put on makeup—but a beautiful lady like you doesn't need makeup." Her natural beauty aroused him, and he wrapped his arms around her. "I wish we had more time before the ball. I'm not sure I can wait until after the dance to be alone with you again." He kissed her.

J. W. was wearing a gray Boise suit with a black suede western trim and black yokes, black western-cut pants, a crisp, well-starched white shirt with a silver bolo tie, and a black felt hat. His black cowboy boots were shiny enough to mirror how handsome he was.

Sunshine brushed an invisible speck of lint off J. W.'s jacket and said, "Julian Coalton Weston, you're the handsomest man west of the Rio Grande."

Julian laughed and said, "Oh, yeah? And just who is the handsomest man east of the Rio Grande?"

"Oh, well, that would have to be my brother, Blue, of course."

J. W. laughed. "Of course. Miss Sunshine McFadden, I'd be honored if you'd accompany me to the nineteen hundred and sixty-ninth New Mexico Cattleman's ball." Pausing to straighten his tie, he added, "Shall we go?"

Sunshine smiled and nodded her approval.

J. W. nobly escorted Sunshine into the crowded ballroom. All eyes were on the handsome couple as they walked among the crowd. J. W. stopped several times to say hello to friends and old acquaintances. Each time, he proudly introduced Sunshine.

Sunshine sweetly listened to all his conversations and respectfully responded to questions asked only of her. She was content listening to J. W. and his friends talk about ranching, old rodeo tales, and rough stock.

One of the gals in the group asked Sunshine where she went to school.

Sunshine said, "I went to Manzano High School here in Albuquerque, and I am currently taking correspondence classes at UNM. I'm working toward getting my teaching degree."

J. W. listened in on their conversation, suddenly ashamed

for not knowing that about Sunshine. A band played country music, and several people danced. J. W. saw her interest in the dancers and asked if she cared to dance to the waltz that was playing.

Sunshine was suddenly concerned. *J. W. asked me to the ball. He probably expected me to be able to dance. I feel so stupid. It never occurred to me that I'd have to dance.* She said, "I'm sorry, J. W., but I don't know how to dance to this music."

It didn't make a difference to J. W. whether or not they danced. He was busy playing the role of a true businessman: networking, bullshitting, and talking ranch with his friends.

As Sunshine was just beginning to relax, Rebecca appeared. Dragging her date along with her like a puppy dog on a string, she marched right up to J. W. and Sunshine, ready to put on a show. Using the voice of a little girl, she said, "Well, J. W., my luck must be changing. I've seen you three times in one day." She released her puppy-dog cowboy and gave J. W. a big hug. "I see you've brought your little hippie rag doll along. I must admit you clean up well; it must have taken you hours to scrub the filth off yourself." Still holding onto J. W.'s arm, she leaned toward Sunshine and said, "Tell me, sweets, how much does he pay you for his entertainment?"

J. W. pulled away from Rebecca and hissed, "Miss Warner, this is hardly the time or place for your games."

A cowboy came up to J. W., grabbed him into a bear hug,

and picked him up off the ground. The two men growled at each other. Just as Sunshine was beginning to become concerned, J. W. and the cowboy began laughing, shaking each other's hands, and patting each other on the back.

J. W. smiled. "Mike, old buddy, if you ain't as unexpected as a fifth ace in a poker deck. I was hopin' I'd be seein' you here, and now that I have, I'm sorry I did."

Mike said, "J. W., I've missed your ugly face." He hugged Rebecca and said, "And I see you and Rebecca are back together."

Rebecca gave him a big superficial smile.

Tossing Mike and Rebecca an irritated frown, J. W. said, "No, Mike, we ain't back together—and you know that we never were together." He gently pushed Rebecca away and then pulled Sunshine next to him. "Mike, I'd like to introduce you to the lovely Miss Sunshine McFadden, who by the way is the most beautiful woman I've ever had the pleasure of accompanying me to the ball!" He was hoping Rebecca would get the hint and leave him alone. "Sunshine, this is my old rodeo buddy, Mike Web!"

Sunshine was still stunned by the whole ordeal, but Mike was eminently likable. "It's nice to meet you, Mike."

Mike was a true lady's man and quite the charmer. Immediately tuning out everyone around him, he took Sunshine's hand, placed a sweet gentle kiss on it, and looked into Sunshine's green eyes. "Well, your beauty is as shiny as your name." He winked and added, "I don't suppose I could steal you away from old what's his name? Gawl-damn, how on God's green earth did he ever find such a beautiful woman?"

J. W. growled and gently pulled Sunshine's hand from Mike's. "No, you don't, Mike. You're not goin' to sweet-talk this lady away from me."

Rebecca grabbed Mike's arm and pulled him off to the dance floor. "Come on, Romeo. Let's dance." The bright red dress that Rebecca had squirmed her way into clashed obtrusively with her red hair. Her dress was so tight that she looked like a cooked Jimmy Dean sausage that could explode at any moment. The bright shade of red lipstick didn't match her hair or her dress, and the combination made her appear to be all lips and ass. Her chubby calves were exposed by yet another shade of red ankle-high cowboy boots. She wore an outdated, early sixties bubble hairdo, which must have been water-resistant from all the hair spray she had lacquered on, leaving her hair looking like a football helmet. She had the potential to be pretty, but she was way over-detailed. She looked like she was wearing the all the shades of red from an artist's palette. Sunshine giggled to herself. *Rebeca should change her name to Red.*

J. W. went off to the bar, leaving Sunshine to try to make conversation with Rebecca's inarticulate puppy-dog date, whose name she found out was Kipper. Sunshine could tell by Kipper's gay mannerisms that he had not come out of the closet yet—and she soon figured out Kipper wasn't the sharpest spur in the tack shed.

Mike and Rebecca returned from the dance floor at the same time J. W. returned with the beers and a soda for Sunshine.

Rebecca laughed. "What's wrong? Doesn't the rag doll drink beer? Oh! I know, she must be tripping on that LSD stuff." Caught up in conversation, Mike and J. W. didn't hear her comment.

The group found a table and quickly began sharing stories from their old rodeo days. Sunshine enjoyed hearing their tales and enjoyed Mike's charming humor. She easily joined in with their laughter, but Rebecca never missed the opportunity to voice her lust for J. W. and her disapproval of Sunshine. Sunshine was confused about the relationship between J. W. and Rebecca. She kept reminding herself that J. W. had brought her here tonight and that little bitch, Rebecca, had come with the puppy dog Kipper.

Sunshine whispered in J. W.'s ear, "This is one of the few times I wish I had Yogi here with me. Now that would be a sparring match worth seeing!"

J. W. laughed.

Mike said, "Hey, gang, I feel as out of place as a cow on a

front porch. This place is too civilized. Why don't we leave this stuffy ball and go down to the Caravan East Nightclub for old time's sake?"

They all agreed and scampered off to meet up later. J. W. gallantly escorted Sunshine out to his truck, and as a true gentleman, he helped her in, kissed her, and told her how proud he was to be with such a beautiful lady.

As they drove down Central Avenue and pulled into a parking lot, he asked, "So, you don't know how to dance to country-and-western music? I guess we should have practiced a bit beforehand. Hey, I've got an idea." He put his truck into park, turned up the radio, got out, walked over to Sunshine's side, and opened her door. "Could I have this dance, sweet lady?"

Sunshine's heart skipped a beat. With unabashed happiness, she said, "Yes, I'd love to dance with you."

They practiced dancing in the parking lot for fifteen minutes. Sunshine even had J.W dance a quick dance to rock-n-roll. They laughed and teased each other. Giggling as they got back into the truck, they drove to the nightclub.

It was the first time Sunshine had ever been in a nightclub. The place was loud, smoky, and packed. The atmosphere was an odd combination of a country feed store and Elvis. The walls were covered with vintage boards that appeared to have come from a lumberyard that had gone out of business years ago, and the bright red vinyl chairs clashed with the booths, which were adorned with gold-studded buttons. Old wooden broken spoke wagon wheels lined the stage for the musicians. It was hard to tell if the band's lead vocalist had graduated from singing in the shower to singing in his pickup truck— and now to the stage.

They were playing a rendition of Ernest Tubb's "Walking the Floor Over You." The tunes vibrated the dance hall floor, which was covered with boot-scooting cowboy boots, and echoed on up above the sea of bobbing honky-tonking cowboy hats.

J. W. and Sunshine managed to find the others and squeezed in with them.

Mike said, "Sunshine, do you care to dance a two-step with a poor old cowboy from Ruidoso?"

J. W. said, "Mike, if you ain't slicker than calf slobber, you poor old cowboy. My heart bleeds for you! You can't dance with Sunshine until I've had a chance to." He escorted Sunshine onto the packed dance floor, and after a few dances, she quickly caught on to the steps and started enjoying herself. The two danced several dances with ear-to-ear smiles.

When they returned to their table, Mike said, "You two danced so close to each other that I bet your belt buckled is shined."

J. W. agreed and beamed with pride.

Rebecca said, "I was just telling your buddy Mike here about your rag doll, Sunshine. That she's a hippie from a commune in Taos."

Mike handed J. W. a beer and said, "Now can I dance with this beautiful, uh ... hippie?" He tipped his hat, winked at Sunshine, and held out his hand for a dance.

On the dance floor, Sunshine could see Mike's crystal blue eyes and radiant smile. He was taller than J. W. and had a thick body, brown hair, and a mustache. He was a true cowboy dandy—all steel and leather. "J. W. sure has good taste in his women."

Sunshine laughed. "How long have you and J. W. been friends?"

He laughed. "Oh, I'd say from puberty to present."

Sunshine laughed again. "So, the two of you rode in the rodeo together?"

"Yup! J. W. sure can ride the broncs. Why, he can break a horse while shavin', holding a small mirror in one hand and a razor in the other."

When Mike escorted Sunshine back to the table, Rebecca was trying to hang all over J. W. He kept fighting her off and was sick of her games.

To calm the storm, Mike asked the now-drunk Rebecca to join him on the dance floor.

Slurring her words, she giggled like a teenager, "Mike, baby, I'd like to join you in bed—to hell with the dancing!"

Amused by its energy and the lively twang of the music, Sunshine watched the cowboys and cowgirls. She laughed as one of the cowboys was interrupted by the cowgirl next to him; she grabbed his hat, placed it on her head, and danced around him. She grabbed another cowboy's hat and switched it back and forth three or four times from their heads. Another cowgirl grabbed it and placed it on her own head for a moment. She then danced around and placed the hat on a passing waitress. After the waitress quickly delivered her drinks, she danced back over to the original owner of the hat and placed it back on his head.

J. W. had certainly been tipping the bottle as well and said, "Well, Sunshine, how did you and my buddy Mike hit it off? Let me guess. He's captured your heart away from me ... like he has all the others."

Sunshine could see this was a sore subject. She had never seen this side of J. W., and it scared her. She tried to listen to the music and the other conversations at their table. After J. W. put down a couple more shots of tequila and a few more beers, she finally got enough courage to say, "J. W., can we leave now?"

"Sure, sweet lady, anythin' you ask, but ... you'll have to drive because I love my truck ... and I'm too drunk."

Without saying goodbye to his friends, J. W. walked with Sunshine out to his truck, handed her the keys, patted her on the ass, and said, "Drive careful, sweet lady."

Sunshine was very uncomfortable. She hadn't driven in months. She felt like she was in driver's ed back in high school. She had to adjust the seat all the way forward to meet her legs. She adjusted the mirrors and then turned on the ignition. She gave it too much gas, and the engine screamed its disapproval.

J. W. laughed a full belly laugh. "Down, boy!"

Sunshine was not amused. She cautiously put the truck into drive and drove up the street like an old lady.

"Sweet Sunshine, could you pull over at that liquor store so I can get a six-pack to take back to the hotel?" He went in and quickly returned. "I'm all set with the six-pack of beer and a bottle of Jack Daniels for me—and I picked up a six-pack of soda for you."

CHAPTER 18

SANDIA: TESTIMONY

"I'D WAIT A MILLION YEARS," THE GRASS ROOTS

When they arrived back at the hotel, Sunshine cautiously parked the truck and escorted the staggering J. W. to the room. She opened the door and once inside, she released a big sigh.

Smelling of stale beer, J. W. pulled Sunshine into his arms and gave her a hard, demanding kiss.

Sunshine pushed him away and then stepped back from him, not wanting to taste or smell sour booze.

J. W. began quickly pulling off his clothes and throwing them to the floor. "Okay, it's dark out. Now we can go skinny-dippin'."

Sunshine giggled. "Are you serious?"

J. W. put his finger up to his lips and whispered, "Yeah, we can do this. We just have to be quiet." He laughed.

Sunshine removed her clothes, and they walked outside to the pool and slipped in. They tried to giggle quietly and continually hushed each other.

J. W. held Sunshine close and wrapped his arms around her, whispering, "Damn! Sweet lady, you've tamed my heart just like you have that wild rusted gelding of mine." He gave her a gentle, loving, and seductive kiss and said, "Sunshine … you're such a beautiful woman … both inside and out … Sunshine, I think I'm falling in love with you!"

A loud voice called out, "Hey, you two! The pool closes at ten o'clock—get back to your room."

J. W. called back, "Yes, sir! Right away, sir!"

They giggled as they grabbed their towels, wrapped them around themselves, and ran back to their room.

J. W. flung his drunken body onto the bed and began to sing off-key, "You are my sunshine … Sunshine, you are the most beautiful, sweet woman I've ever met." He guzzled more whiskey from the bottle. "Sunshine, I've got something horrible I need to tell you." He took another swig. "Sunshine, I … I was the guy … uh, I … do you know how you said your mom drowned? Well, I was out riding the fences on the ranch when I found your mother's body on the side of the river." After another swig, he added, "You know, to this day, I still see her cold, dead eyes staring at me." He shook his head as if he was trying to get rid of the image.

Sunshine sat in silence on the edge of the bed.

Running his fingers through his hair, he said. "That damn ranch. What a spoiled brat I am. I should be horsewhipped for being so ungrateful. I mean … how many men are fortunate enough to inherit a thirty-eight-hundred-acre ranch?" He was talking purely from his conscience now. "I'm sure my dad is rolling over in his grave. Ha! Your dad and my dad are up in the heavens, shaking their heads at me. Damn, I'm fucking drunk. It's been a long time since I was this drunk. Damn it, I don't want a rancher's life. I want to go back to the rodeo. And to fucking top it *all* off, I'm in love with a fucking hippie. She sure is beautiful, but she's a goddamn fucking hippie." He then passed out on the bed.

Sunshine swallowed hard with a riot of feelings coursing through her. The way he said it and the way he looked made the hairs on the back of her neck stand up.

Upon daylight, Sunshine wrote J. W. a note and left it on the table. She was going back to Taos. She gathered her things and quietly left while he was still sleeping off his drunken state.

At noon, J. W. was awakened by the maid opening the hotel door. When the maid discovered that he was still in the room, she bid her apologies and left. J. W. sat up in bed and began raking through his mind the events from the past night. *Where the hell is Sunshine?* He held his head and staggered into the bathroom. "Sunshine?" Squinting through the blinding light, he looked out the front door and then checked out by the pool. When he went back to his room, he found the note. An ocean of shame washed over him as he read it: "I hope you can learn to touch the world with a gentler hand. May miracles and blessings shower you always."

He stared at the note and then sang a faded verse from the tune that was left in his head from the night before: "You are my sunshine." He hurled an empty beer bottle at the wall, and it shattered along with his heart. "Goddamn it! What the fuck did I do now?"

CHAPTER 19

KIRTLAND AIR FORCE BASE

"WHAT A LONG, STRANGE TRIP IT'S BEEN," THE GRATEFUL DEAD

Mentally licking her wounds, Sunshine walked down Central Avenue. It was two and a half miles to the Wyoming Base gate, and she extended her thumb to hitch a ride, not noticing or caring if anyone stopped. She remained incognizant to the fresh, cool, early morning breeze; she was entranced by her emotions. She kept pushing his memory away, trying to convince herself that the real reason she came to Albuquerque that week was to visit her father's lifelong friend and fellow airman, Master Sergeant Robert Woods.

There was another protest at the base gate when she arrived. This protest was a sit-in with around twenty-five people. A nerdy-looking guy with glasses sat in the middle, singing and playing his guitar, and the rest of the group sang "I Feel Like I'm Fixin' To Die," also known as "Vietnam Rag," which was a new popular war protest song by Country Joe and the Fish. It had been introduced at the Woodstock concert in New York just one month earlier.

The nerdy Bob Dylan wannabe sang, "Give me an F!"

The group screamed, "F."

"Give me a U!"

"U."

"Give me a C!"

"C."

Give me a K!"

"K."

"What's that spell?"

Everyone screamed "Fuck."

Again, "What's that spell?"

"Fuck."

"Well, come on, all you big, strong men. Uncle Sam needs your help again, he got himself in a terrible jam, way down yonder in Vietnam, put down your books and pick up a gun, we're gonna have a whole lotta fun.

"And its one, two, three, what are we fighting for? Don't ask me I don't give a damn. The next stop is Vi-et-nam."

"And it five, six, seven, open up the pearly gates."

"Well, there ain't no time to wonder why."

"Whoopee, we're all gonna die."

"Now come on, Wall Street, don't be slow, why man mean this's war a go-go, there's plenty of good money to be made, supplyin' the army the tools of the trade, just hope and pray that when they drop the bomb, drop it on the Vietcong."

"And its one, two, three, what are we fighting for? Don't ask me I don't give a damn. The next stop is Vi-et-nam."

"Be the first one on the block to have your son come home in a box."

The last part of the song upset Sunshine as she thought of Blue in Nam.

After the shakedown and rejection she had experienced the day before when she tried to get onto the base, Sunshine decided to try another approach. Adopting the straight-world values through her careful attire, dressing as conservative as possible, she stashed anything society would freak out on or brand her as a hippie. She walked up to the base entrance and proudly stepped into the guard office as though she was meant to be there. She stopped to take a deep breath, straightened her stance, and walked up to the guard's desk.

Noting the name and rank of the guard on duty, she said, "Good morning, Private. I need a temporary pass so that I can get to my new job at the officer's club."

The young guard looked at Sunshine and said, "Can I see some ID, ma'am?"

His strange nasal voice startled Sunshine, but she maintained a straight face. "I was unaware that I'd be required to bring an ID. I left it at home." Looking at her watch, she said, "You see, it's my first day on the job."

This time, he added authority to his nasalized tone. "Ma'am, you have to have a base ID and or a driver's license to enter Kirtland Air Force Base."

Sunshine wanted to roll her eyes and pinch his plump little pink military cheeks. She pictured him playing with his little plastic toy soldiers on the floor. She added more authority to her tone, saying, "Once again, Private, I do not have my ID with me—and you are going to make me late for work."

The guard picked up the phone, and with every dial he turned, Sunshine became more and more alarmed. "What is the name of your boss at the officer's club?"

Dumbfounded, she responded, "Mr. James."

Slamming down the phone, Private Walker said, "The line to the officer's club is busy."

Whew, she thought.

Her luck continued as two cars pulled up the gate, impatiently honking their horns.

The guard sighed. "Miss, I will permit you entrance this

time, but the next time you come to work, you must have an ID."

As she walked onto the base, Sunshine's memory flooded with thoughts her childhood when she lived on base with her father and mother. She thought of the day she heard about her father's death. She stood at the front door at the puny base house of Rob Woods. All the drapes were closed, and the house was quiet and lifeless. She knocked several times, but there was no answer. Disappointed, she thought, *Well, he probably doesn't even live here anymore—or he's away on assignment.* She knocked one more time and sat down on the front step to leave a message.

The front door opened slowly, and a raspy female voice said, "Goddamn it! Who the hell comes visiting this early on a Sunday morning?"

Sunshine stood and said, "Oh … hi! Sorry to wake you. I was hoping to find an old friend of mine—Sergeant Robert Woods—does he still live here?"

The woman had only opened the door an inch or two, and Sunshine couldn't see the woman.

"So, who the fuck are you?"

Before Sunshine could answer, Rob said, "Who's there, dear?"

The door opened, revealing a skinny woman with straight, mousey-brown hair. She was wearing a see-through yellow ruffled and ribboned lingerie. Changing her tone dramatically, she sweetly called back into the house, "It's a girl asking for you, sweetheart."

Sunshine could smell the alcohol on the woman's breath.

Rob appeared at the door and said, "Sunshine, baby! What a wonderful surprise." He picked her up off her feet and gave her a huge bear hug. "What brings you here? I haven't heard from you for so long! Did your buddy Blue bring you here? Look at you! You're beautiful—and all grown-up. Oh! Gosh! I have a million questions for you."

The skinny woman stepped next to Rob to claim her possession. "Robby, who's this?"

Rob's eyes smiled and shined for Sunshine. "Sunshine, this is Dee-Dee, and, Dee-Dee, this is my best buddy's little girl, Sunshine."

Dee-Dee faked a smile.

Rob said, "Please come in."

Their house reeked of cigarettes and booze. Dee-Dee walked behind them with a look of immense irritation and sat down practically on Rob's lap. Her long, shapeless frame slouched onto the couch. She had lifeless pale brown eyes, and her patchy complexion resembled a blank puzzle.

Rob said, "What brings you to Albuquerque? I haven't heard from you since your mother's funeral. Are you okay?"

"Oh, yes, I'm fine. I came to Albuquerque with a friend of

mine. I hadn't talked to you for some time, and I was hoping to see you."

Dee-Dee examined her nails and said, "How nice."

Rob echoed Dee-Dee's response with true excitement, "Yes, how nice!"

Dee-Dee held out her hand to show Sunshine her rock. "Robby and I are engaged."

Sunshine was overcome with a flashback of the numerous women who had lived the same scenario. She smiled, remembering how Rob had been engaged at least five times—that she knew of. "How wonderful. Congratulations."

Rob said, "Sunshine, what do you say we go over to Uncle John's Pancake House for breakfast like we used to? For old time's sake?"

Sunshine said, "Strawberry pancakes with tons of whipped cream and strawberries! Sounds yummy—let's go."

Rob stood up and said, "Well, then, let's go. Dee-Dee, honey, quick, go get dressed."

Dee-Dee said, "No, sweetheart, I'll just stay here." She walked slowly toward the bedroom and yawned, "Nice to meet you. Enjoy your pancakes." She gave Rob him a big drooling French kiss and said, "I'll be waiting for you."

Master Sergeant Robert Woods was the Hugh Hefner of the Air Force; he was the pinnacle of sweetness and suavity, and he could charm the pants off the women. He had never married, and his playboy philosophy allowed him to screw as many women as he could. He kept an accurate account of them all, and at age forty-seven, he was up to eighty-three women and proudly adding to the count.

He wasn't an overly handsome man. He was very plain and ordinary: plain brown hair that he kept heavily Brylcreem-ed, plain brown eyes, and a small, plain physique. However, there was one exception to his ordinary demeanor—his huge dick—and he was known for how well he used it.

He had a generous intellect and generous heart. He always dressed well, and he never lost his composure with the ladies. His polished chivalry and unusually large penis often ignited the ember of gossip and women's curiosities.

A seventeen-year veteran of the Air Force's Special Training Division, and a dedicated career military man, Rob would never make a high-ranking officer. He had too many blemishes on his yearly OERs (Officers Efficiency Report). In 1966, he was busted fucking the HFMICs (head motherfucker in charge) base wing commander's slutty eighteen-year-old daughter.

He spent the entire year of 1967 in military confinement after he was caught in the training barracks banging a sweet blonde over the classroom desk. When they were discovered by the base security, she screamed rape so that her husband wouldn't find out about her infidelity. After Rob spent three weeks in jail, she finally confessed that she consented to the affair and asked her husband for a divorce.

Rob found himself up against a court-martial after he was busted for indecent exposure in the Cibola National Forest by the forest ranger. The stage was set for the court-martial when he was discovered naked, sucking on a barmaid in an Air Force vehicle. The heat to the bust was added when, unbeknownst to Rob, the barmaid was carrying an ounce of marijuana in her purse.

The only reason the air force didn't bust his balls and get rid of him or ship him off to Vietnam was because he was one of the few trainers with a solid academic background and his true concern for the need in developing the course syllabi and class training objectives for the turbulent, explosive, and confusing racial issues bursting throughout the United States and the air force. The brass in the Pentagon wanted him to work for them, but they couldn't afford the risk with his tarnished record. Numerous times, the board of inquiry met to weigh out Rob's excellent workmanship and his dedication to the air force against his rocky, tarnished personal record. Even though he was continually busted for improper sexual conduct, he couldn't keep his dick out of trouble.

The Pancake House was filled with the usual Sunday family crowd. Sunshine ordered the strawberry pancakes, and Rob ordered his all-time favorite, pigs in a blanket.

Being with Rob again, Sunshine felt caught in an odd sense of timelessness. She felt like a carefree child again.

Rob had to snap his perverse thoughts back to reality when he found himself imagining himself licking that whipped cream off Sunshine's now beautifully developed body.

"Where is your buddy, Blue?" Rob asked as he slurped down his coffee.

Sunshine licked the whipped cream off her lips. "He enlisted into the army last year. He's at Fire Base Fanning in Vietnam. Rob, how come my mother wouldn't let me keep in touch with you after we moved to Taos?"

Rob tried to change the subject. "Sunshine, how is your painting coming along? Are you still painting?" During their conversation, Rob's conscience kept screaming at him to take this opportunity to tell Sunshine the truth. He sighed and said, "Sunshine, I have something I have to get off my chest. You're a grown woman now, and you know I would never do anything to hurt you, but I've got to tell you what happened the day we heard about your father's death. Your mother and I were having an affair when your father was killed in Vietnam. The guilt was too overpowering for your mother, and I think that was why she began drinking so heavily and taking drugs." He closed his eyes, trying not to remember the strange elusive dreamlike event that he wished were someone else's memories other than his own. It was all so vivid, and he could recall so many exact words, actions, smells, and sights. Sunshine was in school. He had just finished banging Marianne, doggie-style in her room, his dick still stiff when the base chaplain came knocking on the door with the horrible news of William's plane being shot down in Nam. Jesus Christ! He had only offered to console and comfort her loneliness. Fucking a, he just couldn't keep his dick in his pants.

He carefully watched Sunshine. The comprehension struck her with stunning force, but she remained calm.

He looked at her apologetically and said, "I tried to get your mother to go for counseling, but she wouldn't listen. I even offered to marry her so I could take care of the two of you." He held his breath and looked into Sunshine's eyes. "My apology is sincere."

She took in a big breath to clear her mind of the shock waves and said, "Rob, my mother had more problems than this affair. She continually surrounded herself with cheap drama—and she was very insecure and extremely selfish." Her eyes misting, Sunshine swallowed hard. "The bitterness I've developed for my mother after her drowning only contributed toward my hatred of her. Seeking to heal the emotional wounds, I've learned my best defense against her is through forgiveness. Forgiveness is like the martial art of consciousness. Relationships are God's assignments to us." Her heart was lodged unpleasantly in her throat. "My mother ... she ... I have to laugh off all the stupid things she did in her lifetime. Life is too short to freeze our feelings around a moment of wrong." This pain—along with the countless other pains her mother had left her—would take a long time to dwindle from her memory. Sunshine knew that forgiveness was a blessing. Forgiveness takes great strength of the mind and heart. When she experienced the process of forgiveness, it allowed her to feel whole again. She refused to let the burdensome feelings weigh down her heart.

Rob looked at her and said, "Are you okay?"

"I'm okay." She smiled, trying not to appear freaked out. "I've worked too damn hard for the past few years to make this my own life. And I refuse to let my mother set me back. Yes, I'm fine."

CHAPTER 20

TINGLEY RODEO

"THE RACE IS ON," GEORGE JONES

The rodeo coliseum was bursting at the seams with fans as they restlessly waited for the Rodeo Championship to begin. The master of ceremonies, Lewis Cryer, interrupted the bustling roar of the crowd. "Ladies and gentlemen, welcome to the 1969 New Mexico State Fair Rodeo Championship." An electrifying air of excitement exploded, and the crowd applauded and cheered.

The gate opened with the well-rehearsed, traditional grand entry with a parade of horses, pretty cowgirls, and cowboys. The emcee introduced the riders to the audience.

The crowd stood, the men held their cowboy hats over

their hearts, and the bright-eyed rodeo queen rode into the arena, majestically introducing the American flag.

The emcee called out, "Ladies and gentlemen, please stand as our rodeo queen, Miss Yolanda Romero, proudly presents our American flag—the most beautiful flag in the world!"

The incoming riders entered the arena.

"Miss Yolanda is followed by the New Mexico County Queens."

A lengthy prestige train of horse and riders galloped into the arena in a single-file line with dozens of riders cascading into the arena, glimmering in their silver and gold.

The emcee's voice echoed through the grandstands as he said, "Ladies and gentlemen, we are joined by a special guest tonight—the man who has provided our rodeo's rough stock and New Mexico's own 1967 National Rodeo Champion Bronc Rider—Mr. Julian Weston."

J.W. gave an unenthused wave to the crowd and dutifully followed the riders. His mind was flooded with memories from his rodeo days.

The procession stopped to pay respects to the flag. The National Anthem was gallantly sung with spirit, undeniable pride, and glory.

J. W. thought about the men in Vietnam who were fighting under that flag. His mind flashed to the letters Sunshine had shared from Blue and the tragedies he was encountering. J.

W. thought of all the losses and profound suffering as a result of this war. Last spring, one of J. W.'s rodeo buddies had been killed in action in Vietnam. His thoughts wandered to Sunshine, the pain she endured from the war, and the impact it had on her life.

The emcee said, "On behalf of the Rodeo Association and the New Mexico State Fair Commission, we want to thank you, folks, for coming here tonight. And special thanks to the cowboys and cowgirls who are here to compete."

J. W. followed the parade out of the coliseum, dismounted his horse, and tethered him. He quickly returned to the side gates to watch and help his buddy prepare for the bareback bronc-riding event.

The gate's bolts and latches rattled, the dry hinges moaned, and the plank gate clattered as the bronc jostled against the fence. A staccato of moans came from the boxed-in horses as they pawed the ground and kicked at the chutes, sending crashing tremors through the stalls.

J. W.'s buddy, Mike, had drawn a chestnut gelding named Tuff-Stuff to ride.

The chute boss, Dustin Danner, draped a sheepskin-padded flank strap over Tuff-Stuff's hips. The bronc humped his back and kicked at the strap tickling his sensitive flanks. Using a piece of wire bent into a hook, Dustin drew the flank strap under the gelding's belly and secured the ring in a quick-release latch, and then he moved on to the next bronc to follow the same.

J. W. patted Mike on the back and said, "Hey, buddy, you can hold on to this one."

Mike spit out some of the chewing tobacco that was protruding from his lip. "Um-hum."

The other riders stalked back and forth behind the chute, stopping periodically to stretch out taut muscles.

J. W. stayed with his buddy, but out of fairness, he was unable to give any advice as to the habits of his horse since it was his rough stock.

Mike eyed the gelding in the chute between him and the battleground of the arena. There was some stiff competition here today, and so far, his rodeo season had not been a rewarding one. He lowered himself into the chute, mounting the bronc, adjusted the handhold of his goatskin, well-rosined glove, and adjusted his grip to the perfect hold. He moved forward on the bronco's withers.

The emcee said, "Now, in gate number four, is Mike Webb of Ruidoso, New Mexico."

The chute boss lifted the latigo to tighten the cinch on the bronc. The horse exploded, lunging out of the opened gate and bucking high in the air.

Mike kept his right hand held high in the air, and with his left hand, he mastered the jostling dance of the rough-ridin' monsoon—and endured the ride until the eight-second buzzer rang. When the buzzer signified the end of his ride, Mike released the four-time wrapped leather thong around his gloved hand, jumped off Tuff-Stuff, and dismounted safely.

The pickup men quickly hazed the bronc through the gate.

The rodeo emcee said, "Folks, this cowboy stuck on that horse like a postage stamp. Let's give this boy from Ruidoso a hand. His score today is an eighty-two!"

J. W. greeted Mike behind the chute. "Hey, buddy, good ride."

Mike bowed to the cowgirls who gathered at the back of the chutes to flirt with the cowboys, ran up to the gate, and kissed one on the cheek.

Susie Garcia, the Rodeo Queen for Torrance County, said, "Hey Mike, why don't you and J. W. join us after the rodeo at Charlie's Tavern for a beer?"

Mike tipped his hat and said, "Darlin', I'd be happy to." He looked over to J. W. to check his response.

J. W. tipped his hat to the ladies and politely smiled. *Hell, beer is what I need to keep my mind comfortably hazy.* He remembered the drunken fool he had made of himself the night before. *I have an open invitation from those pretty little cowgirls, and it doesn't even interest me. Fuck! All I can think about is Sunshine.*

"Mike, that bronc gave you a better merry-go-round ride than that one you paid for earlier at the fair. Good ride, buddy!"

Mike said, "Yep! I had a good ride, and now I am going to have another good ride on one of these cowgirls." Mike walked into the group of cowgirls and wrapped his arms around one on each side of him.

After congratulating Mike again, J. W. climbed up into the grandstand to join his sister Wendy, Joel, Justin, and the sleeping Kayleigh.

Joel and Wendy had brought horse trailer filled with all the rough stock horses, and J. W.'s paint horse earlier that morning from Taos.

J. W. quietly watched the rodeo, not displaying any emotions or adding any comments or conversation. The rain falling on the coliseum's roof reminded him of Sunshine and the incredible sex they had together. Snapping his thoughts back to the rodeo, he thought, *Damn it! Everything reminds me of Sunshine!*

Wendy said, "J. W. you're as quiet as a horse thief after a hangin'. What's buggin' you? I'll bet you sure do miss the rodeo. I know it's hard for you to sit here and watch—not bein' able to participate."

J. W. gave her a weak smile. "Yep."

Halfway through the rodeo, Wendy said, "J. W., would you please come with me to get some sodas from the concession stand and help me carry them back?"

Joel said, "Honey, I'll help you—"

Wendy laughed and said, "No, thank you, love! My big brother is going to help me."

J. W. blankly followed Wendy out of the arena.

Wendy said, "J. W., your mind is as deep as a well tonight. What's buggin' you?"

"Nothin'."

"J. W., you can't fool me. I know you too well."

"I guess you do, don't you? I just miss the rodeo is all."

Wendy laughed. "And what else?"

"And what? What?"

Wendy said, "And what about Sunshine? You can't tell me she's not on your mind."

J. W. said, "Yes, she's definitely been on my mind." He shook his head in disgust. "I'll bend your ear when we get home. I could use some sisterly advice. For right now, let's just enjoy the rodeo." He didn't offer any more information. Sunshine had been the center of attention in his mind. J. W. loved her childlike senses and her playfulness. She was hardworking, intelligent, sweet, sincere, and honest. The list went on and on.

The emcee said, "Remember, folks, what we are is God's gift to us—and what we become is our gift to God. Good night."

J. W. smiled. He had heard that verse before—quoted by Sunshine.

CHAPTER 21

RIO GRANDE: JOHN DUNN BRIDGE

"PLEASE HELP ME, I'M FALLING," HANK LOCKLIN

After leaving the Pancake House with Rob, Sunshine thumbed a ride to the Albuquerque bus station and caught the next bus to Taos. The four-hour ride gave her plenty of time to think and pray. She tried to completely shut out Rob's confession. Talking to the heavens, she said, "Mother, it's amazing that you are continually surprising me with your bullshit long after you're gone." Her feelings for J. W. made her mind feel like a roller coaster with deep dips and climbs, jolts, and twisting emotions. She kept reminding herself that love is a gamble of not being loved in return. She knew that intimate relationships were a risk and involve tremendous needs. *Oh, damn it! This damn philosophy isn't doing me any good this time.* She still had a vast emptiness gnawing at her heart. "Please, dear God, rescue my despair."

She was embarrassed that J. W. had been the person who found her mother when she drowned after taking too many drugs. She had to laugh to remind herself that it had not been the first time her mother had embarrassed her. Her mother continued to be a splinter in her mind. She knew she had to constantly practice forgiveness; otherwise, the splinter would take away her peace of mind.

She wondered how Blue was doing in Vietnam and said several prayers for his safety.

Sunshine didn't want to go back to New Buffalo today, but she had nowhere to go. She dreamed about moving to Albuquerque and maybe going full-time to the University of New Mexico and quickly finish getting her teaching certificate—or maybe getting a degree in art. She promised herself she would contact UNM when she got back to check on her options.

As the bus route traveled through the center of New Mexico, there was so much on her mind. She tried to calm herself by pulling the energy and strength from the beautiful scenery with its diverse richness, but she just couldn't keep her mind still.

She released so many big noisy sighs that the women in the seat in front of her asked if she was okay.

Her worries turned to J. W. as she wondered where all his prejudices came from. As a "hippie," there were many times when she felt unwelcome *It's okay. Let it go.* She knew people felt threatened by differences, she needed to stay in the light of God, and she needed to keep sharing her love—the kind of love that could ignite the earth. *It is okay.* She hoped to live as an earth angel and a game changer. *Keep shining your beautiful heart to all.* That was her mission. That was why she was here on earth.

When she arrived back at New Buffalo, she said nothing to anyone. She simply went back to her regular routines. Even though there were twenty-five people at the commune, she felt so alone.

Several days later, she received a letter from Blue. Her spirit intertwined with her sorrow for Blue and her heartache for J. W. She missed Blue so much, and through the midst of her sadness, she tried to pull herself out of her spiritual darkness and doubt. She tried to remind herself to put things in God's hands. *This storm will pass.* She had to keep her faith and belief in God. She continually called up to the heavens and talked to God.

Sunshine wanted to brush off the hostilities of the war in Vietnam and the head trips she was experiencing with J. W.

She wished she could pack away his memories in a box and seal it until her heart healed. She decided she needed a walk to allow Mother Nature's peace and harmony to neutralize the negative energy she was holding.

On the path down to the Rio Grande River, Tylor's three sons greeted her with welcoming hugs and kisses.

Raven asked, "Sunshine, are you going down to the river? Can we go with you so we can fish?"

Skylor said, "You should have seen the trout my dad caught yesterday! I want to catch a big one too! Can we please go with you?"

Stretching out his arms as far as they could reach, Neon said, "I want to catch one this big."

Raven rolled his eyes at this younger brother. "Oh, Neon, there are no trout that big in the river. You're so stupid."

Sunshine said, "Hey now, Raven, Neon is not stupid. As a matter of fact, when Coronado and his explorers first came to Taos, New Mexico, he wrote in his journal that he had seen trout the size of horses in the Rio Grande River."

"Wow!

Skylor said, "Can we go down to the river with you, Sunshine?"

"Sure! Run and tell your dad where we're going—and bring your fishing poles. Raven, will you please stop and pick up my pole from my tepee. Maybe I'll have a change of luck today." As the boys ran off, Sunshine realized she didn't need to be alone today with so many monkeys jumping around in her head.

As Sunshine and the boys walked down to the river, they made several stops to check out all the bugs, birds, and lizards, asking questions and anxiously awaiting any knowledge she would share with them. It took them a half an hour to unravel the maze of trails from the New Buffalo through the tangle of volcanic rock hill down to the river.

A jaybird screamed at them, and a squirrel chattered to protest their intrusion to the riverside brush.

Skylor led them to what he proclaimed was the perfect fishing spot. "This is where the Lone Ranger would fish."

Raven dug up worms from the riverbank, and they soon had their lines in the water.

Neon squished the mud from the riverbank through his fingers and toes and said, "Sunshine, if I catch a fish, I'll give it to you."

Sunshine hugged him and said, "Thank you, Neon."

Thinking about how gentle and wondrous he was brought mist to her eyes. He was full of the love, and he shared it so easily.

As they sat on the riverbank and fished, Sunshine basked in the afternoon sun, soaking up the energy and transforming the light around her into continuous flowing energy. She could sense a faint hint of autumn in the air. It would only be a matter of days until the first frost appeared, christening the arrival of the new season. Fragrant wildflowers and moist leaves filled the air. The boys were bursting with energy and curiosity.

Sunshine thought, *how wonderful it is to see the marvels of the world through a child's eyes and to be able to feel and sense all that Mother Nature has to offer.*

Neon pointed to a huge pine tree and said, "Boy! That is a big tree! Sunshine, how old do you think that tree is?"

She answered, "Oh, it's probably several hundred years old. This tree has experienced many years of life and witnessed the history around it. When the tree was born, the Anasazi Indians were here fishing, just as we are. Several years went by, and the pine grew as tall as you, Neon. He stood and watched the Spanish conquistadors as they gave up their search for the cities of gold and became farmers and ranchers. When the tree was as tall as Raven and Skylor, the tree watched the Anglo settlers come and homestead across the river. And when the tree was as tall as your dad, it watched as the mountain men watered their horses and the miners came to pan for gold. Now, when the tree was four times taller than me, he watched as ranchers herded their cattle down to the river for water. This grand old tree has experienced and shared much of life's blessings. And even when this tree dies, it will break down and decompose, blending with the soil and enriching the earth so that other trees can continue to grow."

Neon sprang to his feet and yelled, "I got one. I got one!"

Skylor started to take the fishing pole away from his baby brother, but Sunshine stopped him. "Skylor, let Neon reel it in. He can do it." She laughed. "Neon, you can do it. Reel it in."

Neon ran away from the river with his pole and tried to reel in the line—and he didn't stop until he had dragged the fish ten feet out of the water.

The fishing team danced and cheered their approval of Neon's first-ever catch.

Sunshine laughed and said, "You did it, Neon! Look at the fish you caught."

Neon's older brothers praised their baby brother for his catch. "Yeah, Neon, wait till we show Dad."

Neon was in awe over the trout he had caught. "Wow-wee, I caught a big fish." He jumped up and down. "Let's go show it to Dad."

The boys were eager to get home to show off Neon's catch, and they ran all the way home.

Sunshine was grateful for the morning she had spent with the boys; all their wonder and endless questions had lightened her heart—and kept her mind off of J. W.

Upon returning from the river, she noticed J. W.'s truck

parked at New Buffalo. Her defenses immediately soared, and all the conflict, confusion, and turbulence leaped into her emotions. *What the hell does he want?*

J. W. was talking to Tylor, and the two men stood when she walked over.

Tylor said, "Mr. Weston informs me he's here to see you. Oh! And thank you for taking the boys fishing. Neon is sure proud of the fish he caught." He shook J. W.'s hand. "I enjoyed talking to you about ranching, and you sure brought back a lot of memories from ranching at my family's ranch in Texas. Give me a holler when you need an extra hand on your ranch."

As Tylor walked away, Sunshine's heart was pounding wildly in her chest—half from fear and half from the excitement.

J. W. took off his hat and fumbled with the brim. "Sunshine, I have some things I need to say to you. I ... I've been a fool!" He ran his fingers through his hair. "Damn ... there's some need for some truth here!"

Sunshine felt her anger rising. "I hate to see you lowering your standards by coming to this low-life hippie town to see me. Or, is it a 'fucking hippie' town? Isn't that what you called me when we were in Albuquerque? A fucking hippie?"

J. W.'s temper got the better of him, and without saying a word, he walked away and jumped in his truck. He spun out his tires, leaving a cloud of dust.

Sunshine wanted to burst, but she froze. Her mind was a collision of emotions and confusion. *Why did he come here? Damn it, J. W.*

J. W. stopped his truck at the bottom of the hill and thought, *What the hell am I doing?* He threw his truck in reverse, spun out the tires, and backed up the driveway again.

With tears in her eyes, Sunshine started to walk away. J. W. walked up to her, grabbed her arm, and gently swung her around. "Please, Sunshine, let me try this again. Would you just hear me out? Damn it, Sunshine! I'm sorry. You're right. You see, I was raised with some powerful prejudices. Yes, I had some ridiculous hang-ups with you bein' a hippie, but that doesn't matter to me now. I am over it."

Sunshine pursed her lips and said, "And what *does* matter to you? Your material wealth? Your fancy truck? Your fancy horse trailer? Your brand-new hat? How about your expensive, sparkling clean, stiff-starched shirts? Hell, you even iron your jeans. Wow! Perhaps you have a fetish for perfection? Or, wait, maybe it's your inability to trust anyone?" When she realized her anger would only make his defenses spring up, she watered down her tone. "Your prejudices and hatred have such a stronghold on you. It's moldy in your soul, and it's eventually going to consume you." She was on a roll, and the words were spilling out of her like a turned-over pail of hot, soapy water. "I'm sure it was hard adjusting from your super-stardom-rodeo days to now, but stop living for yesterday. There isn't anything you can do about yesterday. Let go of yesterday. Live for today. If you don't, it will hang around your neck like an albatross and drag you farther and farther down. For goodness' sake take, a look at the beautiful ranch you own. You should appreciate the things you have rather than the things you don't have. And please let your hatred and bitterness go." Her eyes were tearing up. "Please! Otherwise, you're going to die a lonely, bitter old man trapped in a dungeon of wishing you had done things differently."

J. W. shook his head. "Sunshine, I really do know that I'm lucky to have inherited my family's ranch. I really do know." He released a huge sigh. "And I know ... I agree with what you are saying."

Sunshine stared into J. W.'s eyes.

He said, "Look! Can we take a walk? Or we can go for a horseback ride? I can have Rusty and my horse saddled up quicker than spit on a hot griddle. And it's a beautiful day." J.W wrapped his arms around Sunshine. "What do you say? Would you like to go for a ride?"

"Yes! It is a beautiful day for a ride. And I would love to see Rusty." Sunshine made a silent agreement with herself that she would go, but she would be wearing her best coat of armor—and she was going to leave her heart behind for protection.

CHAPTER 22

TAOS GRAND CANYON: THE TRUTH

"WINGS OF A DOVE," FERLIN HUSKY

J. W. and Sunshine rode in his truck in peace toward the Weston Ranch. Finally, after a long draw of silence, Sunshine said, "I'm looking forward to riding Rusty again. She looked at the two saddles in the back of the truck. "Except there's one thing I need to tell you about Rusty."

"What's that?"

"I've never ridden him with a saddle. I've only ridden him bareback."

J. W. started laughing. "I can't believe you. That sweet little butt of yours has got to be as tough as old Rusty."

Sunshine greeted Rusty with hugs, pats, and whispers.

J. W. observed how receptive the old gelding was to her. Her nurturing had established a unique relationship of understanding and trust. J. W. admired that about her and Rusty, and he wondered if he had ever had such a relationship with a horse. J. W. was impressed and amused by the sight of Sunshine getting up onto the horse without a saddle. She swung up in a graceful fluid motion without compromising her balance. It appeared to be somewhat of a gymnastic exercise: stunning, swift, and lissome.

As they started out riding, Sunshine told J. W. about Blue's last letter from Nam. They talked about J. W.'s horse and about some of the places they rode through, but other than that, they rode for several hours with nothing more than small talk.

J. W. watched Sunshine's horsemanship with admiration. He had never seen a cowgirl ride with such grace. Sunshine had a natural awareness of her horse. He knew it took great skill and balance to ride bareback. *It's no wonder she was so great in bed.* Horny flashbacks coursed through his mind and body. *Damn, she's a pretty picture—even if she is sitting up on that ugly horse. Gosh, what an ugly beast that horse is.*

J. W. studied the way she kept her balance by adjusting her center. He observed her very subtle physical cues; Rusty had become accustomed to taking signals from leg pressure.

Her riding skills were natural, practical, down to earth, and unpretentious.

The northwestern trail took them toward the Rio Grande River, and J. W. stopped and looked over the immense, magnificent landscape. With a panoramic sweep, he looked to the north toward the majestic Wheeler Peak with monochromatic conifer mountainsides, the cedar-splashed foothills, and the basaltic mesas beneath. Further below, blackened volcanic cliffs lined the salient rush of the Rio Grande River. To the west, there were azure skies with angelic, billowing rain clouds.

The tranquility of the view brought J. W. to instinctively draw in a big cleansing breath and a huge cleansing sigh. It felt like he was truly seeing this beauty for the first time. Surrendering his ego, he said, "Damn, I really am a blessed man to have all that I have." He felt a fresh sense of peace. "God sure did good work here."

Sunshine smiled and said, "Funny, 'cause I was just thinking the same thing. Yes, indeed, God did good work here. It is truly beautiful."

They continued down the trail to the river's edge.

"Do you want to get down and rest for a while?" J. W. asked.

"Sure."

J. W. helped Sunshine down from her horse. He looked

into her eyes and said, "Sunshine, I never wanted to hurt you."
He gave her a sweet kiss.

His words and tenderness gave her a breeze of whispering
hope.

Tethering their horses, they held hands, walked down to
the riverbank, and sank into a grassy area.

Sunshine took off her boots and nervously played with
her beaded ankle bracelet. "There are so many things I don't
understand … I … I … this is so messed up. What about
Miss Rebecca? What's her trip? What's the story with her?"

J. W. said, "Rebecca is a fucking pain in the ass!"

Sunshine said, "Ya know what? She's no different than my
'hippie' friend Yogi. And, damn it, you can't tell me those folks
at the bar drinking beer and getting drunk are much different
than those partying fools at the commune. It's the same—
they just wear different clothes and different hairstyles. They
are all the same. They're all the same people. We are all God's
children. We are the children of God who has made us up like
a great symphony in which we must all play our individual
parts. Because none of us can hear all the notes, no single
person is suited to play all the musical parts. We need to be
able to play together …"

He rubbed her hand and stared at the river.

"Please, J. W. Can't you see it? Life is an amazing gift from
God. We need to accept it, see it, hear it, touch it, smell it,

and taste it. And for heaven's sake, we need to live it the way God intended us to."

J. W. smiled.

Sunshine put her hand on J. W.'s heart. "You need to free your heart from hatred. You can't keep going through life with so many harsh feelings. The universe is like a great echo chamber. Sooner or later, what you send out comes back. If you love people, that love will be returned to you. If you sow anger and hatred, then anger and hatred is what you reap."

J. W. smiled at her words of wisdom. Her words were a little far-fetched for his world, but he knew what she was saying had a lot of truth. There must have been an angel tapping on his shoulder and whispering in his ear because he felt and heard three words: "Trust this love."

"I ... uh ... damn! I'm not doin' a very good job with this. Damn ... this is hard. Sunshine, Rebecca was never an old flame. She has been trying to get me in the sack for a long time. She's a heartless, self-centered, manipulative, spoiled brat, and the only reason I don't wring her fat little neck is that her father is a powerful man who I still do business with. I don't dare burn that bridge. I like her father. He's a good man, and he's become a good friend.

"Look, I'm sorry. I should have protected you more when we were in Albuquerque." His heart sank lower into his chest. "Damn! I really am sorry for my foolishness. The Cattlemen's

Ball was the wrong way for you to meet my friends. I wish I had done a better job of making you more comfortable with those folks."

Sunshine stared at him.

"Sunshine, please just hear me out—"

"You know what? I hated seeing you drunk. Drunk people remind me of my mother and all the times I had to try to reason with her when she was stoned or crazy drunk or flying high. The countless times I had to put her to bed after she passed out. It hurts me to see anyone that way, and it hurts me to see you that way. Why did you get so drunk anyway? Were you so uncomfortable being seen with me that you had to be drunk?"

"No, no, no, Sunshine, I was right proud to be with you." He swallowed another lump of ego. "I guess it was my own shame and guilt that I was trying to drink away. Sunshine, I'm sorry I put you through that. I promise that you will never see me drunk again. Sunshine, I'm sorry for anything I may have said that hurt you. I should have tasted my words before I spit them out."

Sunshine said, "You have no need to drink away shame. You clearly are respected by your friends and family." Sunshine suddenly felt guilty because she was enjoying seeing him suffer. Uneasy with her own anger, she softened her tone. "Okay then … what's the story between you and Mike?"

"Mike and I have been friends for many years. And I'm ashamed to say that a lot of times, we think with our dicks.

We kinda' played this sick little game to see who could steal away each other's girl and get them into bed." He shook his head in disgust. "I know it's ... uh, uh, pretty appalling, but you're the first woman I really didn't want him to steal away. I know this all sounds hick and is coming out a little bit sideways, and I'm trying so hard for my words be me amazing. Damn it! I'm not good at this."

Sunshine got up and walked to the river's edge.

J. W. trailed right behind her.

She said, "You and I are like a candle in the wind—"

"But, Sunshine, if we both put our hands around that candle, we can keep it lit. Ya know? I hear country-and-western songs that describe love as an emotion that we can't control, one that overwhelms logic and common sense. That's what it's like for me with you. I've never felt this way about anybody before. I didn't plan on fallin' in love with you. I doubt if you planned on fallin' for a redneck ass like me, but once we met, it was clear that neither of us could control what is happening. Despite my hang-ups and our differences, I fell for you ... and ... every minute we've spent together has been seared in my memory and in my heart. Sunshine, you are truly a beautiful woman, but once I got to know you, I realized that you are an amazing woman. You're loving and sweet—and filled with compassion." He was beginning to realize that their love was being strengthened by working through their conflicts together.

They were walking in arm in arm even though they didn't see eye to eye.

His heart opened up from its rusted cage. He put his arms around Sunshine, looked into her sparkling green eyes, and said, "Sunshine, I love you. Damn, I've never said that to a woman before."

Sunshine's heart pounded in her chest. She gave him a long, searching glance, and a tear traveled down her cheek. So many tears of sorrow had filled her heart, but these tears made her smile. She could taste the sweetness of the happy tears that she could savor and treasure. Happy are those who knew the message of happy tears without the tides of sorrow. She offered him a beaming smile. "A hippie and a cowboy? Who the hell is going to believe that?" She laughed. "I guess I could learn to love a redneck-ass cowboy."

J. W. released a huge sigh, picked her up, spun her around, and gently set her back on the ground. "Damn! All this confessing has been some tough shit for me. Damn! I really am in love with you!"

She laughed and said, "That's pretty funny 'cause I am in love with you too, J. W." Sunshine tightened her embrace and rose on her tiptoes.

J. W. gently lifted her chin to meet his kiss—and neither of them noticed that it was beginning to rain.

CHAPTER 23

MAI: A LITTLE BIT OF HEAVEN IN VUNG TAU

"LET'S LIVE FOR TODAY," THE GRASS ROOTS

High above small arms fire, Blue sat inside the fifty-foot-long fuselage of a Boeing CH-47A Chinook helicopter. He was grateful to be alive and grateful to be on his way to another three days in-country R&R. The rhythmic vibration and deafening noise from the tandem rotor blades made it impossible to carry on a conversation.

Blue's mind kept replaying the battle horror he had just come from. His memory kept replaying the sight of NVA dead bodies with their blood flowing and merging into a wretched pool of blood. *Fuck me! I could fill a swimming pool with all the blood I've seen since I been here.* Blue examined his dirt-stained hands and thought he saw them covered with blood. Rubbing his eyes and clearing his mind, he then became grateful it was only an illusion. Shaking his head, then said, "Fuck me."

Blue was exhausted, restless, and in a horror-stricken funk. The aftermath of the battle made it extremely difficult to unwind and keep his mind quiet. Blue was wishing he could just drift off into a quiet meditation. He had lost so much and experienced things he never thought he would—or that anybody else should. Blue had always considered himself brave and a man's man, but he never thought his bravado would allow him to take another life so easily. Witnessing so much deplorable death, along with the terror of seeing friends and fallen comrades. War had always generated serious moral issues in this world and serious issues within himself. Blue wasn't sure when it happened, but at some point, perhaps in a battle, it was as if he had left his horror-stricken body and was watching somebody else who looked like him experiencing and participating in the unspeakable foul terror of war.

The Chinook helicopter, more affectionately known as a "Shithook," banked and then shuttered as it righted itself and bounced onto the makeshift landing pad near the airstrip of Vung Tau.

A crew member stood in the cavity of the fuselage and

told everyone to stay seated until the props had stopped and the rear door had dropped to the tarmac.

Captain Mayer stood and shouted, "On your feet. Follow me through the gate where our bus is waiting to take us to the Fuck-Off Center. For you cherries who are here for the first time, the Fuck-Off Center is also known as the R&R facility. At the facility, you will have your weapons stored until your return."

Blue shook his head at the thought of giving up his weapon. It always seemed so strange to give up your weapon and ammo as you checked in at the center. Their weapons were tagged and stored in secured lockers. It left him feeling so vulnerable. He and most guys hid a knife somewhere on their person. The R&R center was located on the coast, and it was a five-minute bus ride from the airfield. It was heavily guarded and heavily wrapped with several rows of razor wire.

Excited to be out of the bush and on the coastline of Vung Tau, Blue immediately grabbed Doug, Mickey, and Troy to share a Lambretta scooter taxicab into the city. Included in the group was an FNG named Phillip. It was this his first R&R, his first trip to Vung Tau, and his first trip anywhere outside his tiny hometown of Kerwo, Arizona.

Jimbo just waved them off and went the other way to be by himself. "Fuck you guys. Hope you have a fucking good time."

Vung Tau was six miles southeast of Saigon. It was a

good-sized city with a population of fifty-two thousand people. Most of the businesses catered to the armed forces recreation center and the servicemen who were granted leave. There were more than a hundred bars and restaurants—and many other activities—to entertain the troops. The people of Vung Tau spoke Vietnamese, French, and English. The bars all had names of cities or popular American places like Texas, New York, or Chicago.

Deadened and exhausted, Blue and the guys emotionlessly stared off into the distant streets of the bustling city. The FNG could not take his eyes off his battle-hardened platoon buddies. He studied their dark tans, scruffy boonie hats, and battle-worn boots that the mud had permanently stained. The rickety Lambretta taxi made a sharp turn, and the FNG let out a yell that made the guys laugh.

Blue said, "Don't shit your pants here, cherry. You'll become an expert at that in the bush!"

They pulled up in front of Vung Tau's French Grand Hotel on Quang Trung, Phuong Street.

Blue said, "I am heading into the hotel bar; it's usually quieter there. I'll catch up with you there later."

Doug grabbed the FNG and said, "Come on, cherry. We're keeping an eye on you. There are a few things you should know about this place."

Troy said, "Blue, we'll be showing this cherry how to pick the best flowers at the Spring Blossom Bar."

They all laughed.

Prostitution wasn't encouraged by the Armed Forces leaders, but it wasn't remotely discouraged either. It wasn't difficult for any serviceman in Vung Tau to find comfort or sexual emancipation with a call girl or an actively employed prostitute.

Blue wasn't sure if he was in the same party mood as the rest of the guys, and he headed to the hotel bar and ordered a scotch on the rocks. He was so out of it that he didn't even notice that he had sat down next to a young beautiful Vietnamese woman. Hearing a loud group of laughter behind him, Blue looked over his right shoulder and noticed one of the prettiest Asian girls he had ever seen sitting next to him. *How the hell did you not see this lovely creature sitting right next to you?*

Her soft, petite hand reached for a water in front of her, and he was startled by her beauty. He was guessing she was French-Vietnamese. She was taller than most Asian women, with flawless skin, and elegance in her composure. A true beauty.

"Can I buy you a drink?"

"Of course—if you promise dance with me."

Blue stood, offered her his hand, and escorted her to the dance floor.

They began a slow dance to some soft American rock: "Groovin'" by the Young Rascals.

She looked up at him and said, "Hey, GI, are your eyes real?"

"Yes, my eyes are a gift from my mother."

"My name Mai. I call you Blue Eyes?"

"No, please, just call me Blue."

"You handsome, GI. Blue really your name?"

Blue didn't answer. He was just enjoying being able to feel and smell a woman.

Mai pulled herself closer to him, hugged his right leg between her knees, and ran her hand up his shirt.

Blue's cock quickly started stirring.

Mai looked up with a well-rehearsed smile.

After they returned to their drinks at the bar, Mai said, "Are you here on R&R? Where are you staying?"

"I just got to town, and I haven't decided where I will stay yet.

"You stay my place. I make you very happy, bathe you, and cook for you. You very nice handsome GI. You give me sixty dallah, you have best relaxing time ever. Make me very happy too."

Blue was amused by her broken English. She was so pure

and classy, and he quickly became mesmerized. She was gorgeous, with beautiful black hair, and not a hair was out of place. She was wearing a lovely red silk ao dai, the traditional dress of women in Vietnam, and she her light makeup did not hide her natural beauty. He was amused, intrigued, and suddenly very horny. "How can I resist an invitation like that, Miss Mai?" He was hoping to get some rest and sleep while there on R&R, but he decided he could use some female company and sex.

On their way out of the hotel, Captain Mayer came strutting in with a woman on his arm. "Hey, Cantrell, I'm hosting a dinner here at the hotel this evening for a few of our best, and that includes you and your lovely lady. Be here at seven. See you then."

Mai stopped in front of the hotel and said, "So, Mr. Blue, we got deal?"

Blue reached into his pocket and handed Mai sixty dollars in US military money.

She kissed Blue softly on the lips, turned, and hailed a taxi.

It took about ten minutes of winding through an endless maze through the back streets of Vung Tau to get to Mai's place. Chastising himself, Blue realized he had put himself in a lot of danger by not paying attention to how they got there. He doubted if he could find his way back into the city without several hours of navigation. Her neighborhood was third world architecture made from scrap wood, sheet metal, and concrete blocks and makeshift structures.

Mai's place was located in a small alley, and her home was made up of concrete blocks. Her home even had a real front door that locked. The neighborhood was cleaner and neater than most of the surrounding areas. The small house was dimly lit and smelled of soft sandalwood incense. The main room had no dividing walls; it was a living room, a dining room, and a kitchen. The tiny kitchen comprised of a small counter with an icebox below it and a sink, but there was no running water. A single light bulb hung in the middle of the house. She had an old dial radio, and Blue was glad it wasn't on since there were only two stations: the America Forces radio, which he was sick of hearing, and a local station that played American rock songs sung poorly in Vietnamese, which he was truly grateful not to listen to.

Mai escorted Blue around, showing him the bathroom, which did have running water, and a tiled tub shower and toilet. A hanging woven tapestry divided and sectioned off the bedroom, which hosted a small mattress and a wood cabinet wardrobe in the corner.

"Time for you to relax, Mr. Blue. Let me take your clothes off and rub you. Then we will take a bath before we go back to hotel for dinner."

Blue had always been the one in control, and he realized this was completely different. Mai skillfully removed Blue's uniform and respectfully hung it in her closet. She led Blue to the bed and instructed him to lay facedown. She straddled him and started to rub his back.

Blue felt her silk garments caressing his sides as her hands rubbed an instant state of relaxation across his entire back.

She instructed Blue to roll over, and she stood alongside the bed and seductively let her silk dress drop softly to the floor. She grabbed Blue's right arm and continued her massage, continuing masterfully over his entire sore, exhausted body. Blue had never felt so relaxed and so skillfully aroused at the same time.

Mai slowly stood up and said, "I prepare warm bath for Mr. Blue."

Blue was startled from his state of relaxation and thought, *This is only a performance. This is her craft. Holy fuck! She is good at her trade.* He heard the water running.

Mai walked back into the room and led Blue into a lukewarm tub with scented oil. She proceeded to wash him as masterfully as she had massaged him. She lightly stroked him underwater, quietly studying his face for reactions and feedback. She leaned in and softly licked Blue from his chin up over his lips and to the end of his nose. She guided Blue out of the tub, dried him off, led him back into the bedroom, and helped him get dressed.

"Now you go to other room while your date for tonight gets dressed."

As Blue listened to the Vietnamese chatter in the alley, he heard another GI voice go by, obviously about to embark on the same pampered treatment.

Mai emerged from the bedroom in a dazzling turquoise-blue ao dai dress, looking like Vietnam's representative to the Miss Universe Pageant.

Wow, she is a beautiful woman—possibly the most stunning woman I've ever seen. It might have been his dick leading his brain—and perhaps his imagination had kicked in—but nobody could tell him that right then.

As Blue and Mai enter the dining room at the Grand Hotel, Captain Mayer almost broke his neck as his head spun around to see the lovely vision on Blue's arm.

The wine flowed freely, and the guys talked about things back in the States, purposely not engaging in conversation about military life in Vietnam. The GIs were repeatedly and sternly warned not to discuss military information with any of the Vietnamese people, including the prostitutes. It was a known fact that many of the prostitutes were paid for any military information they could give.

Blue looked around the group of GIs and their rented

dates and thought, *These girls are slutty skanks. I guess it pays to find a prostitute in the most expensive hotel in Vung Tau.*

The Vietnamese dates who were among Captain Mayer's group were quiet in the beginning of the night, but as the night went on, their chatter roared faster than an automatic weapon. Laughter echoed freely from everyone.

The dining room service was attentive, and several courses of delicious food started flowing to their table. After a bout of uncontrollable laughter, Blue found himself quickly wiping a tear from his eye before it rolled down his face. It was an emotional slap in the head as he realized that it was the first time he had found the war far from his thoughts. Mai picked up on his emotion right away and kissed him softly on the cheek. Blue was reminded of this lovely woman's humanity as he realized she understood him so well at that instant. His mood turned melancholy, and he was grateful for the moment. Blue lifted her small, soft hand and placed a sweet kiss upon it. He looked into her eyes and smiled the first smile he had in weeks.

On the way back to Mai's place, they didn't say a word. She just rested her head on his arm and softly stroked his leg. When they arrived, Mai pushed Blue's money away when he tried to pay for the taxi. She reminded Blue that she would take care of everything while they were together. She unlocked the door and held it for Blue.

He set aside his manly urges and allowed Mai to take the lead.

Mai locked the door and turned and sweetly kissed Blue as if he were the love of her life. This melted Blue's thoughts, and he continued to experience separation from the war.

Mai understood all too well the horror of this needless war, yet she felt that no American could understand what she had gone through in her war-torn life. Both of them were locked into a mutual escape for a few days; her role was to make him happy, and his was to graciously accept.

Mai led Blue into the bedroom, looked into his eyes, and smiled. She converted the atmosphere into a salacious experience by undressing in front of Blue and gracefully fending off his attempts to touch her. "Just watch me." She pulled her hair draped over her shoulders and down to hide her breasts in a flirtatious, modest gesture. She held Blue's arms at his side and on her toes planted a soft kiss on his lips. She turned the undressing of Blue into a romantic art form and lowered him onto her bed. Mai straddled Blue, leaned forward, brushed her hair over her shoulder, and kissed him deeply. Her tongue invited him into her entire being. She let her lips roam down his neck to his nipples, and the black silky strands of her hair passed softly over Blue's face.

After getting a ticklish pulse from his nipples, she continued down his body until she got to his throbbing cock.

Blue could feel her hot breath over his cock and down to his balls and then back up to the tip. Blue knew what was next—or at least what he hoped was next. Her tongue softly touched the head of his cock. Blue wasn't sure if it was his imaginative anticipation, but there was no mistaking as her tongue became incredibly wet. Her saliva dripped around his cock as she licked her way down the shaft. Her hot breath was again wrapped around the head of his cock, and her lips closed around him. Blue was over the top with excitement and afraid that he might lose consciousness even before orgasm.

Blue couldn't control the urge to take control. He lifted her up to him and rolled over on top of Mai. In a true swift art form, Mai had a condom on his swollen cock. Once again, Blue found himself in an unfamiliar position. He was usually the one in control and confident that his lover was going to be blown away by his lovemaking skills. Mai looked up at Blue with desire, and before Blue could assume command, Mai reached down and guided Blue into her. Blue pushed deep, and she pushed against him; no lovers could ever be thrust together so deeply.

Mai had set an over-the-top erotic—and romantic—mood, but Blue was in the position where he felt in his moment. He was in control, and the mood changed to a macho performance. Reality slapped him into realization that he hadn't the vaguest idea how many American soldiers

Mai had serviced. This thought suddenly caused an obsession with his sexual performance and prowess. His macho ego took flight as he envisioned himself as a competitive gigolo. He thought, *It's just sex—with no moments of sharing and emotion. I'm just fucking her.* Blue was hoping this emotion was not being transmitted to Mai. He didn't even know if she cared; after all, she had already been paid.

Blue's mind was racing, bouncing between the lovely encounter, erotic desire, physical indulgence, and suspicion. Was her goal to discretely—one random word at a time over a few days—collect information that she would pass on to a brother who was Vietcong? Was she getting paid by an agent? Anger started to enter the equation, thinking he was just seduced by the enemy. Unaware that his pondering had control of himself, he harshly thrust into her with extreme aggression. They were wildly fucking. He exploded, and it felt like he had just emptied a magazine of semen ammo, taking her out. *Fuck me! This fucking war now controls my fucking.* He was ashamed of his paranoia and prejudiced accusations. He collapsed on her and softened his kiss before rolling off. *Did she know? Had she sensed this many times before? Did she care?* He deeply hoped not. Mai sweetly escorted him to the bath and washed him in preparation for bed.

Blue didn't get the sleep that he longed for while being far removed from combat. No matter how many times he woke in the night, he felt fear not knowing where he was until he calmed his fears and drifted back asleep.

When he woke up, he was alone in Mai's house. He sat up and jolted ready for action. *Shit—I don't even have a weapon.*

The door opened, and Mai walked in with food, ready to serve him breakfast in bed. Blue had forgotten the disjointed dream and nightmares, but his mean-spirited thoughts while making love to Mai the night before still lingered, covering him with guilt.

Mai had quietly slipped out into the alley to find one of the neighborhood mama-sans who was passing by to sell her food from her thanh tree, a bamboo carry stick with baskets of food on both ends. Mai came back into the house, trying to be as quiet as when she left. Mai set the food down on a little table and divided their food onto two plates. Breakfast consisted of hard-boiled eggs, rice noodles, bean curd leaf with lightly cooked vegetables, and hot tea.

Blue jumped up, pulled on his pants, as started to put on his shirt.

Mai walked toward him with their breakfast and tea and said, "What you doing, Mr. Blue? You take clothes off and get back into bed. I feed you breakfast."

Amused, Blue gladly obeyed, took off his pants, and jumped back into bed.

She used chopsticks to feed Blue, and after every few

bites, she handed him his cup of hot tea. After picking up the last noodle, she playfully slipped it into her mouth and held up the plate. "Mr. Blue, you like being feed breakfast by Mai?" She jumped up and said, "Would like for me to give you more pleasure? Or go to city to do something?"

Blue said, "What would you like to do, Mai?"

Mai straightened her posture, lifted her chin in the air, grabbed an elegant enamel bowl, and placed it on her head. "As queen of Vung Tao, I officially make it Mr. Blue Day." She smiled playfully.

Blue laughed. "Let's go into town."

Mai said, "Time to get dressed and go do something."

Blue said, "I saw a statue up on the hill with a beautiful building behind it. Is that a Buddhist temple?"

With a puzzled look, she said, "Yes, temple to Guan Yin."

"Guan Yin? She is the goddess of mercy."

Mai seemed startled that Blue knew about Guan Yin.

Blue said, "Can we go up there? I would love to see it. I'll bet it is a cool place with a great view from up there"

"Yes, has nice view. Besides, it Mr. Blue Day."

So, they walked down the street and hailed a Lambretta taxicab. Blue realized how lucky he was to have found such a lovely companion with whom to spend his R&R. The vast majority of GIs were sleeping off their hangovers in a shared hotel room or sleeping back at the R&R base. The guys would be waiting for their aspirins to kick in and having to find someplace to eat. More than likely, they would start barhopping again and then have to hunt for more boom-boom girls all over again. In the meantime, he was getting pampered and laid by a beautiful, classy French-Vietnamese woman.

Mai was holding onto Blue like they were on their honeymoon. As they drove through the city, she graciously pointed out all the interesting facts, interesting buildings, and the names of the beautiful flowers blooming. From a higher lookout point, she pointed out the R&R base in the distance.

Damn, Blue thought. *I wish she hadn't pointed that out. It was a slap in the face reminder that this will all be over tomorrow morning. Fuck me. I sure was enjoying this getaway.*

They went through a large, ornate gate and a circular drive with a magnificent array of flowers, a well-manicured landscape, and a radiantly majestic statue of Guan Yin. The taxi came to a stop at a lookout place with a lovely view of the city below and the temple gardens above.

"Let's get out and look around," Blue said.

While strolling around the immaculately clean grounds, Mai pointed out several places, including the area where her house was.

Blue turned her around and headed back to the entry of the temple.

Mai stopped at the steps and said, "Mr. Blue, you want

go into temple? It sacred place of honor and worship—not curious place to go look."

"I understand very well. I have been in a Guan Yin temple before. When I was young, my father was stationed in Hawaii for a few years. My teacher was Chinese and took our class on a field trip to the botanical gardens that had a Guan Yin temple. My teacher noticed that several of us had an interest in the temple and its beauty. She said if we wanted to go in, that we could go in one at a time. She gave us strict instructions as to the proper etiquette for going into the temple."

"Your teacher was Buddhist?"

"Yes."

Blue progressed up the steps and stopped at the entrance of the temple to look around. *Over time, man has built majestic temples, monumental cathedrals, mosque, synagogues, and extraordinary buildings to worship God. They are brilliant monuments crafted with astonishing intellect and exquisite expressions to lead you to the majesty and mystery of God. However, just like the words chiseled in the Ten Commandments, they are ultimately creations of stone. These structures don't get us closer to the presence of God. We must find God's presence within ourselves.* He remembered seeing graffiti on a public bathroom wall: "Sell the Vatican—and feed the world."

Entering the temple, he placed several coins in the open mouth of the lion statue that served as an offering vessel.

He took three sticks of incense, lit them, and held them in his hands in prayer fashion. He walked to the altar, bowed, and said, "Revering the light of Buddha, reflecting upon my imperfect self, I shall proceed to live a life of gratitude." After chanting three times, "*Namo Amida*, Buddha," he placed the incense in the sand.

He faced the altar and reflected on his faith. While his father was alive, Blue was raised in a loving faithful Christian home. As he got older, his interest had led him to read and study many of the holy books. He continuously compared and analyzed the marvelous undeniable commonalties of each. Blue discovered that all of God's faiths—Christianity, Judaism, Islam, and Buddhism—had similarities. Through these similarities, he couldn't help but question why such strife had been wrought upon the world in the names of each. He educated himself with readings and scriptures from the Holy Bible, the Hebraic Holy Books, the Buddhist Sacred Text, the Hindu Gita, and the Koran. He found that each stated in every case—and every religion is based on the experience of God and his energy of love.

Each religion's description of the death experience and the dual judgement referring to the eternal afterlife in either the nether world or heaven, hardly varied in any significant way. Each stated that all had begun and returned to the same place with God—and with God's unending love. Blue couldn't understand the divisions and prejudices that people perceived in each other's religions. He knew that they are purely human-made—and how ridiculous humans must look to God. He wondered if God looked down at us and was amused or disappointed by our goings-on here on earth. Blue knew that the love of God was profound, awe-inspiring, and unconditional.

All organized religions scurry for Gods "number one spot" with a golden trophy that reads: "This is the only true religion that leads to God." All of us are staking the claim of having the favor of his eye.

Blue felt with all his heart that God's gift to mankind was a life filled with love, joy, serenity, and peace. The problem with religion is that each claims to be the real agent of God and that only through them can it be attained.

He became startled as his thoughts suddenly took him back to the putrid war he was living. He shook his head and said, "Fucking war."

When Blue walked out of the temple, he was surprised when he saw Mai standing there with a tear running down her face. Blue walked up to Mai, brushed the tear away from her cheek, and looked at her curiously.

Mai said, "I never seen American do respect like that to my culture." She was consumed by the hatred created by this scathing war. She was having to live with an unprotected heart and soul by making a living selling her body. At twenty dollars a day, she probably earned more than the mayor of Vung Tau. Twenty dollars a day was a good income in Vietnam. Prostitution was such a harsh profession. She couldn't afford to open her heart to anyone, and she was continually exposed to bad energy and health dangers.

They rode most of the way back into town in silence.

Mai smiled and said, "I have all your money, Mr. Blue. I want to buy you drink at Grand Hotel bar where you found me. It Mr. Blue Day, remember?" She rubbed his thigh.

"That would be great."

They sat at the bar and talked about silly stuff to keep the mood light and carefree. After two drinks, they headed back to Mai's place.

Blue suggested taking a short nap.

"Take nap? Good idea, Mr. Blue." She undressed him, laid him down, and cuddled up next to him with her head on his shoulder.

The relaxation allowed them both to drift off to sleep. They awoke having slept for almost an hour.

"I think the honorary Mr. Blue is very hungry, yes?" said Mai.

"Yes, I am very hungry for both food and Mai."

Mai smiled and put on slippers and a silk robe. "Mr. Blue,

relax. I get us some dinner. It okay that we stay and relax here tonight?"

"Yes, that would be good."

After ten minutes, she returned with a large bowl of food and a bottle of red wine. Mama-san must have been waiting in the alley with food and drink.

At that point, it didn't matter what they did. He was feeling like the war never existed, and he was enjoying his short R&R with Mai.

Mai placed a second drape over the brightest window, started the water in the tub, and lit several candles. "Mr. Blue, I will feed you dinner and wine while we take bath together."

Blue thought, *Wow, do kings even live like this?*

They ate, drank, and laughed in the tub until the water started to chill and their fingers and toes were shriveled. They climbed back into bed quickly to find the gates of temptation reopened.

The next morning, Blue woke up to Mai's nudge. She had already brought in breakfast. Blue realized that it was the first time he had slept a full night without waking since he left the commune in Taos.

After breakfast, Blue got up and dressed. "God damn it. Has it really been three days already?"

The mood was quiet and sober as they dressed and headed out of the house to hail a taxi. Two taxis pulled up, and Mai signaled for Blue to get into the first one. She kissed him sweetly on the cheek and got into the second taxi, and they drove off in different directions.

Blue looked back for a parting glance, and Mai smiled, blew him a kiss, and gave him a peace sign.

Before he knew it, Blue was back at the R&R base, being reissued his rifle and ammo, and boarding the bus to be hauled off to the chopper pad to board a Shithook—back to the war.

In the air, Blue looked out the small porthole window and took a final peek at Vung Tau. Questions and concerns darkened his mind: *Will these wonderful Vietnamese people ever be free of war and fear? Will they ever live in peace? Will Mai ever live with peace? Fuck this fucking war."*

Blue was boiling with a wave of deplorable, gut-wrenchingly anger. His vile anger molested his thoughts and crawled over his body until it totally crippled his being. He instantly felt any and all relaxation from the past few days with Mai ripped from his body as if they had never happened.

"Yes, Mai was a little bit of heaven in Vung Tau."

CHAPTER 24

HONOLULU: COMING HOME

"WASTED AND I CAN'T FIND MY WAY HOME," BLIND FAITH

Dear Sunshine,

I don't even know what day it is anymore. Just a quick letter so you know that two weeks ago, I was wounded. I've been at Third Field Hospital in Saigon and haven't a clue how I got here. This letter is to let you know I'm okay.

I'm still in a trance, not sure if it was the intense combat or the morphine, probably an unhealthy dose of both ... but, really, I'm okay.

Don't be frightened.

The good news is I am coming home soon.

I feel so helpless, lying here in bed, among these crippled and lifeless forms. They tell me I was the luckiest one out there 'cause I'm going home. Other survivors like Troy and Mickey are going back to the bush to start all over again. The funny thing is I wish I was going back with them. They are my brothers, and I feel like I am betraying them by not being there for them when the shit hits the fan—and it will.

My buddy Little Joe is dead. It's for that reason that I'm still wading through the emotional debris. A dead buddy is some tough shit.

Today, some bigwig came down from his fancy division office to see us. He pinned medals on my god damn pillow and said I was "the best." Jesus, I thought that ugly motherfuckin' lunatic was going to kiss me. I wanted to open the pin on one of the medals and stick it deep into his chest where medals are supposed to be worn and tell him that he was the fucking best.

I guess I took a pretty good beating. They cut a huge piece of shrapnel out of my left leg, and the blast broke it in two places. Shit, if that doesn't make you hate surprises. I have a cut on the back of my head that goes almost from ear to ear. I've lost the hearing in my left ear, but they say my hearing will come back. In the meantime, I have a terrible, nonstop ringing in my right ear. They have to remove my cast next week to remove my stitches, but then they'll put it back on again for two months or so.

I'll be seeing you in a month or so ... they'll be sending me home to completely recover at the Kirtland Air Force Base VA hospital in Albuquerque. They recently opened a new wing to handle wounded New Mexican soldiers still on active service.

But please don't worry 'cause I really am okay.

Love,

Blue

The battle had happened more than three weeks ago, and it was coming back in and out of sequence. Blue did not even know if what he was recalling was the way it happened.

Blue's squad had been out on a recon assignment. His platoon had been inserted by helicopter and instructed to hike three clicks over the worst terrain they had yet to have the misfortune of encountering. They traveled up an endless, monstrous, muddy hill to the edge of the DMZ to make observations of the NVA troops below. Unfortunately, political restrictions had been put in place by the higher commanders, which his patrol had enforced, and they ended up giving privileged sanctuary to enemy forces. The ill-conceived military tactics and the callous irresponsibility of some of the senior officers resulted in creating needless casualties to Blue's platoon.

Their squad, plus one army machine gunner, and a corpsman-medic went on a patrol into a real bad area. They were short on men, so Blue was carrying the radio. Having that cumbersome radio on Blue's back may have saved his ass because it shielded him from the blast. The NVA set off ten mines, which were spread out on the trail below the ridgeline, near where they were left. The bombs all went off at once, and the killing dance began.

The blast sent Blue down into his boots for his breath and sucked his youth right out of him. Every other man in the ten-man patrol was hit. Blue was a moving target survivor. The corpsman behind Blue was blown fifteen feet over a cliff. The army machine gunner was blown to pieces—to an unrecognizable state.

Doug, Mickey, Troy, Jimbo, and Blue tried to take care of the wounded while fighting off the gooks at the same time. The NVA was throwing grenades at them and firing automatic rifles. It was fucking hell! Blue eyes were wider than a horse's eyes caught in a fire. The horrifying battle happened so fast like a strobe light, flashing faster and faster, but it seemed to happen in slow motion. The seconds seemed to have taken minutes.

Blue had never been so scared in his life. His adrenaline was spiked to an all-time high. Blue called for help to get a medevac while trying to shoot his rifle, which jammed up after only sixty rounds. He crawled over to the blown-apart machine gunner's rifle and had to remove what was left of the gunner's hand to use it. His hands were shaking uncontrollably, and he was having trouble reloading. He could hear the dry hard rattle of shrapnel scudding against the surrounding debris. The acrid smell of cordite hung in the air, making it impossible to get a clean breath.

Blue watched Little Joe explode. He was in the brush twenty feet away when the bomb went off. Locked into breathtaking concentration, Blue crawled over to him. Little Joe was lying on his stomach with his pack blown over his shoulders. Blue turned him over; his face was grimacing in anguish. He helplessly watched blood gush from his arm that had been blown off. Blue franticly wrapped a makeshift tourniquet around Little Joe's arm to try to stop the blood.

It felt like an elephant was standing on Blue's leg. He knew he had been hit and that something was wrong with his leg, but his attention was totally on helping Little Joe. They waited for what seemed like hours for the helicopters to come pick them up. A sick surreal song played over and over again in Blue's head, a song by the Animals that Blue had heard on the radio before they left for recon. "We gotta get outa this place if it's the last thing we ever do." It was raining, and Blue could see his blood mixing with Little Joe's blood in the puddle of water they were lying in.

The medevac finally came and tossed Little Joe into the chopper. Blue tried to stand up to run over to the chopper, but he was overcome by an out-of-control grasping spasm. It felt like a misfire in his nervous system, and he fell back hard onto the blood-soaked ground. Out of nowhere, Jimbo appeared and tossed Blue's helpless mass into the chopper.

In the air, Blue stayed next to Little Joe, trying to help him. Blue even tried mouth-to-mouth resuscitation a couple of times. Blue's face was covered with Little Joe's blood. Blue kept trying until the medic pulled Blue away from Little Joe. The medic kept shouting, "Leave him. He's dead."

Blue kept screaming, "No, don't you die on me, Little Joe! Don't you fucking die." He sobbed so intensely that the sobs came from deep in his soul. He cried so hard until he couldn't get anything out. He finally passed out from the loss of blood, a concussion, and physical and emotional exhaustion.

A week later, Blue woke up in the Third Hospital bed in Saigon. The only thing Blue had to do was sit in bed and think. *Being here in Vietnam is like sitting in an electric chair and waiting for someone to pull the fucking switch.*

Everything he had seen there was blown through smoke. *It won't matter if my memory distorts what happened here because every image and every sound keeps coming back out of the haze with that horrible stench of destruction.*

Blue decided to write down some of the events. Perhaps this would help him to ease his mind—even if he wasn't sure who he was writing to. During the first nights in the hospital, when he had still not awakened from the battle, Blue's friends and family members who had passed on, including his dad, came from the other side to see if he was still alive. They all looked so youthful and alive, but when he looked at himself, he was a hundred years old.

Blue said, "Dad, is it my time to go?"

His dad's bright blue eyes shined happily, and light around him was overflowing with love. He smiled and said, "No, my son, it is not your time." His visit left Blue with an unremarkable amount of peace. That peace carried over to his awakening, and he knew it would carry over him for years to come:

I've seen some things happen here in Vietnam that have stirred me so much that I've changed my whole outlook on life. It's all so totally mind-blowing. I've changed to a new chapter in my life. Because of this putrid side of life that I have witnessed, I'm a different person now. I have seen things I'll never be able to forget.

Everyone who has been here, both the living and the dead, will never make it back from Nam. We will always be here.

One of the nurses asked me if I was scared. I gently replied, "Yes, ma'am, I am scared." I wanted to yell at her. "Fuck yes! I fucking am scared." The truth is I was damn-fucking-straight scared. And I'm still picking through the layers of fear. I'm very proud to be a part of the 1ˢᵗ CAV, but right now, I don't care about all the fucking brainwashing patriotic-duty bullshit we've been taught. The truth is we are all scared.

I went to Vietnam committed to following in my father's footsteps and proudly fight for my country, but right now, currently, the glamour of "Ooh-rah" is missing. I know I'll have it back soon. If anything, I have to get back my respect for the 1ˢᵗ CAV for my buddy

Little Joe—and for all the Americans who lost their lives in battle.

Anyone who has lost a loved one here in Vietnam will never be able to forget or recover from the shrapnel left in their hearts.

Blue had to convince his platoon buddies and the hospital staff that he wasn't going out of his mind when he started practicing Tai Chi exercises to improve his circulation and increase his internal energy to help get rid of his hostilities and hatred. He also practiced some of the meditations he and Sunshine had performed in clearing his chakras to help relieve the stagnant energy he'd ingested from the war.

Three weeks later, while sitting in the Honolulu Airport and waiting for his flight home, a man walking past him accidentally knocked over Blue's crutches. "So sorry!" The young man picked up Blue's crutches.

Blue looked up to the man and saw Little Joe's face attached to him. Blue felt a sharp freezing pain in his chest. He wanted to tell him it was no big deal, but he was horror-struck, and his words were locked into him. Blue forced himself to look again; he took a second look at the man and noticed that it wasn't Little Joe. There hadn't even been a close resemblance.

Blue buried his head in his hands, his eyes tearing up. "What the fuck! Now you're seeing people walking around who you watched die." The last time he saw Little Joe's face was watching the body being zipped into a green rubber body bag. Blue worked his lips futilely to ease the dryness. "Nothing to worry about—it's only your sixteenth nervous breakdown." His breath was gummed up in his throat, and his face was cold and white. "Shake it off. Fucking shake it off." He shook his head frantically. "Fuck me! Come on, man. Don't let this swallow you up." He ran his fingers through his hair.

A pretty girl passed by Blue and offered him a big bright smile. Blue forced the best fake smile he could in return. *People will never know what PTSD vets are fighting underneath something as simple as a smile.* Rubbing his eyes and shaking his head in disgust, he thought, *Fucking war!*

Later, while sitting over a steak in the airport restaurant, Blue made a nasty meat connection as he was cutting into his T-bone steak. Pushing the steak away from him, he once again reminded himself that it would take years to be debriefed from the nightmare he had just lived in Nam.

The Vietnam War

For those who understand, there is
no explanation necessary.
For those who don't understand, there
is no explanation possible.

SONG REFERENCES

The Fifth Dimension. "Aquarius/Let the Sunshine in." *The Age of Aquarius*. Wally Heider Recording, Los Angeles and United Recording, Las Vegas. 1968.

Jimi Hendrix. "Purple Haze." *Jimi Hendrix Experience*. De Lane Lea, London Olympic London. 1967.

Simon and Garfunkel. "Mrs. Robinson" *Bookends*. Columbia, 1968.

Jefferson Airplane. "White Rabbit." *RCA, Hollywood, California*. 1967.

Jimmie Davis and Charles Mitchell. "You Are My Sunshine" 1939.

Peter, Paul, and Mary. "Leaving on a Jet Plane." *1700*. A&R studios, New York City. 1967.

Tommy James and the Shondells. "Hanky Panky." *Hanky Panky*. Roulette Records, 1966.

Tommy James and the Shondells. "Crystal Blue Persuasion." *Crimson and Clover*. Roulette, 1968.

The Beatles. "Magical Mystery Tour." *Magical Mystery Tour.* EMI and Chappell London, 1967.

The Zombies. "Time of the Season" *Odyssey and Oracle.* Abbey Road Studios, London. 1968.

Peter, Paul, and Mary. "The Cruel War." *Peter, Paul and Mary.* Warner Bros Records, 1962.

The Beatles. "Please Mr. Postman." *With the Beatles.* EMI London, 1963.

The Fifth Dimension. "A Stoned Soul Picnic." *A Stoned Soul Picnic.* Soul City Records, 1968.

The Archies. "Sugar, Sugar." *Sugar, Sugar.* Calendar/Kirshner/RCA/Water Tower Music, 1969.

Buddy Holly and The Crickets. "Peggy Sue." *Buddy Holly.* Coral 9-61885, 1957.

Edward Bangs. "Yankee Doodle." 1776.

The Beatles. "Magical Mystery Tour." *Magical Mystery Tour.* EMI London, 1967.

Creedence Clear Water Revival. "Bad Moon Rising." *Green River.* Heider's Studio, San Francisco California, 1969.

Rolling Stones. "(I Can't Get No) Satisfaction." *Out of Our Heads.* (US Release). RCA Holly. California, 1965.

Ray Price. "Take Me as I Am (Or Let Me Go)." *Take Me as I Am.* Columbia, CS 9606, 1968.

Bob Dylan. "Blowing in the Wind." *The Freewheelin' Bob Dylan.* Columbia, 1963.

The Beatles. "Come Together." *Abbey Road.* EMI London, 1969.

Merle Haggard. "The Fightin' Side of Me." *The Fightin' Side of Me.* Capital 2719, 1969.

Jimmy Davis and Charles Mitchell. "You Are My Sunshine. 1939.

B.B. King. "The Thrill Is Gone." *Completely Well.* Bluesway/ABC Records, 1969.

John Newton. "Amazing Grace." 1779.

Merle Haggard and the Strangers. "Working Man Blues." *A Portrait of Merle Haggard,* Capital 2719, 1969.

The Loving Spoonful. "Summer in the City." *Hums of Lovin' Spoonful,* VEVO, 1966.

Marty Robbins. "I Walked Alone." *I Walk Alone,* Columbia. CS 9725, 1963.

Johnny Cash. "Ring of Fire." *The Best of Johnny Cash.* Mercury Records, 1963.

Grass Roots. "I'd Wait A Million Years." *Leaving It All Behind.* ABC/Dunhill, 1969.

Ernest Tubb's. "Walking the Floor Over You." *Walking the Floor Over You.* Decca, 1941.

Grateful Dead. "Truckin' What a Long Strange Trip It's Been." *American Beauty.* Warner Bros, 1970.

George Jones. "The Race Is On." *Get Lonely in a Hurry.* United Artists, 1965.

Country Joe and the Fish. "Cheer/I-Feel-Like-I'm-Fixin'-To-Die" (also known as Vietnam Rag). *I-Feel-Like-I'm-Fixin'-To-Die.* Vanguard Records, 1967.

Hank Locklin. "Please Help Me I'm Falling." *Please Help Me I'm Falling.* RCA Victor, 1960.

Ferlin Husky. "Wings of a Dove." *Wings of a Dove.* Capital, 1960.

The Young Rascals. "Groovin'." *The Young Rascals.* Atlantic, 1967.

Blind Faith. "Wasted and I Can't Find My Yay Home." *Blind Faith.* Polydor, 1969.

The Animals. "We Gotta Get Outa This Place." *The Animals.* Columbia Graphophone, MGM, 1965.

BIBLIOGRAPHY
GRATEFUL ACKNOWLEDGMENT OF SOURCES

Cobb, Ahad. *Life Unfolding: Memoirs of a Spiritual Hippie*. 2018, Albuquerque, Night Sky Books.

Rose, Ten Doug, *Fearless Puppy On American Road*, 2008. Ann Arbor MI., Edwards Brothers. ISBN#978-0-615-18308-4

Rose, Ten Doug, *Reincarnation Through Common Sense*, 2013. Ann Arbor MI., Edwards Brothers. ISBN#978-0-692-01952-8

Herr, Michael, *Dispatches*. 1978, NY New York, Avon Books.

Gawani, Pony Boy. *Horse, Follow Closely: Native American Horsemanship*. 1998, Irvine California, BowTie Press.

Maddow, Norman. *Rodeo*. 1985, Los Angeles California

Pointer, Larry. *Rodeo Champions*. 1985, University of New Mexico Publishing.

Klein, Irwin. *Irwin Klein and the New Settlers.* 2016, University of Nebraska Press.

Miles, Barry. Hippie. 2004, New York, Sterling Publishing.

History Channel. *Vietnam War.* Web URL. historychannel.com.

Your Dictionary. Web URL. yourdictionary.com.

Named Campaigns-Vietnam. 2007. Web URL. www.army.mil/CMH/reference/vncmp.htm.

Taos Pueblo. Web URL. Taospublo.com/about/.

"Glenn Dean." By Dana Joseph. *Cowboys and Indians.* August/September 2019: 103, 104, 106–109.

"Year of the Commune." *Newsweek,* August 18, 1969.

"Optimists Eager for Banner Age of Aquarius," Lydia Martin. *Albuquerque Journal.* January 26, 1995.

Daily Word. A Unity Publication. Monthly Devotionals: 2017, January/February, March/April, May/June, November/December. 2018, January/February, September/October. 2019, January/February, March/April, May/June, July/August. 2020, March/April.

AUTHOR'S NOTE

In writing *Love and War in the Age of Aquarius*, I recalled events, places, and people from my personal involvement in the Vietnam War. However, I realize that other Vietnam veterans had different experiences. I understand that there were as many different perceptions and impact of Vietnam as there were soldiers who participated there. So, if this in no way represents another Vietnam veteran's experience, I completely understand. Yet, I am sure that all vets can agree that a war is never over when the shooting stops. Those who have seen combat will never stop seeing it. My sincere respect goes out to all veterans of all wars.

Through sentimental bar talk, reminiscing, literature, and movies—along with the countless times I waited for prescription refills and doctor appointments at the VA Hospital—I have listened to the heartfelt stories of other veterans and found that they related to my experiences in Nam in no way shape or form. I hope there is enough accuracy in this story for veterans to connect and identify with.

My other goal in writing this story was to try to bring our readers a little more understanding of the Vietnam War and to educate those who were never there. Through this story, I share an experience of Vietnam veteran's tragedies, healings, and unanswered questions.

Once again, I remind you that this was my account and experiences. Please know I sincerely have done my best to portray the character Blue by stitching together what happened to my brothers and me in Nam.

Geoffrey Carroll
1st CAV, 1st Team, 3rd Brigade
21st Artillery, Recon Sergeant, 2/8 Infantry

ABOUT THE AUTHORS

Set against the gorgeous mountains of Taos New Mexico, a rich literary vision is found by authors Am**aia Joy & Geoffrey Carroll**. This story evokes you to take a vicarious trip in our layered compelling writing. As a husband and wife team, both adding their individual perspectives and imagination.

Amaia has lived in New Mexico her entire life, and as a cowgirl roving throughout the high deserts and mountains. She can brand a calf, shoot to kill a rattlesnake, and ride a horse with ease. Amaia has lived the life of Annie-Oakley on the wide-open spaces; howled with the coyotes in the high mountains, harvested marijuana with neighboring hippies, hunted wild game along the Rio Grande, and waved and smiled at the crowd as she rode in the grand entry of a rodeo. She has waltzed in perfect step at the Cattlemen's Ball; danced the Ranchero at the Fiestas and danced to the Native Corn Dance with the Jemez Pueblo Indians. Amaia knows the people and places has lived the history amongst the many colorful cultures of Nuevo Mexico. Amaia Joy holds the honor of being awarded the Distinguished Governors Award for Outstanding Women of New Mexico.

Geoffrey is an honored disabled Vet, a true American— Vietnam Veteran, 1st Air Mobile CAV artillery assigned to an infantry company as their Recon Sargent. He has been recognized for his heroism, fortitude, and valor, and is a recipient of many Vietnam Service Medals, and Meritorious Citations.

Geoffrey inspires the story with his reflections and experiences as a Reconnaissance Soldier in Vietnam. The events and emotions of Geoffrey's experience in Vietnam had been sequestered in his subconscious for many years. Wanting to report the truth and facts, Geoffrey uses this story to portray a factual representation of Vietnam.

Geoffrey had a firsthand grasp on the year 1969, as it

was the year he graduated from high school, hitched hiked around Europe, returning to his home on Oahu to enjoy surfing, partying, and the life of a hippie at a commune at the nearby neighboring island of Maui. Upon returning from Nam, Geoffrey lived in the Haight-Ashbury district in San Francisco and Big Sur Coast of California until his calling lead him to the land of enchantment—New Mexico. The fun perspective in Geoffrey's writing style is born from his personal experiences and viewpoints.